FULL MOON OVER KABUL

ALSO BY BARBARA KASTELIN

Novels
THE PARROT TREE
WHEN SNOW FELL
HOTEL BELVEDERE

Short stories
A BAD LOT
JUST IMAGINE
IMAGINE THAT

Full Moon Over Kabul

Barbara Kastelin

Copyright © 2024 Barbara Kastelin

The moral right of the author has been asserted.

Apart from any fair dealing for the purposes of research or private study, or criticism or review, as permitted under the Copyright, Designs and Patents Act 1988, this publication may only be reproduced, stored or transmitted, in any form or by any means, with the prior permission in writing of the publishers, or in the case of reprographic reproduction in accordance with the terms of licences issued by the Copyright Licensing Agency. Enquiries concerning reproduction outside those terms should be sent to the publishers.

This is a work of fiction. Names, characters, businesses, places, events and incidents are either the products of the author's imagination or used in a fictitious manner. Any resemblance to actual persons, living or dead, or actual events is purely coincidental.

Troubador Publishing Ltd
Unit E2 Airfield Business Park,
Harrison Road, Market Harborough,
Leicestershire LE16 7UL
Tel: 0116 279 2299
Email: books@troubador.co.uk
Web: www.troubador.co.uk

ISBN 978-1-83628-050-7

British Library Cataloguing in Publication Data.
A catalogue record for this book is available from the British Library.

Printed and bound by CPI Group (UK) Ltd, Croydon, CR0 4YY
Typeset in 11pt Aldine401 BT by Troubador Publishing Ltd, Leicester, UK

For my husband, Geoffrey

London, 1997

It was October, rust-coloured and mild; a day when the opalescent moon was visible in the morning sky, and two women had agreed to meet for lunch in *Little Sicily*. Davina Lewis was already sitting under the wooden pitchfork fixed to the wall above her. With her black hair and dark-brown eyes, she could easily have been wielding such an Italian hayfork during harvest a hundred years ago. Here in 1997, however, she had ordered a small bottle of San Pellegrino sparkling water and was watching the bubbles rise in her glass, while waiting for her friend to arrive. Whenever near St Pancras station, Davina tried to find time to eat in *Little Sicily*. The primitive farming antiques displayed on the walls, the warmth, the soft murmur of conversation, and the hypnotic down-to-earth smell of garlic competing with grilled cheese were worth tossing carb-free resolutions to the wind.

And a chill wind was indeed felt, as the door of the restaurant opened. In came a tall, young woman. She wore a grey, rollneck sweater over a black, calf-length skirt which made her body look slim and lithe. Covering her head was a Hermès scarf, tied the French way: two corners of the triangle crossed under the chin and brought back to a knot over the third corner at the nape. The pale face framed by the scarf, the narrow nose and heart-shaped chin gave her a classy air, not unlike a titled lady wearing a cowl in a medieval portrait. The calm and very blue eyes scanned the room, which was too rustic for her refined appearance. At the sight of Davina, a smile spread; it seemed to lighten up the restaurant. The woman now walking towards the small table was called Colette Fontaine, a French name for, while her mother was British, her father was French.

'I'm late.' Colette grabbed the chair next to Davina and sat down.

'You're always late.' Davina looked sideways at Colette.

'Not always. Remember at the college summer ball: I was there so early, Jack Wilson invited me to do the opening dance with him.'

'You get it wrong every time. First, his name was Watson and, second, he only whirled you across the decking, because you were standing in front of the floodlights.'

'Yeah, you're probably right,' Colette said with ease before focusing on her friend. 'How are you, Dav? You look unchanged.'

'So do you. How long has it been?'

'About three years. I was in Malaysia teaching French at a French government institute for the last two, can you believe that? Now, I've moved back in with Mum in Highgate until I get a new assignment.'

'I guess thirty is looming for both of us then.' Davina sipped from her glass.

'Come on, we're not there yet. Why are you drinking water?'

'I'll tell you in a minute.' Davina screwed the top back onto the San Pellegrino. 'The last time we met, I think it was in St James's Park, summer, sitting on the grass—'

'Yes, you were just beginning your PhD on plant science. What became of that?'

'I did it; it took time, especially since I chose Central Asian flora to make sure my thesis would stand out. I handed it in two months ago and am still waiting to defend it.'

'Well done, Dav. So, why did you insist on meeting today?'

'Because!'

Colette fixed her eyes on her friend's, and brought in her head in a slaloming move until they were face-to-face – the way she had always wheedled information from Davina.

A broad grin made Davina look younger. 'That is not going to work any longer.'

'Yes, it is.'

'Someone round-robin'd that you were back from Malaysia, but you didn't call: no e-mail, nothing. Not even Jack Watson, who has already made partner in his law firm, had news. I wanted to see you again, for old times' sake, a reunion, just the two of us. Lots to talk about.'

'A reunion it is,' Colette decided.

'What my PhD made me do is so amazing, I had to tell you in person.'

'I'm listening.'

'A year ago, I got back from Afghanistan. I was there for four months researching pre-desert plants.'

Colette frowned. 'There is a war going on in Afghanistan. Aren't the Russians still there?'

'They had already left, but there was turmoil afterwards.'

'Bombing, fighting. Women not safe from their own kind.'

'They say the West did not put enough effort into protecting the Afghan nation, and the damage caused by the Russians is still everywhere, of course. Apart from the scars of the civil war before the new regime took over.'

'I wouldn't have had the courage to forage amongst plants under those circumstances.'

The waiter in a large, white apron came up to their table, close enough to press his thighs against the table edge, just below the place where a well-brought-up girl should not look.

'This is Tony.' Davina introduced him.

'You,' Tony pointed at Davina, 'come here from time to time. I remember because you look Italian.'

After short and meaningful glances at each other, Davina whispered to Colette, 'Don't tell him I dye my hair.'

The women ordered carbonara. What did they want to drink? Tony was rocking his body slightly forward and back. The canvas apron bulged and slackened.

'Don't show you're looking,' Davina whispered behind the hand over her mouth.

'Don't show you're thinking about it.' The women giggled. Tony stepped away from the table. 'What about a glass of Chianti?' suggested Colette.

'I can't,' whined Davina.

Tony's solid-looking mother, Maria, came to the rescue. 'A little bit of wine is good for two beautiful, young women, especially today.'

'Why today?' asked Colette.

Maria glared at Tony. 'What day is today?'

'Thursday, 23 October, Mamma.'

'Such beautiful signorinas.' Hands came out as if to clasp Davina's face between them.

'She means me,' Colette said. 'Not you.'

'She means Tony, her son.'

'He is probably still breastfeeding. I had this friend—'

'I bring the ladies some bread and olive sauce. The best olives from Ragusa, where I come from, green and plump, only small stones inside.' Maria walked away to talk to people at another table.

'It saves money not having to go to Sicily, I suppose,' said Colette and put her elbows on the table, the heels of her hands supporting her chin. 'Back to Kabul. Please tell me more.'

Davina lit up. 'I so wish I were able to describe it with the right words the way you probably could, having done English and French Lit.' Descriptions then came in a rush. 'It is an amazing city. There's like a crown of mountains around it, some high ones. Not like the Alps, called majestic because of their aggressive, sheer rock formation. The Afghan mountains are more like obstructions in a rather monotonous landscape of infertile earth mixed with sand. People can hide in them; animals seek shelter in the mountain caves. The city of Kabul used to be called a city of gardens. That's what caught my interest in the first place. Afghans move about their business at a slower pace than ours. And yet it is not the way we think of laid-back Mediterranean cultures. The Afghans move about as if they did not fear time the way we all do. Many smile but not at each other, sort of at their destiny with which they are in harmony.' Davina needed to take a breath. 'And the sky over the city. It is wide and changes mood and colour continuously. In the evening, birds fly west into the sunset, and the firmament at night is fantastic.'

'What about the rights of women? How safe were you, walking around looking for interesting plants?'

'Dogs and women are beaten sometimes. It's just what happens. Men are born superior to women. That, too, is just what it is.'

'It is unacceptable, no matter how much they accept it. Or you for that matter.'

'It does not feel unacceptable when you are there. In the seventies, lots of hippies travelled to Afghanistan because of the free-spirit atmosphere.'

'Having listened to you,' said Colette, 'I now desperately want to go to Kabul.'

'You are a globe-trotting civil servant of the French Government. What's holding you back?'

'You're right, it is time to gird my loins. A twenty-seven-year-old should not live with her mother any longer. All I do at Mum's is avoid getting suckered into playing bridge and deny that I am a novella writer.'

'You, a writer. How come?'

'While in Malaysia, I wrote a journal of what happened during the day and how I felt about it. There was nothing else to do after teaching and correcting papers. Mum thought I should show it to someone she knew in publishing. After that, she pushed for it to be edited. She went as far as paying for the publishing of it. I am still mortified. Nobody bought it.'

'Hey, you are full of surprises. I must read this novella. What is it called?'

'*The Orphan Boy from the Kampong.*'

'Can you get me one?'

'There are two boxes of them still in the loft.'

'See what you can do with words.'

Two large plates with deep dells arrived. They were heaped with spaghettini snaking around bits of garlic, chopped bacon and creamed eggs. Elbows came off the table.

'Enjoy,' exclaimed Tony, with a falsetto ring.

'How am I going to manage all that?' Colette contemplated the carbonara with badly hidden eagerness.

'Start at one end of a cooked worm and the rest will follow.'

'Pepper.' Tony had returned, holding a tall wooden pepper mill. They both nodded. Tony's clumsy way of flirting was part of the charm of the place, especially when he started to grind, his masculine hand cupping the bulbous top of the mill. He felt their mocking, grabbed the mill by its midriff and stalked off.

'Do you see why I like coming here?' asked Davina.

'Without your boyfriend. Are you still with what's-his-name?'

'Simon, my ginger-haired companion. We are now flat-sharing in West Hampstead. But it's not what you think.'

'What do you think I am thinking?'

'It was just a cost-saving move. We still have a lot to work out between us.'

'I can't comment because I wouldn't know.'

'Still no boyfriend, then?'

Colette blushed, pressed her lips together and shook her head.

'Your hair problem,' Davina remembered. 'Better no man than the wrong one. That brings me to why we are drinking water today and not wine. I might be preggers.'

'Might?'

'No period for two months, and my boobs feel like bursting. Besides, I threw up yesterday morning, although that could have been the Szechuan Simon and I had the night before in the Golden Lotus.'

'Buy one of those pregnancy test sticks.'

'I've got one but don't dare use it. I am scared to find out. I haven't told Simon. He's talking about skiing at Christmas.'

'Would you like to be pregnant?'

Very slowly, Davina shook her head. 'It would be a disaster. No, it would be a monumental disaster. We are not ready for this, probably never will be. Simon can only think about get-rich-quick schemes. These modern start-ups obsess him.'

'Why don't you find out whether you have or don't have the problem of a pregnancy?'

'Would you help me?'

'Now I understand why it was so important we had lunch today.'

'I brought the stick with me.'

'Do they have loos in this place?'

'Basic,' said Davina.

And basic it revealed itself to be: a wooden latticed door, a pull cord for light, a mottled sink with candle wax-coloured soap moulded around a fixed metal stick. Two steps led down into a tiny space into which was wedged a low toilet.

'You hold the stick and I pee on it.'

'We won't both fit in there. I will try to squeeze round.'

The latticed door opened. Maria said, 'It is a toilet for one person at a time, you understand.'

'We'll be out in a jiffy,' tweeted Davina, while Colette just stood there grinning.

The door closed. Maria was gone.

'Here, the stick. I'd better stand astride over the loo. I'll tell you when I start piddling. You've got to be ready.'

'Don't pee on my hand.'

'Just make sure some of it gets onto the red strip on the stick.'

The door opened again. 'It is not good what you are doing in my restaurant. One person using the toilet. Normal good people. Not two, doing things which are wrong. You have to leave.'

'We can't leave. She needs to pee on my stick.'

'Holy Mother and all the saints, not perversion. What have I done to deserve this?'

As she waited for the colouring on the stick to show,

Davina's fingers were clamped onto Colette's arm. A single pale blue line appeared. Not pregnant.

Davina started to weep.

They emerged into the passageway. Tony shouted, '*Scusi*' and squeezed past, holding a tray high on his palm.

'This is such a relief.' Davina wept harder. 'But now I feel so sad and empty.' She blew her nose into a paper napkin, snatched from a table on the way to theirs.

Under the pitchfork, they sat down again.

'Sorry about the emotional me,' Davina apologised. 'Would you have liked to find out a baby had started to grow inside you?'

Colette did not hesitate. 'Not without a father for the child. Besides, there will never be a question of me being pregnant. Don't get me wrong: I enjoyed university life and particularly the teaching in Kuala Lumpur. The students were so eager to learn a new language, which will enrich their lives.'

'Yes, I understand.'

'Mum has lived alone since my father left and went back to France, fourteen years ago. She is a much happier person.' Colette drained the last of the San Pellegrino. 'And, I have you as my best friend.'

'One who pees on your hand.'

'One who gets the restaurant owner to call the police to arrest us for indecent behaviour!'

'Maria is Sicilian. She is used to such things.'

And right Davina was.

'Desserts.' Maria came over to try and tempt them.

'Not today. Please bring the bill. We both have important jobs to go back to.'

Outside the restaurant, Davina challenged Colette, 'What important jobs?'

'I, for one, have to go to the French Embassy and put my name down for a teaching job in Kabul.'

'Are you really going to do that?'

'Wild horses couldn't stop me.'

'And I...' Davina tapped her chest. '... have had enough plant studying and academic papers. Not far from here is a florists called Blooms4You and I intend to work for them.'

'With your hands – tying bouquets, creating baskets, getting mud under your fingernails?'

'Getting mushrooms on my feet standing in dirty water for hours on end.'

'Good for you.'

'I've got to do a floristry course first and will probably apply to several flower companies, perhaps even the flower shop in Harrods. But I would prefer to join one of these new online companies, like the one not far from here.' She pointed in a westerly direction.

'Because it is close to *Little Sicily* and sexy Tony.'

'Of course.'

At the Underground entrance, they said goodbye.

'You be good.' Colette tapped Davina's shoulder.

'Don't do anything I wouldn't,' came back, as it automatically did.

They became separated by the mass of people at the station.

'Let me know if you get Kabul,' Davina shouted.

Colette stopped and turned back. 'Let me know if you get that blooming job.'

Kabul, January 1998

The cold mist above the city which nestles against the Hindu Kush mountain range was tinted in the pale grey of a new day. Down in the Sevom Akrab Road, one of the main avenues of Kabul, those plane trees which had survived the brutal history of the city stood proud, coated in the silver sheen of frost.

On closer inspection, much damage had been done to the city: mortar shells had set houses on fire; a tank barrel had broken off the corner of an old house causing the upper floors to collapse; part of a masonry balcony had been blown away, and so many windows were still without glass. Cardboard and jute sacking protected the rooms from the worst of the elements. There was scaffolding. Repair work was progressing slowly; money was lacking. It was nine years since the Soviet Union forces retreated, giving way to nine years of civil war and power struggles.

Colette yawned and shivered. She had slept badly because of the *muezzin* calling to the faithful from a nearby mosque, because the radiator had been switched off during the night by a timer somewhere in the building, and, mostly likely, because of the unfamiliarity of it all. She sat up in bed. Her unzipped suitcase, from which she had dug out her pyjamas and washbag last night, lay still open on the floor.

Before departing England the previous day, she shouldn't have left things with her mother the way she had. There was no medical cure for *alopecia totalis*. Neither did the holistic remedies, hot stones or soothsaying, which mother insisted on, make any difference. Perhaps Audrey felt guilty for having given birth to a baby which, as a small child, lost every hair on its body. Tension and misunderstandings flared up between mother and daughter over this awfulness. In the end, it was up to Colette to find the strength to step over it, and to work and function like any normal woman.

And that normal woman was now here in Kabul to start a job as French language teacher for two terms in the French Institute. *France* was another sensitivity between mother and daughter. Colette's father, a Frenchman from the Loire valley who left them when Colette was thirteen, had convinced his ex-wife that their daughter should pursue her secondary education in a French boarding school and take the baccalaureate. Audrey never managed to learn the language and felt ill at ease with the often passionate character traits of her French husband, some of which Colette had inherited. If she were honest with herself, Audrey would probably have to admit that she felt challenged by both of them.

Foreign teaching postings resembled long-term adventures. Adventures included discomfort of various styles. Like the bed beneath Colette. The musty smell of the pillow, which she had inhaled through the night, brought back school biology, and the tadpoles which had decomposed in a tank of murky water – despite the science teacher having told the class that growing frogs was easy.

The room in which Colette found herself was on the fourth floor of a small square apartment block on a side alley which didn't even have a name – a narrow and dark habitat. Her predecessor, in an attempt to counteract the gloom, had fixed a poster of Chagall's *Les Amoureux aux Marguerites* to the wall. The couple in the embrace floated in the air. Beneath them, a vase of yellow and white marguerites stood on a table covered in red and white gingham.

There was an iron bedframe with its orphanage-style, thin mattress pushed against an old-fashioned radiator, no bedside table but a small table with a backless wooden stool under the window giving onto the sunless street. The room also contained a clothes rail on casters and a drum-shaped ceiling lamp without a bulb. There was nothing else in the room except a black abaya hanging tilted on a wire hanger hooked over the clothes rail. The teacher Colette was replacing had shed that black skin and flown. It would be wrong to interpret this as sinister. The lack of a replacement bulb and the need to shuffle about in candle-lit darkness were practical issues. Luckily, the lodging also offered a living room and bathroom with shower, the water not just wetting her but also the toilet seat because there was no shower curtain. Teeth had to be brushed at the kitchen sink.

Best of all, the living room had a balcony facing south-west. Balconies are normally attached as an excrescence to the building, but this one took space from the room. Its knee-high, concrete rim held wrought-iron stanchions about five inches apart supporting a wider metal rim. In a corner of the balcony stood a flowerpot the size of a washing-up bowl with a plant like a begonia. Its green leaves were discoloured by frost. Colette carried the pot through the glass door into the living room. She liked flowers and hoped to succeed in making this one bloom for her.

★

Her first day at work was a Saturday, the start of the week in Islamic Afghanistan, as Thursdays and Fridays were their holy days. Eventually ready, Colette left the flat, locking the door behind her. Down four floors she found herself in the short, narrow, nameless alley. Perhaps its position had spared the house damage, apart from a glass triangle missing in the upper panel of the entrance door. A notice written in Arabic letters was pinned to the door frame. She could not read it. Perhaps it said in Pashto, the official language of Afghanistan, 'Burglars welcome. Reach in through the hole and unlock the door from the inside.'

Colette, in her wide-collared, woollen coat, ankle-high booties and knitted gloves, wore a dark-blue hijab, one of several she owned from Malaysia – a headscarf so long that it wraps around the neck and falls down over the shoulders. She never showed her bald head to anyone. On the wider street, the one she could look down into from her balcony, there was a central division possibly meant for foliage during peacetime, but now there was nothing but rubble, dirt and discarded rubbish, even though it was in the Rika Khana district. Kabul was divided into districts, not unlike other large cities. Paris has arrondissements, Manhattan blocks. Colette was interested in cities, the people living in those cities, their cultures, their languages – just people. Perhaps the failed frog experiment had put her off science.

She proceeded along the street, enjoying the freedom of being an onlooker, a voyager through new territory, a new culture with a different faith. Here and there, she stopped to peer into side streets, shamelessly into house openings. A man with an elaborately wound beige turban passed her and slowed. He turned suddenly back to her, and she was alarmed by the intensity of his look and the frightening words which seemed to crackle deep in his throat. She lowered her eyes to the pavement and kept walking. When she crossed a road, a quick glance to the side revealed a little square with a fountain in its middle surrounded by trees under which market stalls were set up. She had to stop and enjoy the charm of it. One stall in front of which a queue had formed was selling naan bread made of wheat flour and nigella seeds. From the tent rim hung green-striped plastic bags containing what looked like cakes. Perhaps they were a Kabul speciality. She would come here to buy food, she thought, and jumped out of the way of a workman chucking soapsuds from a pail.

And then a bus passed her. Why should Kabul not have a bus service? Somehow, she had thought of this city as an emotionally tinted film set.

Following her street map, Colette turned left. More people were about, mostly men walking fast, faster than her. They wore turbans roughly woven in muted colours, wide shawls over their shoulders rather than coats, and thick tunic shirts. Further along, a black huddled female figure could be seen navigating the pavement, her shapeless burqa swaying.

Colette, her eyes drawn up to swallows flying in the morning sky, stubbed her toe against a segment of fresco fallen onto the pavement. It had carvings of flowers on it – jasmine flowers. She looked up to see where it could have come from. There was a building wrapped in scaffolding and netting – obviously a building of importance. Jasmine, with its endearing little white petals and Tudor-style bow-shaped leaves.

Colette bent to rub her bruised toe. To do this, she had to lift the seam of the floor-length blue skirt. It was one of the garments she had bought especially for this assignment. A shrill whistle felt like a spike in her brain. A black-turbaned Talib appeared from nowhere. Colette let go of her skirt and gave him a rueful smile. He reacted by slapping his right hand against his left shoulder to unhook his rifle. She straightened up and slowly lifted her arms in surrender. The barrel was lowered in her direction. She muttered, 'For God's sake.' He pulled the trigger. The gun leapt. A dry explosive noise. The fresco with the jasmine lay in fragments. It had just been a warning shot.

Shaking with fright, Colette wiped dust out of her eye with the corner of her hijab. She could not blame anyone but herself for being here in this battered, unhappy country.

Her previous *madness,* according to her mother, had been to teach in Malaysia, a predominantly Muslim country. She had learned a lot from her students about the ways of their religion. When the post in Kabul had become available, there was a close run between Jacques finishing a posting in Ecuador and her. Even though female, her experience with Muslim students had got her the job in Afghanistan. Davina had been right; there was something about the way one could fantasise about Afghanistan, some romantic conception no doubt misplaced which one was not able to explain to oneself. After eight months here, she would understand her feelings for the country, surely.

Walking on, she came to a sizable roundabout. She recognised the building on the other side from pictures. It was the French Institute and it seemed to have been spared damage as if it had merited it, so proud it stood, yet vulnerable and beautiful, with wooden shutters and a wood-carved balcony wrapped around the first floor. Colette came to a stop as if her excitement interfered with moving her legs. A challenging new job awaited her right over there. Was she up to it? Helpfully, the Muslim faith came her way by insisting she covered her head. Was she as courageous as she made herself out to be? In short, was she a good enough teacher?

A man flagged down a taxi but declined to get in. He preferred to haggle over the fare, while the driver had to lean at an uncomfortable angle over the passenger seat. Colette perceived it as a selfish man who could afford a taxi ride torturing his inferior.

At an open door to an alley between two buildings, a

hungry cat was begging, but the woman in the opening was deterring the animal by flapping a towel at it. Colette walked away from the sight and gave a gasp of surprise. A few more steps and she would have fallen into a large hole in the ground. This made her decide to cross the roundabout to get to the French Institute, but there were no pedestrian markings and no other person could be seen walking across the space. If she dared, she would stand out. The rifle shot had made her jumpy. The pain in the toe flared up.

What a foolish thing to accept a teaching post in such dangerous surroundings. Just because Davina had loved it here…

Her mother's worries had been brushed away by Colette's reassurance: 'They will look after me.' And indeed, the instruction letter from the French Embassy prior to her start today had contained an addendum of rules which made it way down the page and even onto the next. *You must arrive at least half an hour before the start of the 9 o'clock lesson. After the last, at 2 o'clock, you must tidy the classroom and return the books to the secretary. You are not allowed to use the telephone in reception. Important calls may be accepted by the receptionist who will take messages. You are forbidden to become personally involved with students. You are forbidden to bring up religious subjects in class. You may not leave Kabul, nor adventure anywhere further than the shortest route to and from your flat provided by the Institute. You may not give lessons outside the Institute and are forbidden to give private lessons anywhere at any time. The cost of electricity in your flat and any photocopies above the number of thirty a day will be deducted from your salary paid in Euros and agreed upon in the contract with the Cultural Attaché of the French Embassy in Kabul.*

She had signed the contract. She was a French civil servant once again. How likely for her would be a romantic involvement with one of the students?

With fast steps, she started walking the periphery of the roundabout. It was by now a quarter past eight. Traffic had intensified. Motorcycles clattered by on cheap petrol. Groups of cyclists passed, bells ringing, with a female figure in full burqa amongst them. The ample black cloth spread and tightened as she pedalled. Colette did not smile. It could be misinterpreted by the soldier who had suddenly stepped forward from the corner of the French Institute. Of course, the Institute was guarded. Of course, she was being watched.

It was more than half an hour before her first lesson. The blue hijab felt securely tight around her head. The guard, doing his job as commanded, read with concentration the identification he had ordered her to produce, a text in French he almost certainly did not understand. The crest of the French government did the job, for he gave her back the contract letter and mimed for her to walk into the building. The tip of the rifle showing over his shoulder was at a tilt.

She pushed open the wooden door.

The moment Colette found herself inside the historic building, she felt as if the house was part of her heritage. Standing in foreign territory, it had been built with European craftmanship and for a higher purpose – the promotion of French culture. The entrance hall was a big space between two stone staircases. It was rather dark, as no lights had yet been turned on. Despite this, there was a glitter in the stone tiles on the floor. Through glass double doors, at the very back under the stairs, she saw the grey light of winter morning, the outlines of skeletal plants.

Just as she bent to touch the gold glitter in a tile, a woman in her early forties appeared from a side door. In her pink face, murky green eyes were magnified behind oversized spectacles, a style which had been fashionable in Europe a few years earlier. Her calf-length skirt sat tight; Colette could make out the edges of her pelvic bones. This severity was counterbalanced by a lilac blouse of polyester, the two ribbons at the collar knotted into a low floppy bow, revealing a dry-skinned neck.

'A splendid house, isn't it? Built more than a hundred years ago in this old part of town. But then our country could afford the best. Now, it costs a fortune to maintain.' She chatted on. 'I do the accounts.' She took breath. 'My name is Laura Lambert.'

'You are also the receptionist,' said Colette. 'The keeper of the telephone.'

'There are rules here. New, you'll have to learn them. The teacher you are replacing never got the hang of them.' Laura dry-coughed several times and then in a cheery voice, 'I'll show you the outside-in. That's what the courtyard garden would be called in Pashto. You speak any of it?'

'I didn't think that was a requirement,' said Colette.

'It isn't. The students' English is surprisingly good.

Corruption from America and England manages to trickle in. I hope your English is adequate.'

'My mother is English. My father French. I am bilingual.'

'That will come in handy for you.'

'May I ask you for a great favour?' Colette made a shy, pleading face. 'Would you let me make two phone calls?' Seeing Laura's reaction, she tried harder. 'My mother, being anxious, needs to know that I made it here safely.'

'Three minutes, no more. What's the second call about?'

'Equally important. A friend. Practically my sister. I promised to let her know.'

'I have to assume that she also suffers from anxiety.'

'She does.'

'Sorry, but the answer is no. I can give you paper and an envelope.'

Bitch, Colette did not say out loud. She expected Laura to take her into her office and the telephone to call Mum, but this did not happen. Instead, Laura set off towards the outside-in. Reluctantly Colette followed, daring to remind her of the phone call.

'The international telephone lines often don't work. You'll have to write.'

'That'll take two weeks at least to get there.'

'Months. Most international flights are cancelled these days.'

The two women were now in an inner courtyard garden about the size of half a tennis court. It was a wintry scene, with frosted earth and a stone slab bench. Some evergreen bushes were struggling to survive, more stems than leaves. A bush from which emanated a shy, sweet scent was the only plant flowering. Colette cupped some of the flowers and bent her nose to them.

'It blooms because the rooms around it offer heat.'

'Like a hothouse,' said Colette.

'Careful. The pollen will get on your clothes. That bush reeks. A gardener is supposed to come and dig it out before it gets more enthusiastic in spring.'

'No!' escaped Colette, louder than she had meant to. 'It's the best thing I've smelled since I got here. Please. Please, don't destroy it.'

'All right. But you look after it. The temperature will stay sub-zero for months and then we don't have rain in the summer.'

'I will have to find out more about it.'

'Look, all I asked you to do is water it.'

'In Malaysia, I learned a lot about orchids. Learning about the vegetation in a country is part of integrating with it.'

Laura gave one of her nervous coughs. 'Your eagerness is reprehensible or admirable. But then you are new here. Novelty is one of life's treats.'

'Please show me the classroom.'

The women went back into the house and up the stairs.

'We have two rooms; one is used to store stuff and the photocopier.'

'The other?'

Laura's pale, puffy hand lingered on the brass handle before she pushed.

'In this room, I used to teach. I came on a two-year

contract. All the way from the Limousin I came, just as the Soviets were withdrawing. But then came the real trouble and the Institute closed, and I sat here twiddling my thumbs. Endless trouble. A mortar bomb landed right across the roundabout. It killed three. There is still a deep hole in the ground.'

'I saw it. Why didn't you go home at the end of your contract?'

'Home is my parent's – Papa fancying himself enough to flirt with every woman in the village, Maman with a fag in her mouth even when she takes a shower. I stayed put. Eventually, some normality returned and the shops in Chicken Street had some things to buy. Imagine.' Laura moved her head closer to Colette's. 'Imagine,' she repeated and her green eyes widened. 'Women were allowed to come here to learn French.'

The classroom which Laura had revealed was of a generous size. There was some natural light from the two windows, but it was limited by one of the shutters being closed.

'It's ancient carpentry and stuck.' Laura sighed. 'A carpenter was supposed to come, but two days ago he was found shot in his workshop. Recently we've had a wave of cleaning out former rebels in the city – *rebel* in his case because he had helped us westerners. He wasn't the only one sacrificed to the new Taliban regime.'

The ceiling light which would illuminate the classroom consisted of two neon strips. The desks were like rough kitchen tables, pushed end-to-end in three rows of three. Each table had two wooden chairs facing the front – room for eighteen students.

On the wall next to the door was fixed a large old-fashioned blackboard in a wooden frame, as if it were a picture of a blackout. From a string to its side hung a sponge, so dry it resembled a crisp wasps' nest.

'Does the ceiling light work?'

'It is not nine yet and the class has not started. I am in charge of the electricity bill.'

Colette went into the dimly lit room, feeling Laura's judgemental eyes on her back. Laura was not just the telephone-keeper; she was the Doberman defending its territory. The times the floor had rocked and tiles flew must have had an impact on her.

Colette trailed her finger along the surface of the little square table right next to the blackboard. It had one chair pushed against it, facing the class – the teacher's. The only objects on her desk were a plastic screw-top lid with a few stubs of white chalk, and a Coca-Cola bottle filled with water to moisten the sponge.

In the corner, she noticed one concession to modernity: a slide projector on an elevated stand, the plug hanging at the end of a long cable.

Colette turned back to Laura. 'Nice,' she said. 'It is a traditional schoolroom. The projector will be helpful.'

'The slides get stuck every time one uses it. The five-year guarantee has run out. What can I say, except that you won't last? Since I stopped teaching, seven years ago, six teachers have come and gone. You're the seventh. These grown men are difficult to handle. Right after potty-training, they are enrolled in boot camp, survival exercises, shooting practice, endurance gymnastics, I don't know. The syllabus and teaching aids in your table drawer are not exactly targeted at such dark-skinned, brutal and very hairy men.'

'Hair, or lack of, should never be an issue,' Colette said forcefully. 'Some people have no hair at all.'

Laura started with one of her little dry coughs, while Colette closed them into the room by shutting the door. She checked the time on the clock against the wall. 'As we are going to work together for some months, I think I should show you.' Colette pulled the blue scarf off her head.

'Oh my goodness gracious me. You've given me a fright. It looks... I have never seen anything like... It is so pink, so bald.'

Colette wound the scarf back over her head. 'It is called *alopecia totalis*, an unexplained condition which I developed as a small child. The capillaries are destroyed everywhere in the body.'

'Poor you.'

'I paint my eyebrows where they should be and glue lashes onto the rim of my eyelids.'

'I noticed them. Long and shiny.'

'Synthetic.'

'Poor you.'

'Can we stop this conversation? I don't want anyone to know. Do you understand? Nobody.'

'I promise.' Laura pushed Colette gently out of her way and left in a hurry. Her nervous cough could be heard down the stairs.

'Poor me,' said Colette, left alone. It was important to befriend Laura for many reasons. So many teachers had come and given up.

Laura reappeared, more composed. 'Just to tell you that I will keep your secret. But why don't you wear a wig?'

'In this Islamic country, I have to cover my head at all times, so I don't need one. Wigs are itchy and tricky to wash. I have two of them: one short, one shoulder-length. Both blond.'

'I see.'

Laura still only shot Colette furtive glances. Colette tightened the scarf, which calmed Laura enough to start gabbling. 'You must have been born with blond hair. Your beautiful large eyes are so amazingly blue.' Laura gave up trying to make amends for her dismay. She changed tone of voice. 'I have to warn you about your students who will shortly arrive. Currently, there are twelve enrolled. They are between the ages of about twenty-five and thirty. They are trained to be strong and dangerous. The last teacher was punched in the face by one of them and her black eye got worse as the days passed. And we are halfway through Ramadan, so they will be hungry and even meaner. Good luck to you.'

After the sarcastic *luck*, Laura was gone, back down to reception. Colette felt abandoned. Imminently, she would be faced by adult Muslim students. Should she stand near the door? Perhaps that would look too eager. Remaining seated at her desk, head down, she could read the names on the roster left for her in the drawer. Perhaps too detached. She decided to stand at the blackboard, a chalk in her hand. That would convey *teaching*. She wrote *Samedi, dix janvier* as the first two students arrived.

'*Entrez*,' she invited them, the dry sponge curled

in her hand. Neither of the young men returned her greeting. They sought the table at the very back, stood there and embarked on a conversation rather loudly. Was it one of them who had punched the teacher?

The next to arrive was short and stocky. The hair on his head and around his pink lips resembled the fur of a black poodle: tight curls with a greasy sheen to them. The scarf wound around his thick neck could well also serve as his turban. He gave his name as Mukhtar. With jerky head movements, he looked around the classroom as if danger might lurk in the corners.

She heard the laughter of men in the corridor. A group of four burst into the room and totally ignored her presence. The door clacked shut behind them. Their complexion was not dark as Laura had said; it was the abundant facial hair which shaded their faces.

She wrote her name on the board to establish her presence. A next student arrived; he was in the same age group as the others but his personal presentation was messy. 'Edris,' he announced himself. His straggly hair was too long and the untrimmed beard had grown wild. Small eyes darted about in a coarse and surly face. She did not like the look of Edris. She noticed on his forearm, below the rolled-up sweater sleeve, the crisscrossing of white scar tissue. Her *bonjour* came out only as a whisper. He grimaced and changed place three times without replacing the chairs before he was satisfied, took out a gadget on which he moved around squares, and folded into himself. Would she dare give him back his work with red corrections?

She sprinkled water on the sponge and managed to

wipe out the date. She had to keep to the lessons planned in the curriculum and not branch out into her own ideas. It had been the same in Kuala Lumpur. These students had to pass the proficiency exam at the end of the school year in August. Four students were missing and, on the clock at the wall, the big hand was jerkily edging closer to nine o'clock.

Laura's head appeared at the door. The women exchanged glances, before Laura ran across to Colette, hands raised as if she feared being shot. She whispered, 'Ahasam and his brother, Mutil, will not attend today.' A pause, and her head nodded gravely. 'Ali has arrived fully armed. He is downstairs. He said he had no time to change. He is one of the scary ones.' She used the word in French *terrifiant*.

'Send him up,' Colette said. 'He will realise that he can't write with his rifle, when I give them the written task.'

'It's not the rifle. That, I was able to convince him to leave at reception. It is that ugly bullet belt and the two dangly things which, to me, look like hand grenades.'

Before Laura had finished speaking, Ali, the terrifying man, came into the classroom.

'I'm off.' Laura fled, slightly colliding with Ali and emitting a high-pitched squeak.

Yes, on Ali's leather belt was a row of full bullet pockets. There were also fastenings for two hand grenades of ribbed metal with ring-pulls, which hung alongside his khaki trousers. From a string around his neck dangled what looked like a magnifying device, probably a telescopic sight for a sniper. His eyes measured Colette from head to toe and, in a tick, right back up again.

'Give me your name and please choose a seat,' she said as if everything were normal. Wrestling a hand grenade away from a trained soldier was a bad idea. For him, of course, to be armed was normal. Born into nothing but army training, conflict, and death and destruction. Why on earth did he want to learn French? She had to ask him that. He might be here under cover to blow up the French Institute. Oh God, maybe Mum was right. It was too dangerous. Even his name spelled danger: Ali Haterami.

In Malaysia, her male students of a similar age had been shorter and softer. They wore pillbox-shaped hats, neatly embroidered. They wrote in their exercise books with hesitant gentleness. Colette had guided them through the maze of French grammar and rewarded them with French poetry, which may have meant no more to them than tepidly dripping rain, but they were polite and smiled often. When she left, they had given her a gift: the Koran translated into French. Every section started 'In the name of Allah, the compassionate, the merciful'.

Kabul teaching was obviously different. By now, nine students were in place, two would not be attending. It was one minute past nine. And number twelve, Abdul Hannan, without a tick next to his name, had not yet arrived. Perhaps he had given up on French.

Colette distributed photocopied sheets of pictures of a French farm, cows in the field and sheep, scattered poultry, the traditional French woman hanging up laundry, while – in some perspective-obeying distance

– the farmer rode on a tractor. In the foreground was a well-fed, pink French pig.

Colette began. 'The lesson today is about *La Ferme*. You must know the word: the farm. And I can't tell you how irritating it is to know that such farms do not exist in Afghanistan but that you have to learn it anyway, according to the syllabus. While, on one hand, teaching you French has to include the French way of life, on the other, one must ask how helpful it will be for you to learn about things which will probably never be part of your life.'

The men watched her agitation with detachment.

'The French Institute is not just about language. It is a facility for communicating culture.' She thought, *A safe plank over a hole in the ground*. 'The French, as you were probably told, came to Afghanistan more than a hundred years ago, and your king visited Paris in 1928. Maybe we will talk about this during another lesson.'

The last student, number twelve, had obviously arrived in silence behind her back. It was the reaction of the students at their tables which told her. She turned round. Thirtyish, he was taller than her. There was an athletic hardness about his body which showed in his chiselled face – a face which looked exposed, almost vulnerable as, unlike his colleagues, he was clean-shaven. This exceptionally handsome young man said, *'Bonjour, Professeur,'* he checked the blackboard, *'Mademoiselle Fontaine.'* He scanned the students. *'Bonjour, mes amis.'*

'Well, bonjour to you, Abdul Hannan.' She dared go on, 'As Abdul means *serving Allah*, which is a given, in class we will just call you Hannan.'

'I am sorry I am late,' he excused himself.

As part of the lesson, she translated. *'Je m'excuse d'être en retard.'*

He threaded himself between the tables, making the round, before pulling out the chair right in front of the teacher's table. Colette sat down and checked the scarf on her head. His smile directed at her was cheeky, but not in any way offensive. His eyes appeared to be black and the lashes around them so dark that it could have been make-up. Omar Sharif wore make-up to emphasise the effect of his smoky eyes.

Hannan laced his fingers into each other and stretched his arms towards her, forcing the hands out. She heard the cracking of his joints and dared look into the bold eyes. There was a steady and encouraging response.

'In France, you called your ruler just Gaulle?' he asked.

At first she did not understand his question. 'Ah, you mean General de Gaulle. Would you prefer to be called Abdul Hannan, then?'

His fleeting criticism of her was gone, almost as soon as she had interpreted it.

The class was now late to start. Mukhtar sat at the table, his face between his dirty hands as if he was furious at the situation he found himself in, while Edris next to him was fidgeting on his gadget. The two at the back had not finished with their argument. Ali had taken some bullets out of his belt; they rolled on the desk like metal suppositories. The student directly in front of him had turned his chair round to admire them.

'Put those bullets back into your belt and come to the blackboard.'

Ali smirked. Women did not talk to him like that.

Colette rose from her chair. '*La Ferme*,' she almost shouted it and closed the folder with the syllabus on the table in front of her. 'Let's just put that *Ferme* to the side for the moment and start at the foundation of the wonderful world of French verbs: *Avoir* and *Etre* – to have and to be.'

'Some people have to possess things, while others are happy with their thoughts.'

'Hannan, we are not discussing philosophy. We are learning how to conjugate these verbs. Who can give me *to be* in the past tense?'

Nobody could.

'That's what I thought.' They were behind schedule in learning. 'Now, let us take this farm setting and make sentences related to the picture using the present, the future and the past of *Avoir* and *Etre*.'

At the back, the two men did not comply and just ignored what was going on around them. Someone was obviously forcing them to learn French.

'Anyone? In that case, you to the blackboard,' she said to Ali. 'Listen to the verbs you hear in the sentences your classmates are going to say and then write them on the board.' Colette reached into the jar top. He caught the chalk even though she had thrown it badly.

She was aware that she was treating trained killers like children. But then, learning a new language regressed anyone to early childhood, to one's first words.

Mukhtar, to her surprise, raised his hand. She gave

him an encouraging smile. 'The French pig is dirty. We have weapons to kill it.'

She was taken aback. They did not eat pork. Who put together this teaching material? 'Change of plan.' In a brisk voice she asked, 'How many verbs ending in *er* have you learned? Do you know the verb *parler*? No. How about *penser*, *tapper*? *Je tappe la table. Nous tappons*.' Colette patted the tabletop several times. They imitated this. 'A simple verb ending with *er*. Conjugate, please.'

All they did was bash the tabletops, chanting, '*Tapper, tapper*.'

It had been a mistake. She stood and lifted her chair up high enough to show the seat. '*La chaise*.' She turned to Ali. 'Write *la chaise* on the board underneath where you have written *la table* with an *a* rather than an *o*.'

They switched to '*Je tappe la chaise*' and the noise increased as they hit their tables with their chairs, fury growing. The door opened.

'What in GGG... Gordon's name is that racket? Less than ten minutes' teaching and you have lost control of the class. They are smashing up government furniture. Take note of those who have broken things. They have to pay.'

Hannan's voice boomed out suddenly. The bashing stopped. The students used their chairs to sit back down.

'I told you it wouldn't be easy,' gloated Laura. 'I can't be expected to come to your rescue. I am not paid adequately for that.'

'I don't need help,' Colette said firmly. 'I'm an experienced teacher and just need to get the hang of them, and you do a brilliant job as a receptionist and accountant.'

'You don't have to rub it in.'

'It was a compliment.'

Laura left.

'Where were we? Ah yes, verbs ending in *er*. And the verb *to be* in the context of *the pig is dirty*.'

While Ali scratched this sentence on the board, she had time to look at Hannan more closely. His shoulders were straight under a chain-knit rollneck pullover. He reclined in the chair and his legs were crossed at the ankle. He wore American-style jeans and trainers. On his wrist was a Rolex-looking chunky watch. His lustrous hair had a soft wave; his chin was smooth. Colette could feel the pulse tingle in her fingertips. There had been attraction at first sight. She had to battle against it.

The time had come for written work. She asked them to write three sentences using *Avoir* or *Etre* – sentences of at least five words each.

There was a lot of sighing and heads looking up as if inspiration were airborne. After a while, Colette paced along the gaps between the tables. Some of them were scribbling. Several sat arms crossed and she could have smacked the two at the back. Next to Hannan, she lingered. Without looking up at her, he tilted his upper body towards her, his ear at the height of her belly, until he almost touched her.

'I came to Kabul to teach French,' she said down to his handsome head, so dangerously close to her body. 'That is all.'

'No, sometimes it isn't…' A pause. '… all.'

Colette checked the first sentence he had written. *Je suis l'homme et tu suis la femme.* Checking her face bent over his writing, he clicked open his pen and drew a heart after the full stop.

'*Etre* is a difficult verb to conjugate,' she said down to him, trying not to sound teacher-ish.

'No,' he said, 'not difficult.' And filled in the heart with ink. She went back to the safety of the blackboard.

'Next, we work on the future of these two verbs. Now I want you to write—'

'Now is recess,' shouted one of them. Chair scraping started. She could not control them. She had to be honest with herself. Saturday, first day, and already a nightmare.

They left the classroom, putting on their jackets for the outside-in. She, at her desk, turned pages in the syllabus, to find out about the next subject to cover. *At the seaside.* Sandcastles built by small children, two people in a rowing boat, yet, in the same sea, a surfer was riding a high wave, gulls flying. In the distance, a container ship; nearby an oversized crab between striped deckchairs. There was a palm tree leaning into the picture from the right-hand side. Afghanistan was an arid and landlocked country. Honestly.

Colette suddenly remembered the endangered fragrant bush and rushed from the classroom. When she got out into the open, the bush was intact and no gardener in sight. The students milled around, large dark figures in a wintry setting, several using this leisure period to smoke. The two inseparables, who had sat yacking at the back of the classroom, now to her annoyance sat on the stone bench in silence, one squinting up at the sky, the other in bent position examining the ground around his shoes.

She could not help looking around for Hannan. He was at the far end of the rectangle, close to the back wall of the house. He was alone. He did not smoke. He was looking at her. She put her hand to her forehead and wondered what she should do next. The silent chatterboxes got up. Out of politeness? Most probably not. Never mind. She sat down on the bench, so cold it bit through her skirt. Her woollen coat was hanging on a hook behind the door in reception, but she did not feel like interacting with Laura again. Colette pressed her legs together, crossed her arms in front of her and pulled her shoulders up. Milky white breath came from her mouth. The miniature lemon or orange tree in a pot next to the bench looked dead. A last leaf on a thin branch was hanging by a thread. Gosh, it was cold.

'Are you going to stay in Kabul?' Edris, the unkempt student, had taken a seat on the bench leaving a gap between them which was correct.

'I have only just arrived.' But she softened her brusqueness with, 'Can you tell me why you are learning French?'

'No, but I can tell you that Hannan is the son of a newly appointed Commander of the Taliban government. You owe him respect.'

'I respect every one of my students and admire anyone who desires to learn a new language so strongly that they do something about it.'

'He is big. His father will be our ruler in the future. Hannan is a lucky guy.'

No politics, Colette reminded herself. 'Do you like the perfume of that bush over there? Isn't it sweet to bloom in the winter? I wonder what it is called.'

He got up. 'I couldn't give a shite,' he probably said in Pashto and left. In French, it would have been, *Je m'en fous*.

Left to her thoughts, she felt proud that Hannan came from a rich and influential family. From the moment she had turned to look at the latecomer, she had perceived him as a cut above the others, one to admire. Now proof existed that her instinct had been right. It was an honour to teach him and a privilege for her to have been noticed as a woman by him. And right now, she could not see him near the wall any longer. The desirable man whom she had to turn undesirable in her mind and body because of rules had come over to her. In Hannan's warm voice, she heard, 'The fifteen-minute recess is up.' He looked down to her and she caught the flash of a smile. She found herself open-mouthed.

'Thank you for reminding me,' she stuttered. Able to get hold of herself, with a deep in-drawing of breath, she stood up. The toe she had stubbed on her way to the Institute pushed to the front of her boot and shot a burning pain into the foot. Turning the foot sideways to ease the pressure on the toe, with an awkward body twist, she ended up plonked back on the bench. Her first reaction was to touch her hijab with both hands to make sure it hadn't slipped, while Hannan's hand was proffered to help her back up. Colette looked at lean long fingers, clean nails. The other students were filing back into the house. The unidentified flowering bush shivered in a waft of cold wind. Colette used her leg muscles to get up without help.

He took his hand back.

*

In her flat that afternoon, Colette spooned up the instant noodle soup and wolfed down the egg and tuna sandwiches – food she had bought at the airport to tide her over. Then she installed herself at the small table in the bedroom. In what had become her habit, she wrote down in her journal what had happened in Kabul so far. She knew that the impact of first impressions dulled as rapidly as black-and-white photographs pale in strong light. Her thoughts had to be captured on paper while still fresh in the mind. Saved from an emotionally crippled life in England with Mum, there was now teaching again, contact with humans her age, the thrill of trying to make a difference. It was a self-indulgence to release her thoughts through words flowing from her hand onto paper, words which would remain hers forever.

Done with that, she made herself a mug of Earl Grey tea and carried it out onto the little balcony despite the cold. She watched the traffic on the road beneath her for a while, then, looking at the facades of the houses on the other side, she became aware of a lit window through which she saw a woman sitting at a desk typing on a computer. The face was obscured by the side of the hijab, except for the tip of her nose which showed from time to time as she worked. Her office was on the fourth floor which was par with Colette's balcony, but of course the width of the road separated them. The sign at the front door of the house was that of an insurance company: an Afghan woman allowed to work in an office, familiar with computers...

Next to the keyboard was a plastic bag with green stripes from the market stall Colette had seen that morning. At exactly half past three, the woman stopped typing, opened the bag and ate a bun she pulled from it. Eating during Ramadan? Perhaps she was not Muslim or perhaps she was cheating. Colette went to fetch her saucepan and watered the begonia. Out on the balcony again, hands stuck into the sleeves of her warmest cardigan, Colette saw the woman typing again, a diligent employee. What was her private life like? Perhaps she had fought to get this job, argued with her husband and won. She had to be childless to work well into the afternoon. A disgruntled, widowed mother pushed her around at home. Colette gave up hypothesising; she would call her Malalai, after the Joan of Arc figure who had brought victory to the Afghans at the Battle of Maiwand.

Much good had come from this interlude on the balcony. Now, Colette had a routine to adhere to when she returned home after teaching. The Earl Grey would have to be replaced with Afghan green tea and the food be local but otherwise...

*

A week later, just when Colette had tidied up the classroom and was ready to fetch her coat from reception, Laura held her back with, 'I need to add to your duties.' She held out a bound document.

'What is this?'

'The new textbook issued in France and sent to us. I have brought one copy to the printing shop we use and asked them to make twelve more copies of it. They will take two weeks to do so. A busy season, apparently. It's just a ploy to charge more. I told them I wasn't born yesterday. They didn't understand.'

'Probably not.'

'What I want you to do is go to the print shop and pick up the books on Monday in two weeks' time – the beginning of February,' Laura specified.

'I'll make a note.'

'That's not all,' Laura continued. 'The next day you bring the books here, and then take one copy to the Embassy for the attention of the Cultural Attaché. His name is Eugene Roux. He has already faxed twice to show his annoyance with the delay. I don't like going to the Embassy; they are all so stuffy in there. Are you on board?'

'Picking up the copies on Monday afternoon is noted. But the day after that, going to the Embassy to deliver one of them, I won't make it there and back in the fifteen-minute break.'

'Don't worry. You can take your time. I will fill in for you.'

'Yes, Laura.'

Laura still did not let her go; she had something else on her mind. 'I guess in your flat you can walk around with your bald head uncovered.'

Colette shrugged on her coat.

Irritatingly, Laura continued, 'But you can't go out on your balcony. I was housed in that flat while I was teaching. But now, as a local employee, I live in a basement room of the Institute and am paid in afghani.'

'See you tomorrow.' Colette left the building. The guard took notice.

★

Saturday, the first day of a new working week, it rained. Colette, leaving her building, held out her hand. Sand, it was raining red sand. And then the rain stopped, but the surface of the road glistened with grit.

During break in the outside-in, she checked whether the fragrant plant had suffered from the sand rain. This bush had become personal for her. Those whom she had asked about it showed no interest. Perhaps it could be planted back in England and survive. She had to find out more about it.

Laura, consulted, said there were *of course* no decent bookshops in Kabul about plants. Seeing Colette's disappointment, she suggested, 'You're better off going to the university library.'

A few days later, Colette hailed a taxi to take her to the university. She paid the fare with the afghanis she had changed from British pounds. As she walked up the stone steps, students ran down past her, shouting and shoving each other. When she found the library, it was disappointingly small. In the section *Nature,* written in English, she searched along dull, brown book spines and realised that many of the books were published academic work: *Mushrooms in Tibet* – obviously not many as the published research was thin.

She imagined the student of mycology trekking through mountainous landscapes, his eyes concentrated on the ground while passion guided him to higher and higher terrains, and then the release, the writing it down, the description, the legacy left for those who will never go through what he had just endured.

She thought that perhaps one day Davina's work would be one of the books on the shelf: Dr Davina Lewis, and a headshot of her friend the way she had looked when younger, the hair lighter in colour and cut short with a bow holding it away from a face in which puppy fat still filled her cheeks. Colette smiled. The first time the two of them had met was in Royal Holloway College library; Davina in her second year, Colette in her first. They had started to talk about the Founder's Building being used in the filming of *Howard's End*. Carried away with the subject and their attraction to one another, they were eventually asked to shut up or leave. Preferring to leave, their friendship had made its first root.

Colette thought that their bond had grown strong, Davina in Kabul working on her thesis and now her in Kabul, probably walking along the same pavements, buying flatbread at the same stalls which might not have changed since Davina was here. One thing was for certain: Davina would be interested in the fragrant plant of the outside-in and know all about it.

Colette went home via the French Institute. She had to ring the bell many times before Laura made it up from the basement to let her in. 'Why are you here?'

'I need a leaf from the bush in the outside-in.'

'What? Now?'

'Yes, right now.'

'You are acting weird about this bush, you do know that?'

A fully grown, dark-green leaf in her hand, Colette left the building and Laura locked the door behind her.

The next day, the leaf, having spent the night flattened between pages of writing paper under the weight of the begonia plant pot, was pushed into a brown envelope addressed to Davina Lewis, Royal Holloway, University of London. It had a note with it:

Dear Dav,

I was not allowed to call you when I got to Kabul. The secretary of the Language Institute is a real dragon.

Yes, I am here. I am in Kabul, walking down the roads you must have done. Looking at buildings you must have looked at. Much is broken but they are rebuilding. I like flatbread with quince jam more than hard British toast.

The leaf I have enclosed is from a bush growing in the inner court of the French Institute. Even now in January, it is in full bloom and the scent is almost overwhelming. Please tell me all you know about this bush. The leaf should help you identify it.

You be good,
Colette.

*

February arrived and the day for Colette to pick up the textbooks. After a morning lesson of verbs ending in *ir* and sheets with pictures *In a Department Store*, more unsuitable material for Afghan life, she headed for the printing firm with the help of her street map. At a stall selling fruit and vegetables, she took out her purse and paid out afghanis for two green apples looking like Granny Smiths. She also bought two carrots and two root vegetables resembling turnips to make a vegetable stew for one. She turned her head away from the stall selling camel brain in brine.

A blue cabbage at another stall pleased her with its cobalt colour and perfectly round shape. It weighed down her shopping net. She turned the corner and had to cross a four-lane avenue, which was in the same district as her flat. Traffic was always busier at this time of day than it was in the morning on her way to the Institute.

The pedestrian lights were red. Others joined her waiting for the green – a sombre silent group of people. The lights did not change. Back in France, there would have been talking, gesticulating and complaining, rather than the resigned way these Afghans accepted the situation.

Colette felt him before she saw him. It had an eerie sensation about it. She stood locked in herself, so how could she perceive the presence of one human being with such definition? She had only known him for a few weeks. He was close to the kerb, spine straight, alert head forward as if to dare the traffic. His black hair had a lustre which reminded her of Grandma Nonnie's polished oriental cabinet. His shapeless brown trousers and thick shirt, with a frayed collar, were those of a soldier off duty, and suitable for class that morning. But over this workaday attire was a gabardine jacket clearly bespoke from a fashionable tailor for a great deal of money. How close to the Institute did he live? Where was he heading? Were there two Hannans?

The stubborn light was stuck on red. Hannan, showing lack of patience, turned to give up and faced the waiting crowd. He was caught in the beam of her admiration. Struck, he challenged her with a widening and focusing of his eyes. To her, it showed that he had an equally strong reaction to their meeting outside the protection of the French Institute. She also realised that it was the most exciting thing related to men that had ever happened to her. It was so precious that she would have to keep it cherished in her mind forever. Any hope for it to develop beyond this was, in her case, not an option.

Somehow, as more people joined the waiting group, the pair were brought so close that they nearly touched. He lowered his eyes and a private smile played around his lips. Nobody in the gathering could be aware that something beautiful had just happened between two people.

Eventually, he spoke out. 'The lights aren't working.' And put his hand on Colette's shoulder, as if the hand had decided to do this on its own. On impulse, she tilted her head until her chin touched the back of his hand – bony, but still body warmth to body warmth. She held the lover's pose as long as it could still be considered accidental between teacher and student and be laughed off.

She felt inebriated, with an out-of-control desire to reach out and pull him against her, to kiss him, kiss him urgently and with desperation. *'J'ai besoin de toi,'* she mouthed. 'I need you.'

Instead of changing to green, the red light simply went out. Had she caused this? Did a nearby guard possess a mind-reading device? She was forbidden to get romantically involved with a student; she had signed the contract.

Drivers took advantage of the situation until enough pedestrians started to cross, and the cars had to stop for them. A driver shouted out of his car window and shook his fist. The raised voice and gesture threatened the fragile magic of budding love, the enchantment at the sensitive core of humanity.

In class, Hannan was always ordering the others to listen to the teaching, obey and show respect. Colette had felt he was a man she could not be equal to, certainly not come to grips with, let alone teach. But seeing now how sensual and sensitive he was, she realised that it was she who had never come to grips with herself. She had assumed that she had mastered the ugliness nature had bestowed on her and learned to work around it, while being generously pleased for others who found love and togetherness. Teaching in Muslim countries offered her the dream of all the things other young women could expect, as long as her head remained covered and nothing could actually happen. But how could compromises and concessions survive such an ardent desire?

Hannan pulled the strap of the shopping net off her shoulder. 'I'll carry that. A blue ball?' he asked with surprise.

'A cabbage. Don't you know to cook?'

'My mother and the maid do the cooking.' He looked at her sideways. 'Where are you going with a cabbage?'

'To pick up a dozen new textbooks from the printers. Tomorrow morning, I will bring them to the Institute, but must take one of them to the French Embassy.'

'The Ambassador, is he interested in such a thing?'

'The Cultural Attaché is. He makes decisions concerning the French Institute. It is the same in every capital in which France has an embassy.'

'Thank you for telling me this. I want to come with you tomorrow.'

'Why?'

'Your bag will be heavy. I can carry it for you.'

'It's only one book. Why do you really want to come to the Embassy?'

He hesitated and she noticed him preparing an answer. Would he confess to his attraction to her?

'I shouldn't tell you,' he finally said.

She felt jubilant. He felt shy about his feelings for her. Maybe he had followed her this afternoon. He wanted to spend time with her.

They were now walking beside a low wall along the river. It did not flow. Water was only visible in shallow puddles amidst a riverbed of sand and silt. A load of empty cans had been tossed over the wall. A man squatted at a puddle, washing a chequered piece of fabric, his turban. A brown dog dug in the silt for food, its tail wagging lazily. Colette took out her map. Hannan took it from her. 'You don't need that. The printing place is on Ali Reza Khan Street. Not far from here.'

He turned left where there was a metal bridge over the river. She tried to keep up with his strides. Her position as woman was demonstrated. All that was lacking was a black burqa. The wind had a mean bite to it. She fleetingly touched the bridge's railing and it felt like dry ice. She pulled her hand off.

Suddenly, Hannan stopped and turned round. 'I want to become a diplomat. I learn French because it is the diplomatic language. I would like to see the inside of an embassy.'

'It's just a building.'

'I would like to see the inside of *just a building.*'

She smiled at him fondly, despite the fact that his answer had disappointed her.

'You agree,' he read in that and beamed. 'That is splendid, absolutely splendid.'

The frown on her face made him confess. '*Upstairs, Downstairs,*' he said. 'My father has a satellite dish on his roof.'

Hannan did not follow Colette into the printing shop. He walked past it for a bit, lingered and absent-mindedly peered into the display window of a toyshop. A battery-operated locomotive went round and round, risking derailment each time where the tracks had been badly laid. When Colette joined him, he gallantly carried the box, heavy with textbooks.

'I will leave the Institute for the Embassy at nine o'clock tomorrow.'

'Isn't that too late?' He gave away his eagerness.

'Civil servants start work late. To get there by nine thirty should be right. Abdul Hannan,' she said, 'I should go there by myself and you should go to class. Laura will be teaching.'

'Right, nine o'clock. I don't want to be teached by Laura.'

'Taught.' She took the box from him.

'Too heavy for a woman,' he said and took hold of

the box again. She knew that he would carry it all the way to her flat. Somehow this seemed natural. In step, Colette and Hannan crossed another road which led away from the river.

'In the future, on some days I will probably not be able to come to your classes,' he said when they reached the pavement on the other side.

Her eyes asked *Why?*

'The Taliban have selected me for officer training.'

'I don't understand,' she admitted, sounding miserable. 'You're not a soldier.'

'Every healthy young man in the country is given some military training. Some choose it as their profession. That was not my case.'

'Yet,' she said, still dejected, 'they chose you to become a leading figure, an officer.'

'It is an honour.'

Say no, she thought. *Refuse the offer to become an army officer. You don't want to order soldiers to kill people. Let's run away together to somewhere else, somewhere safe, right now. There's a bus coming. Let's get on it and just keep going.*

He felt her agitation, because he put the box on the ground to have both hands free to grab hers and hold them warm and tight.

'Don't frite. I will be working in an office, doing intellectual work.'

'Don't fret. *Fright* is a noun. *To fright* does not exist as a verb.'

'See, you forgot to worry about me, teacher mind. I have a military strategy mind. It is unsuited for physically killing people.'

She managed a lopsided smile. 'I worry about you because I care.'

He let go of her hands, one by one, slowly. 'I care about you too.'

'You'll still be able to come most days to the Institute though, won't you?' She nodded eagerly. 'And I will make sure you pass the proficiency exam at the end of August.'

Flurries of small snowflakes started to fill the air, like pointillism gone mad in a painting. They took up walking again. The cold prickled her scalp under the blue hijab.

Last night she had dreamed about soldiers crossing a frozen lake, possibly a link to the film *Dr Zhivago*. What her subconscious could not possibly have known was that Hannan would divulge, hours later, that he would become part of the Taliban army. She glanced sideways at him, partly to make sure he was real and next to her. The snow danced around his head. His glance back at her had still the clear-cut, clever and knowing glint which she liked so much. 'I love you,' she said and both of them stopped in their tracks.

'I have responsibilities. My family. I...' He decided not to involve her more. They walked on.

She was now close to her apartment building. He had walked alongside her all down Maiwand Road and even turned into the nameless little alley. Once she had gone through the door with the broken glass panel and looked back, she saw him withdrawing, a Taliban army officer. He had not kissed her. It hurt.

★

Tuesday, half an hour before start of class in the Institute, Colette arrived with the textbooks to find Laura sitting on the floor in reception, her back against the leg of a chair and a small rug covering her legs. She picked her glasses from her hair and set them on her nose. Seeing the surprise on Colette's face, she explained, 'That's the way they sit in their homes, on large cushions, which they call floor-sofas. You have to understand and adapt.'

'In Malaysia, they swayed in hammocks. I understood.' Colette looked down at Laura on the floor and asked, 'Out of curiosity, what made you decide to come to Kabul?'

'I just needed to get away from France for a bit.' Awkwardly, she got onto all fours, before getting up and forcing her skirt down. 'If you don't understand this,' she said, folding the rug, 'it's because you are only half-French. Actually, you are mostly English.'

'What brought that on?'

'If you were French all the way, you could have helped me get back to France. We could have become good friends.' She heaved a sigh and slipped on her shoes. 'My parents have sold their house and moved into an old people's village. If we were sister-like friends, we could plan to go back, save up and buy a house together.'

'Maybe.' Colette was hesitant. 'Friendship cannot be commanded at will. Like you, I don't have any friends back in France where I went to a convent boarding school. Teenagers are not generous-minded. The nuns sort of thought that, because of my hairlessness, I had to pray harder to be forgiven for my misfortune. It was not a happy time, apart from holidays back with mother in England, especially visiting my grandmother, Nonnie.'

'But you have friends in England.'

'Just one, but a good one.'

'You know, I'm getting tired of Kabul. There are more roaches down in the basement. The students are all alpha males. And I don't like to eat lamb, and lamb is the cheapest meat on market stalls. And, *oh merde*, it's snowing again.'

'Nine o'clock. Laura, you have to start class and I need to get this to the Embassy,' Colette said, waving one copy of the textbook. 'Have a nice day.'

'Have I told you about their mid-month test?' Laura tried to detain Colette to have someone to talk to. 'I'll help you with that. They cheat. All of them. Have done for the last nine years I've been here. We separate them. Six stay in the room; the other seven go into the spare room. We'll have to move tables in there. You supervise one room and I do the other. Still, they manage to cheat.'

'I'll do my best.'

'Go to the Embassy. Go!'

★

Colette did not find Hannan in front of the Institute. She felt a pang of disappointment. Then she saw him off to the side, near the guard, winding the turban scarf with fast and practised movements around his head. Now he looked the proud ethnic man from the country which had bred sultans. The guard saluted Hannan before running into the busy roundabout, arms waving, the rifle hopping on his back.

A taxi stopped amid the traffic. The guard talked to the driver shortly; the car made the circle and then drove up to the Institute.

Hannan opened the rear car door for her. 'For the Embassy, we need to arrive in a taxi.' He installed himself next to her. Only now did she notice that he was wearing not just the expensive jacket but well-cut matching trousers. 'Do I look smart enough?'

'We are not going to a reception. We bring a document.'

He did not respond. The taxi driver lay into a curve, causing the two at the back to slide against each other. She was too tense to enjoy this opportunity for intimacy.

At the Embassy, she identified herself over the intercom system. At reception, she was told that the Cultural Attaché was back in Paris at the moment but that his deputy would see her. Together, Hannan and Colette went up the carpeted stairs, Hannan gliding his hand along the brass rail as if to record every sensation.

On the first floor, the deputy, alerted by reception, stood at the open door of a small office. Colette went up to him and shook his hand in greeting.

'And who is this individual you have brought along with you?'

'He is a pupil at the Institute. I thought Eugene Roux would benefit from meeting one of them.'

'Unfortunately—'

'I know. He is in Paris.'

'And I am stepping in. Is that the new textbook for me?' The man was clearly not inviting her into his office. She gave him the document, while behind them Hannan walked into the office uninvited.

'Have you had a thorough security briefing?' the deputy asked, looking back over his shoulder with alarm.

'I have agreed never to get romantically involved with an Afghan,' she responded rather facetiously.

The deputy produced a mirthless laugh. 'They blow up buildings. They plant devices. They spy on the activities of Christians.'

At this moment, two armed security men raced up the stairs and slid to a halt on the polished floor.

The deputy shrugged. 'I had to. You, Miss Fontaine, have caused a serious security breach. How can you be so naïve?'

'Don't harm him,' she pleaded, as both guards disappeared into the office.

Shortly after, they emerged, Hannan held tightly between them. 'He is clean,' one of them reported to the deputy.

The deputy took Colette further along the corridor out of earshot. 'What were you thinking?' He was annoyed. 'Bringing a trained spy right into the Embassy. We know that you were chosen for the job because of your experience with Muslims in Kuala Lumpur. Malaysian Muslims are soft stuff; they are not taught to annihilate Christians. Eugene should have made you go through the drill he gives every employee coming out here. You slipped through the net. You have no idea and bring in here the most dangerous—'

'He is not armed. You heard the guard say.'

'There could have been stuff in that turban.'

'There wasn't. And you must have noticed he is clean-shaven and wearing a suit.'

'That's not the norm. That's the uniform of military spies trying to infiltrate themselves into western facilities.'

'With that turban?'

'All the western embassies here are on red alert at all times. You and Eugene should have an urgent talk about that on his return. You are a danger to yourself and others. Why are you not wearing the black burqa?'

'It is not required until the first of May.'

'You could start practising now.' The deputy went up to Hannan, writhing in the grip of the guards. 'What were you doing in there?' he asked straight into Hannan's face.

'Let go of me.' Hannan glowered from one to the other before answering the question. 'I had a look around your office. Not impressive. Can I see the Ambassador's, please?'

'He is studying to become a diplomat. I promised to show him the inside of an embassy.'

'The carpet on the staircase is good,' said Hannan. 'Afghan workmanship.'

'You, Miss Fontaine, leave at once and take this student of yours with you,' ordered the deputy, 'or we will have to arrest him and then there will be so much trouble. We want to avoid that. And,' he added, 'don't ever even think of returning.'

'I've seen enough,' Hannan answered for Colette.

Abdul Hannan

Abdul Hannan, sitting sideways on his army bed, laced his second shoe. The man with whom he shared the room in barracks had just left; only the smell of his cigarette lingered. As it was officer accommodation, Hannan was able to open the window. Taking a deep breath of fresh air, he was relieved of the feeling of claustrophobia induced by being in this spartan room, one of hundreds in rows on the outskirts of Kabul. He had the late afternoon off, because he had been summoned to see his father.

In Commander Qader's house, Hannan was not received by the maid gracefully as usual and escorted upstairs to his father's living room, called the smoking room. Instead, po-faced, she walked him along the back passage to a seldom-used dining room. His father was sitting at the oval table, looking uncomfortable. Mona, his mother, next to Qader, even more so. Hannan's younger brother, Baghish, stepped forward out of the shadow of the drawn curtains. There was little light in the room.

'Power cut again,' grumbled Qader, and only then did Hannan notice the two oil lamps on small occasional tables. 'It's a disgrace that the city can't provide electricity. It is the fault of the Russians.'

'Gas still works,' contributed Mona. 'For cooking,' she added shyly.

'It is an even bigger disgrace that my firstborn son is betraying Islam and the country in broad daylight.'

'Brother,' spoke up Baghish, 'I saw you in town with your western whore. You were carrying her shopping as if you were her servant. You talked to her. You walked close to her. I had to report it; the bitch is now on the red list.'

'She is my French teacher. Leave her alone.'

'The French are immoral, sex-minded and perverted.'

'Wrong. Their language is that of diplomats, culture.'

'I hope you have not touched her, my dearest. I don't want to be shunned by our friends.'

'No, Mother, I have not and will not touch her. She is just a teacher.'

'Next Friday, my cousin, Kamran, will be visiting us from Iran,' Mona said.

'Bringing your future bride with him, bro,' said Baghish in a sneering way. 'You're older than I am. You need to have a wife. That will solve your problem with the teacher.'

'Watch your mouth, Bag. I'm just starting officer training. What would I do with a bride?'

'Straddle her.'

'Don't be so crude, you two,' said Mona before turning to her husband. 'Make them stop. Shabana is a nice girl. I used to brush her mane of hair to plait it and she did not even squeak once.'

'She was five years old then.'

'By now she must be...' Mona could not work it out.

'About twenty,' calculated Qader.

'Whatever her age now, a good nature shows in little girls.'

'Your mother is right. It is time for Hannan to marry and start a family.'

'I can't be forced into a relationship with a woman for the rest of my life. I am too young and want to have choices.'

'Sooner or later, men need women whether they like it or not. You might as well agree to one who is good-natured and still firm. You won't have to be drunk or close your eyes.'

'Did you just say something hurtful about me?' Mona reacted.

'No, I meant the maid.'

'You and the maid?'

'Forget about what I said. It was meant as a joke. You are still desirable, my little swallow. And I am sure Shabana is a good girl. Moreover, her family are Shiite, and we need to bridge the divide between Sunni and Shia, if Islam is going to defeat the West.'

Mona lifted the hijab off her dark hair and flapped it briefly, as if her hair needed air. 'My elder sister married into a Shiite family; they have two children and, as you know, there is no friction.'

With sudden vehemence, Baghish shouted, 'I have just worked it out. Hannan is duping us. The French teacher is not to serve for sex; my ambitious big brother is using her to get information about our enemies. His new training officer will be very impressed.'

'Is that so?' asked the Commander with sudden interest.

Hannan looked down.

The Commander pushed his dining chair back and stood up. 'We men should go up to my smoking room. There are important things to talk about.'

'What about the future bride being driven here next Friday?'

'What about her?'

'The preparation for the family, the meal, the clothes.'

'My little swallow, you are in charge of all that. You have our maid to help you with it.'

Mona, who had also risen from the table, stood helpless behind her chair. 'Can you swear that the maid has never been anything else but a maid for you?'

'Come on, guys.' Qader ordered his two sons upstairs with him.

The smoking room upstairs was dusty. In the sharp light from a bright, cold day outside, disturbed dust particles could be seen whirling in the air. The maid was not allowed to clean this room. There was a glass door to the roof terrace, rarely used as no furniture was on it. The Commander had stood on it during the Russian bombing, like an admiral on the bridge of an aircraft carrier during an attack. Mona, to Hannan's memory, had never set foot on the terrace. He remembered a confused time when his mother had wanted to put plants onto the rooftop, soil even, and his father had said that it was his observation deck. Mother had sat at dinner, her head in her folded arms, crying because he would not let her have flowers on the roof.

'Sit down,' Qader ordered, and then his mobile phone rang and he went out onto the roof to talk. The brothers, used to important calls leading their father away, made themselves comfortable on large plump cushions and Baghish filched a cigarette from a pack in the side-table drawer. 'It's called a smoking room, isn't it?' And the lighter clicked.

Hannan, feeling something hard behind him, reached back and pulled a string of prayer beads from the soft creases. It was such an intimate item that he imagined the warmth of his father's large hand on the jade beads still, but at the same time it felt like an intrusion. If his father performed the five daily *namaz* prayers, he did it in private. In their family, religion was assumed, not questioned or used in casual conversation. It was the mullah at school who taught Islam, going on and on, ignoring the vacant glazed eyes. What Hannan had liked most had been the celebrations at the summer Eid. 'Allah u akbar' blasting from the loudspeaker on the table set up in the park south of the river. Praise for the one and only God. They all sat on the grass, he and his brother in front of their father, who proudly breathed over their washed and trimmed heads. Behind the assembly of men and their sons was a measured gap on the lawn, separating the valued men from the untidy rows of women sitting dressed in their finery. Unrestrained girls ran around acting silly in their lacy dresses. It was a joyous event for everyone – the only time his father talked to the stallholder at the end of their street to wish him *Eid Mubarak*. He even greeted Hazara rubbish collectors in Nehru-collared kaftans. And the family maids who sewed their own Eid dresses were part of it all.

Qader returned from the roof terrace. Baghish stubbed out the cigarette in the ashtray next to him and Hannan pushed the prayer beads back into the fold between the cushions.

'Is Baghish right? Can she be used?' asked Qader.

'Who?' Hannan looked up at his father with unease.

The Commander took his time to answer which was never good. Instead, with a little groan, he lowered himself onto the cushion next to Hannan.

'Dad means your teacher, Brother.'

'Yes, of course,' affirmed Hannan, daring to look boldly at his father right next to him and feeling a hitherto unknown complicity between them.

'Intelligence work will be part of your course. I am pleased to hear that, all on your own, you have already set out on that track.' A strong shoulder nudge from the Commander jolted Hannan.

Hannan, wanting to reinforce this camaraderie with his father, said, 'Two days ago, I was inside the French Embassy. She took me there.' At this, he pulled from his jacket pocket a roll of papers held by an elastic band. 'I stole them from the in-tray on the desk of an attaché who was in Paris at the time. You can find out what the ambassador has been up to and see his agenda for the following week.'

The Commander stroked over the red *Top Secret* stamp on the first page once he had removed the elastic. 'Well done, son. Ambassadors are, of course, not politicians but they lead us to them.'

'We should plant a bomb in the Embassy. Send in one of our hero brothers who do not fear death. Get rid of the undesirables. Pow.'

'Baghish,' the Commander looked up at his enthusiastic younger son who had leapt up in excitement, 'the Americans and English are the main enemies, whereas the French…' Qader said, mulling the words, '… they are a grey area. But then again, some of our Islamic brothers might not make that distinction.'

'They need to be wiped out, all of them. Pussyfooting shows weakness,' Baghish insisted.

'Afghanistan is a nation state,' said Qader, 'and not a suicide unit. We have problems enough with the different tribes in the country. But we are offering temporary domicile in our mountain caves to people more inclined to bomb the enemy indiscriminately. Baghish may well admire them.'

Hannan gave a sudden explosive sneeze, followed after a short tense pause by another. Distaste and irritation distorted the Commander's face.

'It would not be a waste of time and resources to prepare to undermine the French, just so they don't get too comfortable in the NATO cradle. You, Hannan, do good work on your teacher. She is not in any key position, but when you scratch the veneer off, you'll find that they are all linked together somehow. Keep reporting to me and your training officer. We can consider planting a beacon on her person. And if you manage to talk her into showing you the Military Attaché's office, we'll need to prepare you for it.'

'Dad,' said Hannan, tears in his eyes from the sneezes, 'you should consider letting the maid clean your den.'

'Bloody maid, compromising me,' Qader exploded. 'I've just decided. The maid will have to go. A cleaning agency and a couple of new servants will take over. You mother has come up with this idiotic idea about me and the maid. Nobody knows why she needs to invent such rubbish.'

★

Friday, the *muezzin* called out the *azan*. In the Commander's house, Mona rushed hither and thither while the maid sat at the kitchen table, dejected. Muffled moaning came from her. The lamb shoulder had come from too young an animal and not enough good meat was on it to serve to the Iranian family, expected soon.

'Fill the dish up with cooked carrots.'

The maid lifted her head. 'The carrots are old and have black spots. I can't produce something impressive if the ingredients are not here to work with.'

'Do your best. It is now too late to think about chicken with spiced figs.'

The Commander, in a smart, grey *shalwar kameez* suit, his feet still in slippers, tried to calm his household. 'Women,' he boomed, 'stop your panic. These people are not coming for the food. They come to talk business.'

'We don't want to dishonour the household by serving a poor meal to our guests.'

While this was going on in the kitchen, upstairs on the roof terrace, Baghish and Hannan were leaning over the wall to check the forecourt for arrivals.

'What shall I say to Shabana?' Hannan asked.

'Start with something kind.'

'Like?'

'Like, thank you for coming to visit.'

'That's dumb. She is forced by her parents to come here. I'm getting nervous,' admitted Hannan. 'She might be fat.'

'Then don't agree to become betrothed.'

'How will I be able to tell?'

'She will be wearing the full virgin burqa with the smallest mesh window. But you will see her wrists. They are giveaways. If they are very thin, she is not fat. When she crosses her legs sitting in a chair, note the length of her thigh under the cloth and pay attention most of all to the angle where the leg shows with the knee bent. A bony knee shows trim legs. A long upper leg, a tall woman. Besides, if she talks a lot, you can still refuse her. Especially if she talks nonsense. Bring up a subject of culture and analyse how she copes. You'll see part of her eyes and eyelids with lashes even with the mesh screen. If she blinks a lot, she is nervous and therefore probably a real virgin. If her eyelashes are long, the shape of her eyes will be large. Concentrate on her eyes. Whether they smile at you.'

'You have just given me a headache. I don't want to marry yet. I don't want to join the Taliban army. I want to study French and visit Paris and a French farm. I have never been to a seaside holiday. After learning French, I want to learn Latin. It is the basis of Mediterranean languages and of much culture.'

'Whatever. You'll never change, brother,' said Baghish. 'After I shot the dangerous dog, you stroked him with tears in your eyes, hoping to bring him back to life. You've got to toughen up. Father knows confrontation with the West is approaching and it's going to get bumpy.'

In the forecourt below, a car drove up and stopped.

'It's Shabana,' sing-songed Baghish. 'Let's go downstairs.'

'Can I just get a glimpse of her?' Hannan leaned out over the parapet.

His brother next to him leaned out even further. It took some time for the car door to open. 'It's a Nissan, not bad. Why aren't they getting out?' asked Baghish.

'They prepare themselves. It is not so easy for them either, you know.'

'Why do you always care about what other people feel? As a soldier, you shouldn't give a shit.'

A car door opened and a woman appeared.

'Oh no,' escaped Hannan.

'That's the mother, you idiot.'

The father emerged. He wore white, as they do in Iran, a tight-fitting hat on his head. Finally, the father opened the rear door. Hannan started to breathe heavily. A foot showed briefly, before the hem of the dress concealed it again. More fabric emerged. A hand at the door handle to help her get out of the seat.

'She does have five fingers. I counted them. On her right hand at least,' joked Baghish.

The bent upper body straightened up outside the vehicle. She was wearing a light-coloured abaya, with a veil covering her face. The robe fluttered in the breeze.

'It seems the Iranians are much less strict with their women,' noted Baghish.

'That's a good thing,' said Hannan.

'That's the wrong thing to say, brother. Let's go downstairs and be sociable. The way it looks, you can just walk up to her, blow away the veil and kiss her on the mouth.' Baghish made a smacking noise.

★

The lunch was awkward. Mona felt obliged to embrace her cousin's wife with hospitable warmth, but Fariba became as stiff as an effigy. The guests sat at the table covered by a *sofrah* and were offered very sweet tea. Shabana still had the wild hair, which Hannan remembered from their childhood, but it was not sufficiently tamed under the flimsy head covering. The abaya she wore had prints of small flowers on it.

The lamb was, as feared by the hostess, not a success, nor was it helped by the Commander noticing a thin, gold chain on Shabana's wrist. He could not contain himself. 'Shabana is not pure,' he stated, helping himself to more stew juice. 'She is wearing jewellery. Only men give women jewellery. My firstborn deserves an untouched bride. I am sorry you had to drive such a long way to get here.'

'So what?' retorted Kamran, taking the sauce ladle from Qader. 'She wears a little gold chain. I gave it to her on her thirteenth birthday to celebrate her reaching puberty.'

'I can take it off, Hannan, if you prefer,' Shabana fluted.

Hannan wiped his forehead. 'Look, Shabana, it is your jewellery, your wrist, your life.'

'Are you saying it that way because you don't want to… to…?'

'Of course he wants you to become his bride,' said Qader.

'More lamb stew anyone?'

'Please no,' said Kamran. 'I did not come here to eat.'

The Commander looked at Mona. 'Didn't I tell you?' he muttered. 'Perhaps it would be better if the fathers settled the business amongst themselves.'

'I had planned *jalebi* in syrup for dessert,' Mona said, almost in panic.

The maid, who was collecting the plates off the table, muttered, 'The dessert is better than the stew.'

A sharp 'Thank you' shut her up. Qader by now was annoyed; it showed in his brusque movements. 'Women eat dessert. They like sweet things.'

'Very well.' Mona sounded relieved. 'Just to point out before you disappear, the two guest rooms are prepared for you. I hope they will be satisfactory and, when evening comes, that you will spend a comfortable night in our humble home.' Mona obviously doubted whether the men would reappear downstairs.

'By the end of the day, we will let you know about the deal done for Shabana and Hannan to become man and wife.' Hannan, Kamran and the Commander left, the last closing the door firmly behind him.

'My husband is angry,' said Mona crestfallen. 'It is all your fault.' She turned on the maid. 'You blabber about things which do not concern you, things you don't even understand. Please get back to the kitchen.'

Baghish took this cue to lead his aunt to the living

room to show her old photographs, leaving Mona and Shabana alone.

'Aunt Mona,' said Shabana, timidly. 'The stew was not that bad. I am glad to be here and see you again. I don't remember you, but I was told about it.'

'You are still the considerate child I knew then.'

'But, Aunt, if I may tell you this, I don't really want to be a bride yet. I think Hannan is spiffing but not for now.'

'What is *spiffing*?'

'Oh, it is from one of the TV dramas I watch. You see, I am only just twenty and, when my child is twenty, I will be forty and after that… I can sit on the circular bench around the tree in the square and fight over who can sit where the sun does not hit. Round and round, until one of us falls off dead.'

'Shabana, how morbid. What do you want to do instead?'

'Women have no choice, in Iran or here, but my father predicts the Taliban will become increasingly hardcore. It is of course out of an inferiority complex and fear of women.' Seeing her aunt's puzzled face, she quickly said, 'I want to study psychology.'

Mona felt threatened by the young woman's misguided ideas. She had to find a way to tamper down her sudden fear. 'As you know,' she started, 'Hannan is attracted by the way they live in the West. He is learning to speak French. And you want to study… what did you say? Well, both of you want to burst out of what we have here. At least you have that in common.'

'You understand us, Auntie *jan*.'

'No Shabana, I don't,' admitted Mona, folding those napkins which were unstained.

'Pretending to understand might be the beginning of getting the hang of it,' suggested Shabana. 'I love you, Aunt Mona.' Shabana hugged her aunt.

'You will become a clever teacher somewhere else in the world. I just hope Afghanistan does not lose its brightest young people. As for Hannan, he is supposed to serve in the Taliban army. I don't know what to make of it as his mother. He is so wrong for it.'

★

Later in the afternoon, the three men came downstairs. Hannan joined his brother on the bench in the window. Shabana moved close to her father who stood, his head hanging. The Commander was so distressed that he had to wipe his face with a cloth he had dampened under the tap in the kitchen.

'What happened?' asked Fariba.

'Hannan does not want to marry our daughter. That is what happened. And he waited until now to make that clear.'

'Not *yet*,' Hannan said, with courage. 'I have to do other things first.'

'What other things? The most important thing in life is choosing a wife and starting a family. Other things can be done at the same time.'

'My poor Shabana. How can she be so insulted?' wailed Fariba.

'Don't forget I have another son, Baghish. He does

not suffer from stupid ideas. In two years' time he will have made a rank in the army, if Shabana can wait that long,' suggested Qader.

'Now, I am insulted for myself and my wife,' erupted the Iranian father. 'A replacement son. A cheap solution. Not that I am trying to put down the qualities of Baghish. I object to the way you Sunnis comport yourselves towards family members.'

'Does anyone want to hear what I think?' Shabana was almost whispering.

'No, Shabana. We are leaving right now. Hardly ever have I been treated so ungraciously.' Legs astride, Kamran stood in the room, his hands on his hips.

'If I may say,' Mona started, 'Hannan is at the moment undecided, confused almost. He has just started advanced army training and he is still studying. Perhaps it was a mistake to meet today. In a few months' time, I am sure everything will fall into place and we can agree about the two young people's plans for their future.'

'And you expect us to drive all the way from Iran back here in case the Commander's elder son brings himself to consider my beautiful Shabana as his bride?'

Into the silence came a cackling laugh from Baghish. All eyes on him, he saw the need to explain himself. 'This meeting of two families arguing about marrying their children is like a soap opera.'

'I remember forbidding you to watch foreign television. And especially Western television. Most of it is insulting, if not pornographic.' Qader vented his pent-up anger.

'I agree with my husband,' said Mona. 'Earlier,

Shabana used the word *spiffing*, which she says comes from the television. She also said she was too young to be married off and wants to study psychology. Our Hannan is not the only one hesitating to become engaged.'

'One must not ask what young people want,' stated the Commander. 'One tells them what one wants them to do.'

Hannan sidled up to Shabana and whispered, 'You don't want a father-in-law like that, do you?'

'Whose side are you on, Hannan?' Her large eyes were hazy under the veil.

'You are a beautiful, clever young woman,' he complimented her. 'Far too good for me. To be honest with you, because you deserve it, I have become attached to a French woman.'

'You will marry a French woman?'

'No, that is not possible. It's just that she occupies my mind all the time.'

'Who occupies your mind, son?' The Commander had overheard the end of the conversation.

'A French woman,' said Shabana, unadvisedly.

'Oh, that French teacher.' Qader laughed it off. 'She is only in the picture because we need her to be useful to us.'

'Useful,' Shabana repeated, before telling her mother that she was ready to leave Kabul for home.

Baghish, for whom this family gathering had offered much amusement, sprinted up to the roof terrace to watch the departure, taking his brother with him.

Once the Nissan had driven off, the Commander appeared at the glass doors and asked Hannan into his den. Unpleasantness would follow, just when Hannan had come to terms with his mixed feelings for his father, the man who prayed in secrecy, the man who ordered around his subordinates and the man for whom fighting-fit sons were his oxygen. Instead, Qader asked Hannan to help with something which he had ordered for the smoking room. Hidden in the top-floor storage room, it was large and covered by a cloth. Qader pulled that off to reveal a moss-green armchair. Both men moved it from the tight room and along the corridor. In the den, they pushed it into position and stood back to look at the effect – a throne amongst a gathering of stuffed cushions.

'Many important men pride themselves on sitting in easy chairs for relaxation; it is supposed to be the thing to do these days. I tried it out at the carpenter's shop. If you ask me, it's uncomfortable and many important people are wrong. Who can relax on something which destroys their back?'

Hannan consoled himself with the thought that Father had confided in him about the purchase of a chair before anyone else, shared with him this surprising purchase. Surely it was not just because he needed someone strong to move the piece of furniture. Hannan forced a smile. His father looked away.

Sitting in the chair, his spine so stiff and straight that it did not touch the upholstered back, Qader finally focused on Hannan. 'The squabble with the Iranians must have been painful for you.'

'No, Baba. It wasn't. I focus on what is important to me.'

'That bloody French teacher.'

'She is part of that.'

'She'd better be. I will only forgive your indiscretion with the western bitch if you prove that you can run her as a spy for us.'

'Father, I—'

'Otherwise, Son...' The Commander's stern look was on Hannan who forced himself not to cringe. The sentence remained unfinished but it had meaning enough. 'What can you show for it so far? Out with it. We are not fools either of us.'

'I have decided to ask her to take me back to the Embassy when it is closed.'

Qader lifted himself out of the green chair. At the little table, he took out the cigarette packet and shock it once. His lips closed over the one who stood out. Hannan observed this with painful clarity.

'And she told you she could get you past the night guards?'

Hannan nodded eagerly. Smoke came from his father's nostrils as if he were smouldering inside. Realising his father guessed that he was fabricating, he persisted, 'I did make it inside the Cultural Attaché's office, didn't I?'

'I've had a word with your training officer about you.'

'You did?'

'About you being more suitable for intelligence work than combat. Remember the dog your brother shot?'

'The dog story. Always the dog story.'

'From now on, we must be guarded in our conversation. Fully trained, you might be of good use to us, the way your brain works. Obviously not the clumsy student-teacher infatuation stunt. But,' and the word sounded like the pop of an airgun, 'you have to be made aware that, if you aren't doing the dirty deed, the enemy will. Your French teacher has been sent to the French Institute for a reason. Have you thought of that?'

'I know she has.'

'Good. You prove more alert than I gave you credit for.' The Commander even briefly smiled at his son.

'She wants us to become familiar with French verbs.'

'Allah, give me patience. My firstborn is a nitwit. Say something, Son. Don't just stand there frightened. The world is a shithole. Either you shit or you are the hole. Make your choice. Do that and it will make the rest of your life so much easier.'

Colette

End of March. Colette had not been able to wish her mother happy birthday but eased her worries: Audrey would be all right; she had friends in Highgate, bridge friends.

Colette lingered on the balcony, still wearing her coat and her hands wrapped around a warm mug of green tea. Her daily routine had been disturbed because, during morning break, Hannan had sat so close to her on the outside bench that their knees touched and neither of them pulled away. His left arm went slack and his hand fell alongside her thigh. Her hand found a way to his. Their cold fingers weaved into each other. At which moment Laura had appeared in the outside-in. A space appeared between the legs and the hands separated. Had Laura seen them? If she had, she did not show it. The cold after the separation from his body felt cruel. He had given Colette a rueful smile. She had shivered. His arm did not come around her to warm her against him, the way she had described in her journal a moment ago. Soon it would be April and then May. Surely this country would warm up.

Colette put the mug on the flower stand, approached

the balcony railing and, arms crossed, focused on the building across the street. In the insurance company office, her friend "Malalai" was sitting at her desk, but something seemed wrong. The green-striped bag was unopened. She had not eaten the pastry and it was nearly four o'clock. "Malalai" turned away from the computer screen and, with a tissue, wiped her eyes. She was crying. Colette watched with concern as the woman rolled her chair away from the desk and blew her nose, before discarding the tissue in a wastepaper basket. She untied the hijab and pulled it off her head. A mass of thick, dark hair uncoiled to amply cover her shoulders and half of her back. Colette pulled a tissue from her coat pocket and wiped away her own tears, tears of jealousy, before turning abruptly to go back inside, forgetting the mug on the plant stand.

*

End of April. Colette, who had slept wearing socks on her hands as well as her feet, woke to find that ice had formed inside the window. Munching on a jam-spread flatbread which was breakfast, Colette admired the beautiful curly ice patterns on the glass, resembling miniature fern leaves.

At the Institute, the wind blew in from the north so fiercely that those in the outside-in for break fled. Scampering up the stairs, Hannan manoeuvred himself right behind Colette. She slowed. His hand drew down her spine in a possessive way. She continued upward at a much slower pace. He encircled her with his arms and pulled her back against him, so closely that the side of his face brushed against hers. She felt his hot ear and the stubble of his shaven beard, and then it was gone. He let go. She stumbled on the stair; others pushed past them. The consolation was that the magic would survive in Colette's mind forever.

At the end of the working day, Laura called Colette to reception. Was this related to the staircase incident?

With trepidation, Colette entered Laura's office to find Laura business-like. She boasted that she had approached the Embassy and asked that employees of the Institute be permitted to get away with wearing the black chador, instead of the full body-and-face-covering burqa. Only two days ago had she heard that this exemption had been granted by the Taliban government.

'Aren't they both just like wearing a long, black evening gown?' asked Colette.

'The chador is a large, half-moon-shaped, black shawl made of light material, while the burqa is something much more substantial. The part covering the head is formed by fold-over-fold of material sewn onto each other and turned into a stiff headpiece, a weighty one too. Through the opening, you can just about see in front of you, but not sideways. One tires wearing it, especially in the heat and walking uphill. There is also a feeling of suffocation; sweat on the face does not dry as there is no air circulation. I've seen women in the pharmacy, showing their faces, begging for acne cream.'

'For women, another deterrent from leaving the house.'

'Yes. They put leather hoods on falcons so they don't fly away.'

★

Second of May. The class was showing surprising interest in Molière's plays, when Laura appeared looking like Zorro and produced a second black cloak which she almost ceremoniously wrapped around Colette. The students applauded loudly. Laura bowed. Molière would have been baffled.

Colette thought these students of hers were human, born open-minded and with a sense of humour. What right did a government have to take that away from them?

★

The next morning, Colette opened the door of her flat and the draft in the stairwell caught under the chador, as if she were about to fly off. Afghan women were of course used to walking around under such coverings. Perhaps they felt safe underneath it, even comforted. An older woman could be younger, a bra gone grey could be pink and lacy. Make-up was not needed. As for hair… Suddenly, Colette realised she shared something of the same feeling of protection that Afghan women felt. With her hand lifting up the long cloak so she would not be tripped up, she started down the stairs.

On the third-floor landing, she was confronted with the problem of a distraught cat – a kitten more like, or perhaps a starved adult.

Colette sighed. 'You poor thing,' she said to the pitifully crying animal. 'You stress me because I can't help you. I have to tell myself that you are only a small cat and that there are thousands, no, millions of small cats everywhere on earth, and how can I help you with a statistic like that?' The kitten drew itself further into the corner. 'I haven't seen you. I haven't seen any cat.'

Colette bolted down the rest of the steps, out of the door and into the street. In front of the insurance company building, "Malalai" was unlocking the door. She was shorter than Colette had imagined, the seam of her burqa touched the floor. When she kicked against the door panel which seemed to be jammed, it revealed a fat ankle and strange orange-coloured shoes.

Colette was disappointed by the encounter. The magic of imagining the life, desires and despair of this Afghan woman had now been destroyed by reality. Walking down the road, Colette felt renewed guilt about the abandoned cat, but they sold kitten meat in Peru as an appetiser, didn't they? She kept walking, the light chador's seam undulating around her body. Frost gone, there seemed to be a lot of dust in Kabul on this morning. Her lash-less lids failed to protect her eyes.

In class, she lifted off the chador, leaving the hijab in place. The heap of black material on the table in front of her resembled the black flag of Islam. Colette gathered it up and slipped it under the table.

She started the lesson with, 'I saw a small cat on the staircase this morning. I wish it was not abandoned.'

Hannan's arm shot up. 'I wish it *were* not abandoned.'

'Subjunctive, well done. By the way, I gave you an A on your exam paper. You deserved it.'

He held her with his strong stare. It was only because

of the attraction between them that she could see the outward corners of his eyes creased in a soft smile, which betrayed his feelings for her. Colette forgot what she was going to say next.

After the break, she made Edris read a simple French poem, which he managed although with a strong accent. It was called *Déjeuner du Matin* and started with *Il a mis le café dans la tasse*.

At the end of it, she dared disturb the dense silence in the classroom with her question, 'Can anyone tell me what Jacques Prévert, the writer, tried to tell us with his poem?' The silence returned. 'Ali?'

'The guy is alone somewhere and made himself a coffee.'

Colette encouraged him to elaborate. 'What is your *guy* thinking, Mukhtar?'

'How should I know? His mother died and now he has to make his own coffee.'

'Perhaps. Edris?'

'His woman showed herself to another man. He is a French sissy and cries into his coffee instead of taking the man down.'

Many laughed at that.

Colette changed tone. 'In a week is your exam. Please do some homework. I want you all to get an A.'

Laura interrupted the class, asking Colette to come down to her office at once.

'I had to take an important message for you,' Laura panted, running down the stairs. Down in reception, she snarled, 'You're not allowed to take your chador off.'

'Even in class?'

'You should be grateful to me for getting the Embassy to let us get away with a chador.'

'The cloak constricts my arm movements. I need to be able to write on the blackboard.'

'That's why women in this country should not get an education. The clothes prevent them from doing an adequate job.'

'That is so the wrong way round.' Colette puffed with irritation. 'I need to get back to class. Who left me a message?'

'None other than our supreme employer.'

'What supreme employer?'

'Eugene Roux, the Cultural Attaché, wants to meet you in the lobby of the Hotel Intercontinental tomorrow at two thirty.'

'Why doesn't he come to the Institute?'

'Ha! He will invite you for tea in the hotel bar. Maybe a brandy for him and sweet cakes. He can put it on expenses.'

★

Colette arrived in the lobby, breathless from walking up the steep drive to the hotel which had dominating views over Kabul. The Cultural Attaché was not there. She sat on an upholstered seat to the side of the room, a foreign occasional piece of furniture few had a reason to sit in. Behind it on the wall hung a large, framed landscape painting of an Afghan village with mountains behind it. She read on the brass plate screwed into the frame, *A. Gh. Breshna*. Colette waited.

At a sudden disturbance, she looked about her. A pair of uniformed soldiers had entered the hotel. They were armed and walking either side of an officer; from his medals, ribbons and turban, he was obviously important – important enough to be protected even inside the best hotel in Kabul. His glance taking in the large lobby scanned over her, his head stopped rotating to go in reverse to scan her again: a young unaccompanied woman in western clothes though her head was in a blue scarf.

Suddenly, she knew who he was. The Commander. He had a similar physiognomy to Hannan's, but in his case much coarser. Chilled, Colette looked down and then back up to Breshna's landscape. If that powerful man knew that the son of whom he had such high expectations was drawing shy little hearts for his French teacher, his reaction would be unimaginable. Surely in the eyes of the guerrilla father, a European woman like her was of as little use as the chair she was sitting on: a woman without the protection of a man, an example of the hated race. The pathetic effort to wear a hijab, and the clumsy way it was held in place by an ugly brooch, could only be understood as a provocation, mocking Islam. These thoughts she put into his head out of fear or, curiously, out of a wish to make herself small, to lie at the man's feet. *I have no right to love your son. I have no right to even dream about him.*

She woke to herself. Love for a man created strange feelings. Loving Hannan was so powerful for her that she almost yearned to be punished for it, kicked by the man's military boot. She looked away from the Commander.

Was her infatuation with Hannan not treason to her race? No, she exclaimed internally. Love is above that, above everything. Love is free and beyond prejudice.

An Asian-looking hotel employee in a burgundy uniform asked her whether she was waiting for someone. He had worked out that she was not a hotel guest. After some brow work, to which she was attentive having none herself, he let her be.

The Commander was still conferring with his army escort. The sobering thought came to her that this frightening man would never accept her as his daughter-in-law, that love was not beyond prejudice. He could easily order his guards to shoot her dead in the lobby, at a quarter to three in the afternoon. Someone would discreetly slide her body out of sight and that would be that.

Heavy boots clapping now, the Commander was led into the dining room by his men. Colette still reeled from the impact of his presence. The furniture seemed to creak, the upholstery giving out dusty puffs. In the painting, there was no sun even though the small herd of sheep in the foreground threw shadows.

Eugene Roux finally materialised. Colette had almost forgotten about him. She rose from the seat and took her time to gather her shopping net with her notes. He had made her wait and did not apologise.

She greeted him with '*Salaam Alaikum*'.

'Same here,' he said offhandedly. 'I was delayed on the Massoud Circle. The use of animals for transport holds up modern traffic. A donkey stopped to vomit and everything came to a halt. Shall we?'

Did he consider the vomiting donkey an apology? This man without manners guided her into the dining room and to its side, where small tables not laid for lunch indicated that this was the bar. There was a notice in English saying *Conversation Area*.

Colette asked for a Diet Coke with a slice of lemon while Eugene *needed* a whisky on the rocks. Laura had been right.

Eugene pulled a stapled document from the briefcase he had brought. There were new recommendations on health and safety, and suggestions of cultural events to offer given the political situation in the capital. Colette read out loud, '*French choir evening. Ballet performance for children under five.* Oh, no more French film afternoons?'

'Too risky.'

'*Le Ballon Rouge*, 1956, risky?'

Eugene shrugged.

'I guess the balloon is red and plain red is forbidden.'

'As I said, risky.'

Colette changed the direction of the conversation. 'The man in uniform over there is an important Taliban Commander. I teach his son,' she whispered.

'You seem to be already well settled in Kabul, my dear. Be careful. Every day, the Taliban is embracing Islamic extremism more tightly. We have intelligence that they are harbouring Al-Qaeda terrorists. Western lifestyle and success irritate the hell out of them. They wrap their criminal behaviour in religion, Islamism. Too much resentful navel-gazing can only erupt in attacks on those whom they blame for their poverty.'

'I follow your thinking,' said Colette.

'We now have a department of psychological analysis in the Foreign Ministry. When it comes down to it, every political movement can be explained in psychiatric terms.'

'Does that eradicate conflict?'

Eugene laughed through his nostrils. 'You must know that we closed the Institute during the Russian invasion. Anything can blow up at any time.' He flicked his fingers for the waiter. 'Crisps, peanuts, crackers, but no dates.' Turning to Colette, he explained, 'Can't stand the gooeyness of dates. Now, unfortunately, I have to talk to you about something unpleasant.'

Colette's breathing became shallow and rapid.

'Thank you for the copy of the new textbook. My deputy told me you waltzed up to the Embassy with one of your students. Are you mad?'

'No.'

'He is not a schoolkid. He is, as you've just told me, the son of a Taliban Commander. What were you thinking?'

'It sounds stupid but he wanted to see what the inside of an embassy looks like.'

'You are completely insane and I should send you back to France at once for consorting with the enemy.'

'I wasn't... It wasn't... like that.'

'The Taliban certainly already have a detailed plan of the inside of our Embassy. They will want to plant bugs, look for weak spots in our security, fiddle with the phones – who knows? Probably plan how to booby trap the Ambassador's office. Thanks to you, we had to fly in a technical team from Paris to check every inch of the building.'

'He is not like that. He's learning French because he wants to become a diplomat.'

'Who is not like that – the sweet little guerrilla?'

'I understand what you mean,' Colette said, after a shy glance over to the Commander's table.

'You don't. That is why I have brought you this top-secret document, a guide on how to look out for enemy infiltration and how to protect yourself. I hope it is written in a style a stupid little teacher can understand. It is not material to be taught to your students. Once you have assimilated the content of one page, destroy that page before going to the next.'

Colette nodded.

'This area is covered by surveillance cameras. We know that there are no listening devices implanted anywhere. The cameras are supposed to be for the hotel guests' safety. In the Institute, however, there will certainly be listening bugs. Read the instructions and learn.'

Colette touched one of her ears. 'I get it.' But she wondered what the listeners would make of her mundane conversations with Laura.

'How do you plan to destroy the pages?' Eugene tested her.

While she thought about it, he ordered another Scotch from the waiter.

'I'll boil the pages on my stove until they turn to porridge mush. And then I'll knead the mush into small balls and, on my way to work, throw them into the river, one a day.'

Eugene drained his Scotch in one drawn-out move.

'Wow,' she said. 'Doesn't that burn your stomach?

Ah no, I don't throw the balls into the river. I burn them on the balcony.'

'Yea, where every other tenant wants to know what the smoke is about and calls the fire brigade, which happens to be the army.' He put the whisky glass down. 'You have to become aware and alert. You took a job in Afghanistan, a country with a simmering war going on beneath the surface. You are not here to play fairy godmother in Disneyland.'

'I don't like you, Monsieur Roux.'

'You're not supposed to. And if I may chide you some more, you should be wearing a burqa. Here, take the security instructions.'

Colette leaned slightly forward to rub her back, while her other hand snatched the papers from Eugene's hand under the table. She slipped the document into her blouse.

'Well executed. A first step in the right direction, my dear.'

★

At the Institute the next day, Laura asked, 'How was he?'

Colette gave a shrug, checking the ceiling and walls; everything looked as it should. 'He gave me some security instructions.'

'Better late than never. Can I see them?' Laura searched on her desk for her glasses.

'On your head,' said Colette, handing her the document.

Laura unfolded the pages and read. In the ensuing

silence, Colette examined the base of the lamp, tested along the side of the desk, the windowsill – nothing.

Laura took her glasses off. 'Still the same instructions. I am surprised,' she announced. 'France is clearly slow on the uptake. Technology moves in leaps and bounds. It's all much more sophisticated now.'

Colette made an effort to distract her. 'Roux bought me a Diet Coke which was not diet. He could have paid for lunch.'

'I am glad he didn't. If anyone should be offered lunch, it's me for all the extra work I am doing for them.'

'The recreational entertainment of the Institute will be much reduced. They will let us know officially. Film afternoons are cancelled.'

'It'll change again soon. I am so tired of it.' Laura groaned.

'Eugene thought that' – Colette tapped both ears – 'are in the Institute.'

Laura wagged her finger for no. 'Not the classrooms, I believe.' She curled her fingers into a fist. 'If one lives with it for a long time, one can't be bothered about it anymore.'

'That's when the cat gets the canary.' Colette gave a short laugh.

Laura's finger was wagging again, fast this time. 'Never laugh. To be ridiculed is the button on their detonator.'

Laura pushed her backside onto the corner of her desk. 'Some days, I think I need to leave this place. But I can't. Where would I stay back in the Limousin? Who would I know? Anyway, I have work to do. My accounts for the month are not yet done.' She went behind her desk and shuffled through papers.

'Can the two of us really not just go somewhere for a Wednesday, end-of-week evening drink, talk and relax?'

Laura puffed. 'You must be joking.'

★

Days passed. Despite the arrival of May, the temperature did not rise remarkably. The Taliban were clearly intensifying military activity; she could tell by the frequent absence of her students and by the intense way they discussed things, standing in groups during the break. To Colette's dismay, Hannan was often one of the absentees. When that was the case, she felt the impact of the cold. Colours seemed to be dimmed to a monotonous grey. She envied the secretary of the insurance company into whose life orange shoes fitted. She regretted not having kept the cat as a companion.

And then, with a new glimpse of Hannan, the grey fog lifted and the sunshine had warmth, and she felt sorry for the insurance secretary who had a boring job, every day the same. Colette's life was transformed. He smiled at her, he moistened the sponge for her, he made sure their fingers touched as he returned the chalk to her hand. During recess, he often chose to sit next to her on the stone slab rather than talk to his colleagues. Ever since the knee and leg touching, the precious minutes on this bench recalled that moment for her – the breaking of the seal of chaste conduct and the sharing of a delightful little sin. It made her tremble. He felt it. Despite their superficial conversation, furtive looks spoke of their desire to let go.

Edris presented the class with a poem in French, which he proudly read aloud. He had cobbled together the words of Prévert's poem about breakfast coffee, but the protagonist, instead of putting milk in the cup, put a bullet in his gun, cocked the weapon and fired. Then he smashed the coffee cup in frustration because he had missed his enemy.

'Ten for effort,' she offered. 'Below zero for bad taste.'

Walking up the stairs in a group after recess, Colette made sure Hannan ended up right behind her. He feigned a stumble, grabbed her hand and brought it to his lips.

Another time, he was in high spirits and broke a branch off the fragrant bush and offered it to her as if it were a spread of exotic orchids. Laughing, she accepted the gift and brought it back to class with her. The torturing sweet scent reassured her that if Davina were to ask again, *Do you have a boyfriend?,* Colette could now say yes.

*

Returning to her flat each afternoon, Colette wrote her journal, watered the plant and, while drinking green tea, watched "Malalai" at her desk. Every page of the notepads Colette had brought was now covered with words. For some time, she had continued on single white sheets with faint lines, for which Laura made her pay. She realised that, in her Afghan journal, she did not mention her *alopecia*, because Kabul freed her of the restrictions it imposed, psychologically as well as physically. Once her experiences were in words on paper, it released in her a sense of peace and acceptance.

Throughout May, women in the street wore black. Their body contours were concealed. The little which still showed of their faces made her think of women behind dungeon bars, women begging to be forgiven for being women.

Finally, even the southerly winds bringing sand-peppered rain stopped. Colette turned her head up. The sky was blue. Instead of going straight home after class, she broke the rules and strolled down Chicken Street. She had been paid and felt like not so much treating herself as pleasing Hannan. At a stall selling women's clothing, Colette chose a full-length cotton dress which was the blue of her eyes, with beige embroidery alongside the V-neck and wide sleeve-openings. The stallholder offered two dresses for an advantageous price. Her acceptance was so fast, he resented it and sat down on a little wooden stool, sulking like a child, while Colette walked away with the blue caftan dress and an orange-coloured one. The elation of extravagance was tempered by her finding the secretary absent, the office empty. Perhaps today was the funeral of her mother – the reason she had been crying.

★

It was after the last lesson on a Wednesday, the equivalent of a Friday in the Christian calendar, and shortly before two thirty when Colette, alone in the classroom correcting written work, heard a knock on the door. Hannan came in and asked to borrow the dictionary, not to take away, just to look things up, but as she reached for it, she realised this was not why he had come. From the sports bag he had dropped on the floor next to him, he pulled a much-creased paper bag, came up to the table in two large strides and slipped it in front of her.

Hesitantly, she opened the bag and pulled out a bunch of pink roses, the heads badly mangled by the carelessness with which they had been treated.

'For me, flowers?' She thanked him in a high nervous voice. Just then, silently, the petals fell from one of the flowers. They both watched it happen. He did not reach out to pick up the dictionary, she did not switch on the ceiling light and, as outside rain lashed, darkness filled the room. Words would have spoilt everything. He stood near her desk looking straight ahead into his thoughts, as Middle Eastern people could do for lengthy periods, as if they owned time. Reaching out to her soul, he took her away with him into a timeless moment of delight. For the moment, neither their different cultures nor religions separated them in any way, and it was perfect. She reached a tentative hand out to him and his met hers in a strong grip. They stood together in the darkness. On the table in front of them, the shed petals lay like miniature alabaster cups.

For the rest of the week, Hannan was absent on military training. His classmates knew about it but nobody said anything. During break, she sat on the stone bench alone, hoping Edris would join her again and tell her about the importance of Hannan's father, but he didn't. A new fad had started in the form of a Persian game where small pebbles had to be thrown across a wooden board, so most students remained inside during the break.

As Colette left the Institute, Laura handed her a letter from England. Walking home, Colette dug her thumb into a hole in the corner of the envelope. With the side of her finger, she pushed along, leaving two untidily torn edges. From between them, she pulled a folded piece of paper.

The letter started,

> *Dear Colette,*
>
> *After our carbs in Little Sicily, no news from you. Today, I got a brown envelope from Kabul. You are there, congrats. I am jealous. I would so like to show you the Babur Gardens where I spent most of my time fondling plants. It is remarkable to think that a Mogul Emperor designed it in 1480, strolled in contemplation there for years to find peace when the rest of humanity rolled around in mud and straw, and asked to be buried there. When you visit the gardens, go all the way up to the shrine which contains Babur's remains.*
>
> *As for the leaf, it didn't survive the long journey. I was able to recognise it by veins before crumbling it into the bin. I do appreciate your effort and your interest in botany. There was a cheeky exclamation mark after that. The bush to which the leaf belongs is not a pedigree plant. It is a fusion between frangipani and jasmine. I doubt it would thrive in England.*
>
> *By the by, I got an interview with Blooms4You and am*

enrolled on a fast-track florist course. I have to tell myself every day, come on Dav, you can do this fiddly job.

I miss you. Haven't seen Jack Watson. He is now too important to hang out in our old student haunts.

Colette folded the letter. There existed an important Mogul garden. Nobody had mentioned it. She would have to go and visit it when summer could be felt in Kabul.

★

Finally a new week started and with it the attendance of Hannan. During his absence, she had spent time remembering and fantasising over their intimacy, the roses now in a glass of water, heads drooping. Saturday started with grammar, but when she gazed at him to communicate, he snatched his eyes away. She felt a deep rift between them. He seemed to walk more stiffly as well. He was being taught to hate her race, her society, her politics – was that it? *How can that happen?* she asked herself, knowing the answer already. He had started intensive training and could not both fight the enemy and secretly love one of them.

His detached behaviour hurt her deeply. When she went to the blackboard to write *Acrobat* because the lesson was about a circus, suddenly her right eyelashes stuck to her cheek. It pulled the lid down. Turning her back to the class, chalk in hand, she rushed downstairs towards the bathroom.

Laura shrieked, 'You're having a stroke.'

In the bathroom mirror, it did look as if Colette had suffered a serious stroke. With care, she unglued the lashes from the skin of her cheek, one by one. She wiped the surplus of glue from the rim of her lid and from the cheek, and dabbed it off the lashes before gluing them back on and returning to resume the lesson. It was a cruel reminder that she could not expect a life as a normal young woman. She did not seek Hannan's attention for the rest of the morning; she had no right to do so.

That night, sleep did not come. Her mind did not let it happen; it kept grinding on. But it eventually slowed down and the dark thoughts had a chance to give way to positive thinking: the pleasures Hannan had brought into her life. The looks, smiles, a drawn heart, a caress with his hand passing the chalk, his closeness when they walked up the stairs, the roses, magic she had never felt before. It was romance which for once included her. She had felt no shame, nor worried about it. She did not even wonder at the strange destiny which had brought them together, just as Chagall had not cared that a bourgeois French housewife would shrilly laugh and point out that the objects he painted could not fly.

The truth lay in the fact that her romance was only a dream. In reality, lovers could not fly. Colette tossed and turned on her uncomfortable mattress. Her relationship with Hannan would remain recorded in her journal, but in reality would fade to nothing.

But then a new sensation took hold of her. It started with a fuzzy feeling in her head and, from within this fuzziness, emerged a distinct urge to leave the bed and go out onto the balcony. Hurriedly tying a scarf around her head, she went out into the luminosity of a full moon at midnight.

The road below was lit in parts as if by some magic. In front of the insurance company door, a man stood, looking like a black cut-out. His outline was familiar. His face was turned up to her. When he reached her by some telepathic ability, she gave a surprised, audible sigh. What was the meaning of Hannan's presence? Was it real? If so, why was he here in the middle of the night? He wasn't carrying anything and wasn't going anywhere. Everything was shut. His arms hung by his sides, while his chin was up. Should she run downstairs and throw herself into his arms? Should she shout and wave? She remained on the little balcony bathed in shimmery bluish glimmer. He had been driven by an irresistible need to come here and make sure she was still in his life, despite his efforts to efface her. Please let that be the explanation.

For him below, she probably looked like a gossamer apparition. He pulled his jacket closer over his body, as if the cold light in which he stood made him shiver. She yearned to seize Hannan in her arms, offering him her body heat, the rhythmic rising of her chest. She would reach out for his beautiful hand, bring it up to her lips and ardently kiss the back of it. A more intense telepathic wave coming from him made her sway. She felt a clear sensation of skin to skin, as she nuzzled her face up his strong neck towards the softer features of his face. Prickly heat ran up the inside of her thighs.

'Hannan,' she gently wailed, overcome with the novel sensation of sexual desire.

★

The next day, Hannan did not arrive in time for the first lesson. Her mind worked overtime, inventing reasons for his tardiness. The road was blocked. Donkey-drawn carts prevented the flow of traffic. Electricity cuts held back pedestrians at traffic lights. Then she realised that she did not know where he lived. Given his conscientious nature, he would make up for his tardiness and surely appear for the second lesson. When he did not and Laura had not heard anything, unwillingly Colette had to offer the class breezy brightness when she felt constricted with pain. Only during the last class did she dare ask whether anyone knew why Hannan had not appeared today. Many shoulders shrugged.

'His dad probably sent him to fight. There is serious trouble out there, Mademoiselle.'

On the way back to her flat, Colette had in her pocket a second letter from England, which Laura had apparently received a couple of days before but had only just "found the time" to give her.

Colette noticed that someone had put several sturdy planks over the mortar hole in the pavement instead of filling it. These plagued citizens had become resilient. Somewhat confused about life as well probably. Colette stopped at the window of a women's clothes shop. The pale plastic models displayed short summer dresses, many of them cut low at the neck. Each model had a dark-coloured veil draped over its head, as a concession to the strict dress regime. Perhaps women could go inside and try on some of the short dresses, feeling different for a short while or looking different in a changing room mirror.

Colette moved on but a last glance revealed a figure draped in deep black, only the pale oval of the face showing – a face, very familiar for it was her own, reflected in a narrow display mirror. She was taken aback by how authentically Muslim she looked and how equally restricted her life was. If not turning rounds in her flat, she worked at the Institute. She walked from one to the other and back again, eyes down. She stopped sometimes to buy food which produced some interest. Her predecessor had angered her students, given up and fled this city.

Colette glanced in the narrow strip of mirror again and realised that looking the way she did was strangely reassuring. If she was to have any future with Hannan and diminish the chasm between them, she would have to come his way, accept his way. She felt no qualms in stepping away from her culture, determined to hold on to her first love. If her wearing a black chador pleased Hannan for the sake of his family, so be it. Her love was something so strong and radiant that seven yards of cotton were immaterial.

She smiled at her reflection and immediately flinched because someone's hand landed on her shoulder. Was a guard arresting her because she had stared at herself in the shop mirror?

'Why do you look so thoughtful?' asked Hannan.

'You!' She spun round. 'You did not come to class and I thought I might never see you again.'

'I will come tomorrow and you will see me many more times. I was busy this morning. Important political things. But now I am here. With this for you.'

She took from him a brown envelope which contained something bulky. She felt self-conscious holding it.

He noticed. 'It has nothing to do with political things. A small present from me. An Afghan tourist item.'

She tore the envelope and pulled out a silver bangle bracelet, the type one clipped to one's wrist. In the widest part was set a walnut-sized dark-blue stone in which glittered golden granules.

'Lapis lazuli, a gem from the Afghan mountains. Blue eyes, blue stone,' he said. 'Right? And you always wear a blue headscarf.'

'It is beautiful.'

'It will always make you think of Afghanistan.'

'It will always make me think of you.' She clipped it onto her right wrist and held the arm at a distance to admire. 'Beautiful,' she said again.

'Many semi-precious stones can be found in the rocks of our mountains.'

'I have noticed the stone tiles on the floor of the Institute. They too have glitter in them.'

'Most likely pyrite,' he said.

She admired the bracelet on her arm again. 'I should tell you that I cannot accept this gift and that the only gift I would like from you is for you to get an A in the final exam in August.'

'You and I are friends. I am allowed to give you a small gift.'

'You and I should be pupil and teacher.'

'And friends.'

'You make me happy, Abdul Hannan.'

He smiled. 'You make me happy too, Colette Fontaine.'

'Do you think we could kiss?' she heard herself ask to her astonishment. 'You see, last night in the shimmer of the moon and you downstairs, so real, so strong, so magnetic, I wished we could…' She did not spell it out.

'It was quite a moon. Up on your balcony, you looked like…' He searched for a word while she waited. '… a lamp.' He noticed her disappointment at once. 'A beautiful lamp, a lamp with silver pearls, a magical lamp.'

This made her laugh. He joined in for a short while before approaching his face to hers and kissing her on the nose.

Taken by surprise, she backed off and then her mouth trembled because she had blown the most significant moment in her life.

'You did the right thing,' he tried to appease her. 'We are not allowed to kiss, especially not in town where everybody can see us. My brother passes here often.'

'I lost out on a proper kiss from you. It is upsetting.'

He noticed her dismay. 'Touch your nose with your finger and then put that finger in your mouth. OK? And don't ever cry when you are with me. Promise?' He moved back and clearly something else was occupying his mind now.

'You need to go. Thank you for your kindness. One question, please. Does a botanical garden still exist? Its name is Babur something.'

'Mogul Dynasty,' he said. 'Ziihir ad-Din Muhammad Biibur, end of fifteenth century. A passionate gardener.'

He had lost her.

'Yes, one of his gardens still exists. He designed ten of them during his reign. The Babur Gardens were only partly destroyed during the war.'

'I have a friend who is a doctor in Plant Science in London. She studied in that garden. I would like to visit it. Where is it?'

'It is close to a warlord tribe in the mountains, a dangerous place. They were Mujahidin who fought against the Russians, but are unhappy that Allah rewarded us with the power of government, not them; they have turned against us. Do not go there.'

★

Back in the flat, Colette moved the plant out onto the balcony and watered it. Across the road, "Malalai" had already eaten her bun.

'You are not going to bloom for me, are you? That is not nice. My friend, Davina, would know how to deal with you.'

Out of sorts, instead of writing her journal, Colette stretched out on the bed. The sunset had left a pale light lingering in the small bedroom. She used it to read the letter. As always, her mother wrote in green ink on vellum paper. Elaborate windings of the ink relayed that Grandma Nonnie had not been able to shake off the flu she had caught in the winter. *She kept saying she was all right.* The tip of the pen had moved upward with the last word and returned to base with, *You know her. Clearly she wasn't.* First a chesty cough and then bronchitis according to the GP who referred her to Bedford Hospital. The full stop after that was smudged. *There, it developed into pneumonia. Nonnie talked about you, her little Colly, when she wasn't doped. I visited every day, but the consultant for the elderly said that, at her advanced age, miracles could not be expected. What happened was she caught the hospital bug which ended any chance of her getting better. That's the way things are nowadays in hospitals and one has to…* Colette turned the page. *… live with it.*

A blank space looked odd after that. Further down the ink engaged again. *I am sorry to inform you that Nonnie passed away July 9th at midnight.*

'No, no, no,' Colette whimpered. It was the full moon that night, the moon had killed Nonnie. The full moon had tried to tell her that her grandmother was dying and thinking of her. The full moon definitely had a lot do with what had happened that night.

Colette pressed the heels of her hands against her smarting eyes. Before folding the letter and putting it back into its envelope, she noticed more writing – a short sentence.

My mother, your Nonnie, left you Riverbend and everything in it.
I send you all my love and tell you again to be careful in such a dangerous country.
Come home soon.
Mum

Hannan

Qader made some urgent calls to summon Hannan home at once.

'Dad,' said Hannan, standing taller in the smoking room than he had ever before. 'You can't just command me to come to you on a whim. I am now in officer training. Home visits for me will be sparse from now on.'

'The lace on your left boot has come undone.'

Hannan looked down at his shoes. And up at his father again. 'What do you want from me?'

'Your teacher whore has been tracked to the Babur Gardens. She is, as I speak, climbing up the steps to the praying level.'

'Oh no.'

'Oh yes. It's good to know that bracelet beacon works. The unit leader told me about her whereabouts an hour ago. The woman is meandering around, touching plants and smelling flowers.'

'Shit,' escaped from Hannan. 'I told her not to go there.'

'Serves you right. You had no right to talk to her about anything of that sort. Whose side are you on?' Qader's head was pushed forward.

A call came on the phone. Qader said a few short words only.

'Your verb-spouting woman has made it close to the top of the steps. Feisty western female, isn't she?'

'I've got to go.'

'You'll trip over your laces.'

Colette

The Babur Gardens, eleven hectares of public green space, are the historic resting place of Emperor Babur, a notice at the entrance explained in several languages. It also said that the Emperor believed in 1480 that only flowers could heal sorrow and bring happiness to one's soul.

Colette went in and looked up at the many terraces either side of a dried-up water channel. At the top glinted a small shrine, white against the blue sky, the resting place of the Mogul. One could still imagine him strolling amongst the flowerbeds, shrubs and trees, the noise of cascading water mingling with the chirping of sparrows as his ermine-trimmed coat brushed the soil. Of course, the water cascaded no more, not just because of the two years of drought but because part of its course had been damaged.

Colette proceeded upwards on stone paths and steps, passing from one terrace to another. She saw late-blooming wild cherry trees, intermingled with tough cypresses and mulberry trees.

Halfway up, Colette noticed that a segment of the tall wall surrounding the garden had been blown away. Through the gap, a rugged mountainous terrain could be seen.

On the next level, she came upon a myriad of marigolds. Davina must have walked here and seen those and stopped. What Colette could merely admire in passing, Davina's dedication would have recorded for ever. Mogul Babur would have approved of Davina; the thought was immensely pleasing.

Colette climbed further, to a terrace with many shade trees. This level offered her a panoramic view of Kabul. Drawn on in search of jasmine bushes, hoping the sweet scent would lead her, she heard the agitated twittering of sparrows. An area of grass, tormented by drought and wind, survived as short, tough blades, thinning out to where dry sand took over. It was in that sand the sparrows were bathing. The half-open wings whirred, the softly feathered bellies wriggled, the beaks chirruped. Were these descendants of those who had brought happiness to the soul of Babur?

Still further up, Colette came to vegetation which was charred – another reminder of the destruction war had caused to Kabul. Through burnt branches of fruit trees, she perceived the white marble shrine still further up.

At her feet lay an object shining like newly polished brass. She picked it up and immediately dropped it: a bullet casing. A dangerous place, Hannan had warned her. A ruthless tribe, resentful of the Taliban's success. Colette was now closer to the blasted-away hole in the wall and could see that in the rough cliff face were caves, torn sackcloth over their entrance, a goat here and there tethered to a stick in the ground. Some habitations were even bricked and plastered brown by the desert sand used for the concrete, thus well camouflaged.

She turned away and climbed again, eventually reaching a flat concreted surface. A sign described it as the praying area. The vegetation had changed to coarse-leaved bushes, entangled with each other. They had no blooms or scent, and the leaves were almost leathery.

A harsh male voice shouted from behind the bushes. She returned quickly to the stone path, unable to rid herself of a sense of menace. She noticed the absence of sparrows' twittering and the hot dry air seemed to burn the skin of her nose. She turned about herself, trying to decide whether to go up or down, and realising how foolish she had been. She had come here despite the warning. She might even perish.

To her right, several bushes were shaken and aggressive words were yelled again. And then, to her horror, she saw a man on the ground, one foot turned outward unnaturally. He could have been a student in her class, except that he had a gaping hole in his neck. Frighteningly, no blood flowed.

Robot-like, she went down a few steps, to leave death behind her. Perhaps, she could still go down the terraces and leave the gardens as if she had not been there.

But a shot sounded, short dry and close to her. She put her hands over her head and stopped moving. The bushes shook again and Colette yelped. She slipped the bag from her shoulder. Death behind her, danger around her, and only the steps down could save her. But now shock had set in, and she shivered and her robotic legs refused to function.

'I love you, Hannan,' she whispered and then, 'Love you, Nonnie, Mum.'

At that moment, two things happened simultaneously. Someone threw a heavy sandbag at her which knocked her to the ground, while two more shots rang out, echoing off the mountain wall. Her head felt as if it had exploded, her brain destroyed, her nose broken. She felt the grit of concrete on her tongue. The sandbag crushing her to the ground had arms, pressing down on her shoulders. Moving ineffectively, she tried to rid herself of the dead weight on top of her. Hot breath came from a mouth in a face close to hers. It was a man lying on her, a heavy man.

'*Wabakhai*,' he pressed out, before one of his arms flopped off her shoulder. It was Hannan's voice. It was Hannan's body. She knew and because she knew, his body started to melt into hers as if they were one. He did not say anything more than 'Sorry' in Pashto. He was not dead; his heart pumped with hers still. She felt the taste of blood and grit in her mouth. Hannan had thrown himself over her to protect her. The bullets had been for her. Inch by inch, she managed to crawl from under him, unloading his leaden body. He did not object. His breathing was weak, the eyes closed. If he had been shot dead, she would have sensed the flight of his soul and walked up to the barrels of the rifles, so close as to make sure they would kill her, and she would be with Hannan forever in this garden.

'I love you,' she whispered close to his ear. 'Darling man I love so much.'

But she had to make the best of life, alive still for both of them. 'My body wanted you so much when I stood in the moonlight. I will always love you, even on moonless nights. Don't die, please.'

Suddenly, she realised that if she selfishly held onto him this way, he would slowly die from the bullet wounds. He needed a hospital. She kissed him on his slack lips. And then curled herself away, stood up and fearlessly looked around. There seemed to be a change of mood in the garden. The level of danger had dropped. A tragedy had just happened. Those who had shot him were probably panicking. He was the firstborn son of the great Commander.

Colette had interfered enough. In rapid descent, she worked herself down the terraces to the entrance, her head ringing, thirst clawing at her throat. She dared to turn and look back. Up there, on one of the levels, lay a man bleeding to death. 'Only God, no, Allah, can save him. Please send an ambulance and medical attention to save the man who risked his life for me.'

*

Later, when Colette lay on her bed, Chagall's enlaced couple were twisting in the air and her nose hurt as if someone was drilling into it. She did not remember how she had got home. Her pillow was coloured red from her blood. She must have walked back all the way. What a day. Despite her pain, her head swirling, she made the ultimate effort: she got off the bed to pull the stool closer to the writing table. On faintly lined paper, she began with the date of 22 July 1998 and started to record what had happened in the botanical garden, while holding a tissue in her left hand under her nose. Only when she was satisfied that she had saved every detail of the traumatic episode did she allow herself to fall back onto her bed.

Her brain had retained the sound of twittering sparrows and the whirring of their wings. Her physical sensations too had retained the feeling of Hannan's body on hers.

The following morning, cleaned up, despite a splitting headache and a swollen nose, Colette arrived at the Institute only a half an hour later than usual. Laura stopped in her tracks when she saw Colette's face. '*Quelle horreur*! You've been beaten up.'

'I was knocked to the ground. My head hit the concrete,' said Colette, looking down, which caused blood to drip from her nose again. 'I went to the Babur Gardens, ignoring the rules.'

'Irresponsible and stupid. Of course they attacked you; you stood out like a sore thumb. You are lucky not to be dead, but you will certainly be on their list. Mademoiselle Fontaine from London goes for a little stroll to look at pretty flowers.'

'Abdul Hannan was shot while I was in that garden.'

Laura's hand clasped her mouth. 'Is he…? Is he…?' she stuttered.

'He was not dead when I was able to run away. But if nobody helped him, he might well—' Colette could not go on.

'You had a rendezvous with one of your students, is that it?'

'I went there alone as a tourist.'

Laura's smile twitched in a sneer. 'You don't fool me. There is something going on between you and Hannan. *Was* something. That is so forbidden for them that they are bound to have finished him off.'

'Don't say that. Please, don't say it.'

'You have offended Islam. Whatever was going on in your stupefied mind? They are not people like us. Passion courses through their veins, hidden under the deceit of calm, virtuous religion. Our ordinary blood is merely there to be spilled, like that of *halal* meat. You have to leave, but they may well come after you. With all that, you don't even cry. I don't understand you.'

'I can't cry.'

Laura shook her head in disbelief.

'Without a second row of eyelashes, the tear ducts dry out. Otherwise, I would now be crying a river.'

Uncomfortable with that conversation, Laura moved on. 'So, yet another teacher is leaving me in the lurch. This time Eugene Roux is taking me to the Intercontinental, and for more than just a Coke.' She re-tied the floppy bow of her blouse and clenched her teeth. 'You are lucky to get away without punishment for molesting one of our students.'

'Molesting a student?'

Laura saw the ridiculous side of this. 'Honestly,' she said, 'do you really get turned on by military oafs with hobnailed boots, beards and turbans, reeking of stale sweat?'

'Just one of them. And he does not have a beard and wears Prada.'

'But is as Muslim as they come. Muslim, Colette, Islam. What were you thinking?'

'I have read the Koran. It is not unlike the Bible but written in a more poetic way. Lovely.'

Laura shrugged. 'I guess you are free to go home. Six before you have left, although none of them under such alarming circumstances. I will step in and do the necessary administrative work as I always do.'

'Could you please book me on the next available flight to London? I have no access to a phone.'

'With the Taliban restrictions, there aren't many international flights. Perhaps in three days' time, at the weekend, I could get a seat for you. I'm sorry we did not hit it off. You were different. Once back home, will you forget about me?'

'As you know, I have been writing my journal every day and you are a character in the story.'

'Teenagers write diaries. Some with a clasp and a key so that parents can't read which boy they fancy that particular week. You fancied you know who.'

'Journals record a life.'

'And you want to anticipate your autobiography by writing it now?'

'Better be going,' said Colette. 'My head is throbbing and your class starts in five minutes.' *Without Hannan; with an empty chair where Hannan had sat.*

Colette hugged Laura very tightly.

Early next morning, Colette returned to the Institute. Laura had been able to get her a seat on a flight to Karachi and then with BA on to Heathrow. She would leave Kabul in two days' time.

'Thank you. Sadly, I will not make it back in time for the funeral of a woman who has been so good to me.'

'Who would that be?' There was some undertone of jealousy in Laura's voice.

'My Grandmother Nonnie. In her will, she left me her house.'

'I hope it is big enough for you and your newfound boyfriend to live in, happily ever after.' Laura attempted a bitter joke.

'With my departure from Kabul, the boyfriend part of my life will be over.'

'Are you sure about that?' Laura pointed at the ceiling and scribbled on a scrap of paper. *They will be so outraged, they might come after you.*

Colette took the pen. *I didn't tell you. The bullets were for me. Hannan threw me to the ground to save my life.*

Laura wrote again. *Unbelievable. I have never heard of any Afghan doing such a thing for a Christian, a woman.*

'You have now,' Colette dared to say. 'He and I, we liked each other. Please don't say anything to him about this when he returns to class.'

'When he returns, inshallah.'

*

Colette hadn't intended to go to the Ali Abad Hospital at the university, but once she was there, she went in. The receptionist checked two lists and concluded with confidence that no Abdul Hannan was a patient. She suggested Colette check the brand-new private Shinozada Hospital. A look at her map showed that this was on the other side of town. Her nose throbbed still; her head ached. It took her forty minutes to get across town.

This receptionist, a young man, found Hannan's name on his list. On the second floor, Section D, Room 32. She tiptoed along a dull, grey corridor. The guard next to Room 32 sat on a chair too small for him. He looked unarmed but had the physique of a professional wrestler. A much-fingered and folded newspaper lay on his khaki trousers. The second he spotted her, he pulled the black walkie-talkie off his cross-chest belt. She hesitated. Asking to see the patient might cause Hannan even more trouble. She was the reason he had ended up in hospital. She had no right to make things more complicated for him and his family. But she needed to know how badly wounded he was, and how he felt and so much more. Colette made a full turn and walked back the way she had come and out of the hospital. Once outside the compound, she dared look back over her shoulder but saw nobody following her.

They were more devious than that obviously.

England

When the captain of the 747 asked the passengers to return to their seats as they would shortly be landing in London Heathrow, Colette looked down at the tame fields and houses of England. Nothing blood-curdling had ever happened to her there, nor had tingling sexual desire been awoken. With a lazy move, the pilot tilted the plane this way and then that, as if he enjoyed flying. Somewhere down there was Davina – and her mother, with whom she would soon quarrel. Colette swallowed and her ears popped.

In the cockpit, the radio came alive with BBC breaking news. A terrorist attack had killed thirteen people in Paris the previous night. Gunmen had stormed into La Souricière nightclub and started shooting. There was a rush for the emergency exit, with several falling in the stampede. A pregnant woman was crushed behind a heavy fire door. It took the police fifteen minutes to arrive. One of the terrorists was shot dead; the others escaped on motorcycles. The Paris police confirmed that this was an act of terrorism in the name of Islam. France's prime minister condemned the action as barbaric.

The co-pilot turned off the radio. 'These Islamists are animals. We should bomb them.'

'That's what they are doing to us,' said the pilot. 'Engage for descent.'

'Imagine that young mother – her baby killed in her belly.'

'Let's pay attention to what we are doing.'

Behind them in the plane, Colette peered through the cabin window. Houses had become larger, toy cars ran along roads, and there were occasional glints from the Thames snaking through the density of London.

Perhaps Davina was already at work. Soon they could meet up, go to *Little Sicily* and chat about university days, their lives now, men and, best of all, Kabul. She might even share her traumatising experience in the Babur Gardens. Davina could help her recover. They could go to museums, the cinema. Perhaps a visit to Paris even, showing Davina around. Feeling young.

Her teenage years had been lonely, a bald girl at boarding school and, for weekends, a father who seemed only marginally interested in her. He urged her to go out, go dancing. How could she, without having made friends? There had been just one evening, when she was already eighteen and had gone with a group of girls to La Souricière nightclub. In hindsight, her father had probably been afraid of his daughter, especially as she had no hair. He probably also resented the responsibility, but then he had been the one who had insisted she was educated in France. The theory was probably easier than the practice.

With Davina in Paris, they could go on a bateau

mouche on the Seine. With Davina, they could do so many things. The hardship of having lost Hannan would eventually abate.

The 747 came closer to earth. Multi-chimney properties appeared in large, landscaped gardens… Riverbend. Had her grandmother really left her that whole house in her will? Surely not.

★

Audrey Fontaine, dressed in black, had driven to Heathrow to pick up Colette. 'Hello,' she shouted, once she spotted Colette in the group of arrivals coming out of Customs. Colette lifted her hand from the trolley to give her mother a wave.

'Thank the Lord you are back safely,' Audrey exclaimed, when they were re-united.

Colette thanked her mother for picking her up, but felt sensitive about the word *Lord*.

'You look pale and tired, darling, and what on earth happened to your nose? It's twice its normal size.'

'You know I always look pale and it doesn't mean I am sick.'

'Lady, you dropped this.' A woman held out the bundled chador she had picked up from the floor. Colette blinked and, with a 'how kind of you', took possession.

'A black sheet.' Audrey pulled her head back, which multiplied her chin. 'You won't need that any longer. There has been a lot of black these last few days.'

As Colette brought her arms around her mother in a hug, the familiar Chanel scent irritated her nose. She whispered into Audrey's shoulder padding, 'I am upset to have missed it.'

'The funeral was beautiful. Peter, your Nonnie's Briddleton vicar, spoke well. It's not his fault he has such a strong Scottish accent. The printers got her birthdate wrong in the order of service. With Tipp-Ex, I put every single one of them right.'

'Mrs Hungerfunkle?' A smart-looking young man with a thin neck emerging from a collared shirt was still scanning the arrivals, even though most had already come through.

'How can he think such a person exists?'

'Many people have odd names, Mum.'

'I left the Audi in a large car park. I think it was B3.'

Eventually, they found the car parked in P3. The chador, loose on top of Colette's suitcase, had caught twice in the luggage trolley wheels by then.

'The P looks very much like a B without the belly on it. Sorry, darling, I am not good at these things.'

Colette went along patiently, realising that the culture shock of being back in England was stronger than that she had felt on arrival in Kabul. For starters, today was Saturday, the first day of the weekend, when that Saturday in Kabul was the first day of a week's work.

Audrey managed to follow the arrows to the exit of the multistorey car park and they emerged. She revved the motor. Colette told her to look for the signs to the M25.

'I knew that. I want to talk to you, but I can't drive and chat.'

'Better concentrate.'

They took the slip road onto the M25.

'Now I feel better.' Even large lorries overtook them. 'She died peacefully, you know. Sort of.'

'Mum, you have to put it in fourth gear. This is a motorway.'

'The lungs did not work at the end; she gasped for breath and—'

'Poor Nonnie. I am sorry I could not be with her at the end.'

The Audi started to rattle. 'We've got a puncture,' panicked Audrey.

'No, Mum, don't stop the car. You're driving on the rumble strip.'

Audrey veered away, and an overtaking car hooted angrily and repeatedly.

'Stay calm. We are not far from the exit.'

'Perhaps you ought to drive.'

'You are doing fine, Mum. No, not this exit. This is the northbound M1.'

'I know what I am doing,' Audrey said stubbornly, her fingers gnarled around the steering wheel.

Colette said nothing more, not just because she had a slight nosebleed, but also because she realised that Audrey was driving her up to Bedford and Nonnie's house, rather than home to Highgate. In a wheatfield beside the road, they were harvesting. Dust followed the giant combine felling wheat stems in train-track lines; seagulls tumbled behind it. England looked wonderful.

Audrey glanced sideways at her daughter. 'Take that Muslim-looking headscarf off. Wear one of your wigs.'

'They are in the suitcase.'

'Muslims have just burst into the Souricière nightclub in Paris and cold-heartedly murdered thirteen young people. One very pregnant woman was crushed against the wall like a bug. I want you never to go back and work in a country with such heinous people.'

Colette said, 'La Souricière, are you sure?'

'I don't speak French, but I can remember the name of a nightclub.'

For a while, they did not talk. Audrey paid attention to the heavy traffic and Colette felt weak from dread.

Once they were engaged on the A421, the car-weaving stopped and vehicles rolled along smoothly.

'Let's talk about Riverbend,' Audrey took up. 'I simply want to know whether you intend to live in the estate you were so generously bequeathed by my mother. With everything in it and a wad of money in a deposit account. Leaving me out of the will as if I never existed. You even inherit Nonnie's Swiss housekeeper, a woman who has worked for our family for thirty years now. Trudy was already part of Riverbend when I got engaged to your father. She even came to our wedding in France, wearing the most ghastly yellow dress, but that is beside the point. And Trudy kept on ruling in Riverbend when you were born and when your father and I divorced.'

'She has been part of my life since I was a small child. She showed me how to climb trees. She must be close to sixty now.'

'You don't have to worry about Trudy not pulling her weight. She's strong as an ox and about as sophisticated as one. Nonnie got on with her; I have often wondered how. Now, if you decided to sell the estate or perhaps rent it, which I would prefer, then Trudy would have to go.'

'I am confident I will get on with Trudy.'

'But if you don't, I'll come and fetch her to help me out. I have to do everything myself and it is not a small house. Your father had the decency to leave me the property and enough to see me through. Apart from being French, there were good sides to him.'

'Mum, I don't want to discuss my estranged father when he is not here to defend himself.'

Audrey gave a short snort which was not ladylike. 'It's old hat. What is new and interesting is Miss Colette Fontaine owning Riverbend. Even the caretaker, who left a year ago, got my father's watch. Yes and, how funny, Trudy got the mink coat. Ha!' A short, barked laugh. 'Trudy in Bedford High Street, getting pelted with eggs.'

To Colette's relief, her mother finally stopped the indicator from blinking and clicking.

'Presumably you'll only stay in England until they send you to another French Institute somewhere exotic.'

'I have decided to take at least a year off. There is going to be Riverbend to look after.'

'Playing the great madame in the big house. I saw the silver bracelet on your arm.'

'Please watch the road, Mum.'

'You have never treated yourself to jewellery. You thought you didn't deserve it because of your illness.'

'It is not an illness; it is a failure of my immune system. The bracelet was a gift, a gift from a friend. A good friend.'

'The one who punched you in the nose?'

Colette remained silent for an unnaturally long time.

'You can't possibly stay alone in Riverbend. It has nine bedrooms and four bathrooms. Why is that man making a very rude hand gesture?'

'He might be in a hurry.'

'If you do decide to live in Riverbend, you could rent out two of the bedrooms, adjacent, one turned into a living room, and allocate the nearest bathroom to it. You will still be left with plenty. A good deal in such an imposing property for a single professional woman. She'll be out of your hair during the day, working. Sorry, darling, the hair thing is just a common saying.'

'Get into the left lane now. Renting out is not that easy. Professional people who work in London don't want a long and expensive commute. Riverbend is out in the middle of nowhere, even by Bedford standards.'

'All right then, a professional who works from home. An artist.'

'Too messy.'

'A musician.'

'Too noisy.'

Colette knew exactly who she wanted to share the house with. And with that thought came the familiar stab in her guts. Hannan could be dead, killed while saving her life.

'A writer,' Audrey came up with. 'A famous writer living incognito in a house stuck in the bend of the River Ouse.'

Perhaps Hannan was alive and recovering. It was unnerving to pretend to be her old self, while sitting next to her mother and harbouring the poison of a secret.

Worse, her future might be severely compromised by her relationship with Hannan. Even if he recovered fully, she would remain on the blacklist, to be punished by Taliban fanatics. If he were dead, they could get someone to murder her in the UK, easy as pie. Had such people not just killed thirteen innocent youngsters and an unborn child?

'Don't make that face, darling.' Audrey took the A422. 'Writing is a laudable occupation. You should know. You've asked for diaries every birthday and Christmas since you learned joined-up writing. After Malaysia, you published a novella based on your journals, *The Orphan Boy from the Kampong.*'

'You talked one of your friends into publishing it. And I stayed anonymous. Nobody bought the book, not even you, Mum.'

'You didn't dedicate it to me.'

'To become a professional writer, you don't have to be someone like me, Mum.'

'You were a shy beginner. I presume you kept on with your journals.'

Colette's prolonged silence indicated that the subject had to be changed.

'Don't listen to your mother.'

'Mum, please don't wave your arms around. Hold onto the steering wheel. Either side of it, both hands.'

'Everyone knows famous novelists seek inspiring retreats to let their imagination loose: Caribbean islands, the Orkneys, villas on hills in Italy.'

'Bedford, Mum, up on the panel. Try to get into the inside lane.'

'I just had a brilliant thought,' Audrey warbled and they swerved rather late onto the exit road. 'I've heard of an exclusive writers' club in London. Apparently people like Venetia Morley, Jocasta Richmond and Jeffrey Archer are members. Some genius there is bound to be on the lookout for privacy to write a new novel. Riverbend, with the weeping willows along the Ouse – how much more inspiration can a writer expect? You'll charge her rent and that could help with the running costs of Riverbend.'

'We're here,' announced Colette, in an emotion-strangled voice.

They stopped in front of tall gateposts with weathered capitals. Of the two wrought-iron gates, only one was still standing. The other lay in the grass to the side.

'This entrance is not secure.' Colette sat up in her seat. 'Anybody can just walk or drive in and attack me.'

'Why would anyone want to do that? Working in those foreign countries has given you strange ideas. You are in Briddleton now, Bedfordshire, and you are tired from a long journey. Even if the gates were fixed, the parkland is so extensive, it is impossible to enclose it safely.'

'I will get a guard dog.'

'Bad idea. When you take off again, I will have to come and live here to look after Riverbend. The last thing I want is to be responsible for a dangerous dog.'

They drove through the gap in the gate. Whilst Audrey had been a hesitant driver before, she now stepped on the pedal and they roared up the drive to come to a crunching halt in front of the house. Audrey unclipped her seatbelt. 'This residence is now all yours,' she said, 'incongruous as that sounds. I grew up in this house. I was given a pony and learned to ride in the park. There were Nonnie's birthday garden parties. The caretaker had his boat tied up on the riverbank. One summer, travellers camped on our land. The police and neighbours came to send them packing. You know nothing about the house you were given in a will by a confused old woman.'

'Don't go on, Mum.' Colette undid her seatbelt.

'In the drawing room is a painting of your dad's mother. An impressionistic portrait. He might want it back.'

'Do you still talk to Dad?'

'No, he is not in the picture any longer. But my horrid maman-in-law still is, hanging in the drawing room. I'll come and pick it up another time. There is also the silver cutlery service and the tea set with matching tray – I think I should have that – and the candelabra.'

'You are hurt, Mum. I did not ask to get this house. Thanks for driving me here.'

'You might as well thank me for driving all the way back.'

'You are welcome here anytime. You know that. You can also have the paintings, the silver, the lamps, the curtains.'

'Don't make fun of me, Colly.'

Colette got out of the car, while Audrey reached into the glove compartment. 'Here, the keys to the house.' She passed them through the open car window. A purple pansy was on the keyring. Colette hesitated to take it.

Audrey's tense concentration on the dangling pansy made her features look older, worn almost, with a hint of pain. Colette needed to remember that, with the loss of Riverbend, Audrey had also had to watch her mother be lowered into a grave, only a few days ago.

A cawing rook flew over them.

Audrey pulled herself together. She surrendered the keys. 'I expect you remember the geography of the house.'

Colette realised for the first time that her mother's life had not been easy and that women's lives never were. She set her suitcase down on home ground and patted its side, as if the piece of luggage were an anguished creature, one which had loyally and powerlessly stood by her side throughout Kabul. With the sudden termination of her teaching contract, the bag had been packed carelessly in the small apartment on the alley without a name. Laura and Colette had said goodbye, Laura pointing up to the Damocles sword swaying over Colette's head: 'They will be coming after you.' Laura from the Limousin, left behind in Kabul; her last words would stay with Colette forever.

The noisy rook flew back the way it had come.

'I'd better be going.' Mum started the engine.

Colette bent to the driver's window. 'Drive home safely, will you?'

Audrey hooted the horn by mistake, drove off and down to the half gate, the red brake lights coming on repeatedly.

Left behind, Colette turned to face Riverbend and looked up. In the immediate presence of the imposing house, she felt insecure and small, as small as she had been before being sent to French boarding school. Since then, she had visited from time to time and the house had only grown with importance. Now that it was hers, it was quite overwhelming. In nearby Briddleton village shop, postcards could be purchased, photographs of Riverbend in the summer. On the walking map of Bedfordshire, it was marked as a noteworthy sight from the bridle path on the other side of the Great Ouse. Colette breathed out. Mine, the whole thing is mine, and I am only twenty-seven years old and live alone.

She looked back at the parkland. Evening was dimming the colours and softening shapes. Perhaps the legacy had been a legal mistake and Mum should actually have inherited the home in which she had grown up. But then Nonnie and Mum had not got on that well. Colette's *alopecia* was the cause of it – a heavy burden to carry. Perhaps Nonnie's will had been meant to punish Mum, more than secure her granddaughter's future. People on their deathbed could do with their belongings whatever they wanted.

The late July summer evening was darkening more. Even the rooks had become quiet. Colette suddenly felt lonely and exposed. This is what it had come to: an unfulfilled love suffered in silence and a continuing menace of violence. Perhaps it had been a mistake to return to England and Riverbend, but there was no other place where it would be different. She had to pay the price for those heavenly moments with Hannan, for having created an intimacy in a sinless world of old-fashioned chastity, and for having declared herself free to love despite towering intolerance. This vow could not be broken. He had been ready to sacrifice his life for her. She had to stay strong and record in her journal the preciousness of their encounter in an atmosphere of religious intolerance. A pearl-pink rose petal on a teacher's desk.

Colette left the suitcase where it stood. She clasped the bangle and lay her arm against her bosom. Instead of going into Riverbend, she was drawn to one side of the house. Over the strong branch grown out at a right angle from the trunk of an oak tree, two ropes were still slung. She had to squat down deep to sit on the wood-plank swing. It was so low that her knees were at the height of her chest and her stretched-out legs were barely two inches off the ground. Before her was the expanse of wild grass and beyond was a line of weeping willows, giving away the wide, lazy bend of the river. To the left, in the park, stood a group of three tall, ancient conifers, like wise old men.

Dangling, she felt better connected to her surroundings. Time healed wounds. Nonnie had loved her so much that she left her Riverbend. Her life had to go on. Hannan would not like her to be an ungrateful, weak woman. Colette gave the swing a last push. Under her feet, she noticed the patch of barren soil. As a child, she had used the swing so often that the grass roots had died. Just like the capillaries of her hair.

She got off the swing and steadied the ropes' tremor before returning to the suitcase, which stood forlorn in front of the house. Picking it up, she mounted the stone steps between the plinths with their stone cannonballs, one of which she had once licked, curious about its taste. Colette went into the house.

In the hall, Nonnie's scent of lavender took her back. On her way to the drawing room, Colette looked at herself in the tall mirror. Her faded eyebrows needed to be redrawn. The worn blue hijab and embroidered kaftan dress gave her a nomadic air, as if she belonged nowhere. On her right wrist glinted the lapis lazuli bangle, although, in the mirror, it was on the left.

The drawing room light switch was not in the obvious place, so the paintings crowding the walls appeared to have darkened. When she found the switch of the table lamp, she realised that it was a long time since she had been in this room. In later years, she had always sat with Nonnie in the kitchen. Turning about herself, she smiled at the sneaky drum table she knew to have fake drawers. On its surface were grouped the silver teapot, cream jug and sugar bowl on their silver tray. She lifted the small lid by its knob and bent to smell inside. Earl Grey. Always Earl Grey with a thin slice of lemon. As a child, she had not been allowed to touch the set. The sugar cubes with their sharp corners, when hastily popped into one's mouth, cut into the sensitive palate. And they took their time to dissolve while Nonnie, who obviously had seen her do it, engaged her in conversation.

Colette sank into one of the overstuffed chairs. She was twenty-seven years old and would be living here like her Nonnie, probably for years to come. She could not go and teach abroad again, not after Hannan. A dog as a companion – that, at least, could help pass the days.

The door flung open. It hit the corner of a mahogany

cabinet. This was followed by cold light from the ceiling lamp. 'There you are, Colly. I heard the car and was told you were coming, but then you were nowhere in the house.'

'I went to the swing.'

'That is where we normally found you.' Trudy went on, 'I should probably call you Miss Colette now.'

'Yes, you should. Nice to see you.'

'I haven't slept since Margaret passed, in fear that you will turn me out. The lawyer told me you inherited everything and I apparently am getting Margaret's moth-eaten pelt. "Thank you very much," I said to myself. If I saunter through Bedford town, all the mongrels will chase me.'

'Trudy, I will be living in the house and you will continue to do as you did before. There will be no more talk about turning anyone out.'

'That's good to hear. You've had a long trip. Would you like a cup of tea? We only have Earl Grey.' She lifted the tray from the drum table and, working the door with her foot, managed to leave the room.

'No sugar, please,' Colette called after her and a grin spread, recalling the sugar thieving.

★

The next day was sunny and bright. Colette explored Riverbend as an owner. The kitchen was dated, with grey flagstones, painted cupboards and an oil-fired AGA, but the affection she had felt for this room, warm whatever the season, was still intact. Through an arch was a utility room with a sink which was more a stone trough and a top-loading washing machine. One door led down into the cellar and another to the outside.

She unlocked it and went out onto the paved area under laundry lines. Along the back wall were discarded items, broken or obsolete. In the unsightly jumble, she recognised the pink handle of her tricycle. There were also a rusty pail holed at the bottom, a wire cage with a water-dispensing dish – What had that been used for? One chicken? – a pyramid of empty wine bottles – Had Nonnie been a secret drinker? – a splintered rowing-boat oar… One of the first things she would undertake would be tidying up this mess.

She went around the corner of the house to the east where there was a pebbled gap of about ten metres width between the main house and the old stable block. It had been converted to garages – the doors were locked but urgently needed a lick of green paint – with accommodation on the south side, facing the river. She peered through one of the picture windows. Despite the grime on the glass, she could make out a sofa with a giraffe-neck print cushion tossed onto it, a desk with a lamp, even a framed picture on the wall. She did not remember this as a child, but somehow it made sense. Mr Crocket the caretaker and gardener must have lived in this garage apartment. He was the one with hair on his nose who had owned a rowing boat tethered to a pole knocked into the ground on the riverbank. The blue rowing boat had danced in the current as if its only wish was to tear loose and float away. Back came the memory of her mother repeatedly stating that it was wrong for

Mr Crocket to live on the Riverbend estate. Something to do with women or he had a collection of women? A *mummy wrong*, meaning other people would not like it – other people Mum did not think were wrong.

Colette decided that she would clean Mr Crocket's windows. The premises, with so much light and view over the estate, were more engaging than the grandiose tomb-like drawing room of the house.

She would explore more the next day. Her list of things to put right was long enough for now. She returned to the house and her journal writing.

Hannan

In Kabul's Shinozada Hospital, the Commander walked along the corridor on the second floor. He was accompanied by a nurse who made nervous conversation to a man whose mind was closed. The moment they turned the corner, the guard in front of Room 32 jumped up. The folded newspaper fell to the lino flooring. He did not bother picking it up. His right hand was at his cap in an elongated salute.

Inside the room, Hannan, obviously warned about the visit of his father, sat up against several pillows. His left leg was outside the bedcovers, thick with bandages, and the foot was fixed on a metal stand. Hannan, who did not look pale but rather too flushed, greeted his father in a reserved manner.

'Would you like me to get you a chair?' offered the nurse, but she was silenced by Qader's outraged glance.

'You made any progress?' Qader asked his son.

'Medically speaking, I can't comment; otherwise, I feel stronger and more positive.'

'You shouldn't. You should lie there cringing like a worm. Thanks to you, I have lost all credibility with the army. And your brother is made fun of.'

'I'll get the patient's doctor,' suggested the nurse and left.

Qader started to pace. He touched the pale-green wall with a spread hand and took a deep breath. 'What is most appealing about women is when they serve men with pleasure in their inferior position. It is men's role to bring them that pleasure. And if she smiles behind the niqab, she turns into a treasure.' Qader took his hand off the wall. 'And you, firstborn from my wife's belly, you attach yourself to a naked-faced woman, one who teaches you, one who knows no shame. A product of the corrupted West, where women bellow at men to take out the trash, force them to wear aprons and gloves to wash dishes.' He turned back to look at his son. 'It was the Mujahidin bullets you took. Your teacher was alone in the Babur Gardens which it is forbidden for women to visit. She was not wearing the burqa which we have made the law. The Mujahidin take every opportunity to pretend they too have a say in governing Afghanistan. Of course they wanted to shoot her.'

On the bed, Hannan writhed in discomfort and pain.

'You were fully aware of what was going on, up near Babur's shrine. You rushed to her aid. Penalty is not upon he who slays in the flesh, but he who is himself slain in the spirit.'

The doctor, a man beyond middle-age, appeared. He saluted the Commander. He had served in the army. 'Good of you to visit again and show interest in your son's disability.'

'What disability?'

'The picture has become clearer since your last visit.

To start with, all we could do was operate out the two bullets and stabilise the wounds. Luckily, they hit the lower part of his body.'

'That's because they were aimed at a person shorter than Abdul Hannan.'

'The one in his thigh only caused a flesh wound which we are confident of having dealt with successfully. The second bullet nipped one of his vertebrae. One finger's width to the right and the outcome would have been paralysis from the waist down.'

'Don't babble on about what could have been. Tell me when he can get out of this bed and resume his officer training.'

The doctor sucked his teeth. 'I fully understand your eagerness to have him up and about. A nerve was pushed against the spine. We had to use tweezers and a magnifying mirror to remove the bullet.'

Qader listened but his foot-tapping showed that he was annoyed by the medical talk. The nurse poured water from a jug into a glass and handed it to Hannan.

'Talk about the leg,' Qader challenged the doctor.

'I am. The nerve serves the leg. Abdul Hannan will not lose the leg but there will be impairment of movement.'

'And you think you are doing a good job? Hannan will be limping. Is that what you are trying to say?'

'If he does as well as he has done so far, we can think of starting physiotherapy in a week. We have a gifted therapist from Syria who uses a new method of rehabilitation. Your son has a lot of courage and a positive attitude towards recovery. That helps.'

'My son's *courage* is being brought up in front of the war committee. And you should know what that means. Now walk away,' Qader said to the doctor. 'I want to say goodbye to my son.'

'Please don't exhaust him.' A look shot up at the monitor. 'His BP has risen.'

'A limp. You heard him. You'll be limping along. That's what the infatuation with your French teacher has left you with. We haven't finished with her.'

'Dad, please promise me to leave her alone. She is innocent. All she did was go to the Babur Gardens to look at flowers.'

'But when her beacon showed she was on her way there, you dropped everything to go to her aid.'

'I would have done that for anyone.'

'Even that dog.'

'Dad, if I end up with a limp, it will hardly be noticeable. I will become an officer. Chasing around mountain rocks, I will not be asked to do.'

'Do you want to hear something interesting?'

'I'm tired, Dad. They're giving me painkillers.'

'Your teacher has deserted her job and left Kabul. She has been traced to England, the middle of it. The bracelet works. She wears it day and night and has no idea. We have a cell in the nearby town of Luton and they are ready to do what we tell them.'

Hannan, getting slack and sliding down his pillow pile, pleaded, 'Please instruct them not to harm her.'

'It's out of my hands. Your training officer is responsible for that business.' Qader held up both arms.

Colette

After a restless sleep, disturbed by nightmares of shadowy figures with rifles, Colette shuffled to Nonnie's writing desk, where she moved the chair out of the way to reach the windows. Pushing the curtains aside and opening the middle window, she inhaled air smelling of summer dust and lazy days. She relaxed. She was back in England.

Exploring more of Riverbend could wait. Instead, she sat down, pulled out a sheet from the top drawer and, with her grandmother's old-fashioned fountain pen, she wrote a love letter to Hannan:

My Dearest,

You are alive. Deep down in me, I can feel it so strongly. This letter will not reach you. None of the letters I write to you will. Tonight, the moon over the house where I now am will be full. I will send my messages of love up to the luminous disk in the sky for you to read. The moon is la lune in French, a nice-sounding word. La lune belongs to us, when it shows full. No one knows that; no one will ever know and no one can take that away from us. If astronauts land on the moon in the future, they will find a carpet of loving words we will have sent to each other and ask themselves what it means.

The ink ran thin and Colette's attention was drawn to a small mud-caked white car which must have driven up and was now parked in front of the house. Had the driver come up to the entrance to be let in? Dry knocks on her bedroom door told her that he was already on the first floor.

Trudy opened the door and a stocky, middle-aged man with coarse features entered the room. When he stepped into the triangle of light, she noticed a scar on his chin. His curly black beard had been shaven around it and grown back shorter and lighter in colour, emphasising the shape of the injury.

'What can I do for you?' Colette offered generously, although annoyed with Trudy.

'You have just moved in,' he said, giving away an accent.

She was taken right back to Kabul and her students. 'How do you know that?'

'You were not here before; you now are.'

'That makes only twisted sense.'

A noise was heard from downstairs. He backed away towards the door and checked outside, as if to make sure no one was eavesdropping on their conversation.

'I was passing at night and saw light in the house.'

'Do you live nearby and have a dog?'

'I am from the local council bureau.'

'Communists use the word *bureau* and probably some other regimes.' She put her hand on the receiver of the telephone.

He flinched.

When she took her hand back, he merely began to scratch in his thick hair. 'I must check who lives in houses. Empty houses attract low life.'

'Regular government censuses are made by mail. What is your name?'

'I cannot give you my name. For my security. In case there is a complaint.'

'You have to show identification before being let into a house. I will have to talk to my housekeeper.'

'You have a housekeeper and a very big house. You must know important people. Perhaps they come here to party. Perhaps you plan to travel abroad soon?'

She shook her head at him.

'I say that because the weather is not good here.'

'Where would you say the weather is good?'

'In…' He stopped himself.

'Please leave.' She opened the bottom drawer of the desk and pulled out her camera. She pointed it at him. His hand covered his face. He turned and sprinted from the room. Shortly after, she watched the dirty white car drive off. *What was that man really after? He was surely an Afghan. This must have to do with the Babur Gardens. This is not over, is it? Was he from the Mujahidin or the Taliban, and how did they know where I went after leaving Kabul? But then, no spy would have found it a challenge to follow Mum driving here.*

That evening, Colette skipped supper despite Trudy's protestations, and during the night she had a nightmare of Hannan's shot body weighing down on her. Only when morning light grew and the voile curtains in the open window were dancing to the warm morning breeze, did her worries dissolve.

A bee had found its way in and was flying about, trapped in the room. Colette lifted the curtain for the insect to find a way back to pollen flowers. The bee stubbornly missed the way out. Colette suddenly thought, there were no flowers planted in Riverbend. It was all rough grass, summer grass now, tall and bleached to a faded yellow. Why had nobody ever thought of enhancing the surroundings of Riverbend with flower beds? Indoors, flowers were on the duvet cover, on chinaware, in paintings. The bee landed on her desk and with busy legs moved over the last page of her journal entry.

'Jasmine,' Colette said. 'Wouldn't you love the dizzying sweet nectar of jasmine flowers?' The bee flew out of the room.

It was decided: she would plant flowers in Riverbend. Jasmine and frangipani. Perhaps a few pink roses like the ones Hannan had given her. The person who could help her do this was Davina, whom she had not yet contacted. There had been too many other things to be dealt with since her return.

Colette dialled Davina's number and the familiar voice answered. 'Hi,' said Colette.

'Oh my God, you're back.'

'I've been back three days now.' Colette told her friend about her grandmother leaving her Riverbend, but not why she had left Kabul. Davina told her that she had finished her florist course and finally had an interview with Blooms4You in three days' time.

'The place near *Little Sicily*.'

'Wish me luck,' Davina squeaked.

'Just be yourself.'

It's easy for you to give advice to poor struggling florists. You are the lady of the manor now.'

'Don't say that. My mother does.'

'What is the place like?'

'Apart from tough grassy things, there are no flowers anywhere in the parkland.'

'Parkland! Colette, you said parkland. What have you inherited?'

'You have to come and see. Please do come and see. I feel out of place. I think planting some jasmine would help.'

'Of course, I will come. But first I have to get the job with Blooms4You.'

'I understand. Just talking to you helps me feel calmer.'

Colette was still smiling minutes after the conversation had ended. She decided to forget the incident with the intruder and live day by day, grateful to be alive.

Trudy told Colette that thunderstorms were predicted. She embellished it with a description of lightning bouncing off Alpine cliff faces and cows dying from seizures. Colette went outside, heading for the swing, and nothing dramatic was about to happen.

But that night, another nightmare sapped her strength: she was lost in a deserted place and stumbling around in the moonlight trying to get her bearings.

Wednesday, going downstairs for breakfast, she found Trudy in the kitchen lifting the cast-iron pan off the stove with both hands and pouring a heap of scrambled eggs into a silver dish which had a domed lid.

'Why are you making such a huge amount when there are only two of us?'

'Half a dozen,' Trudy said. 'Every day we get six eggs. Another six are just about to arrive.'

With that said, the back door opened and a familiar woman with grey streaks in her short, wavy hair came into the kitchen. At the old pine table, she put down a six-pack egg carton. 'Welcome to this neck of the woods,' she said, looking at Colette.

'I told you,' grumbled Trudy.

'Elizabeth Worship,' Colette guessed tentatively.

'Of course it's me, but only your Granny called me Elizabeth. For the others, I am just Liz. We've all heard that you inherited the estate. Well done.'

'It was entirely my grandmother's wish.'

'Keeping it in the family makes sure things stay the way they were. With investors, you never know. This is such a lovely, quiet place. Nobody wants upheaval. I've known you since you were that high.' Her flat hand was lower than the tabletop.

Trudy spoke up. 'Liz was kind enough to do a weekly shop for Margaret.'

'We should keep this arrangement going, if you are happy to do it. We are also grateful for the eggs and will pay for them, if that is all right with you.' Colette felt for the first time like taking some control of her inheritance.

'They're a gift. Our hens are enthusiastic this season.'

'I know,' said Trudy. 'One of your plucky cluckies ended up in my kitchen.'

'Probably not without your helping hand,' Liz said.

'No one is to judge the actions of others. The vicar said that in church last Sunday.' Trudy shrugged with some disdain.

'Bob and I are happy to give away eggs. A dozen a day go to the SPAR Post Office and it's still omelette for us three times a week.' Liz picked up the egg carton which Trudy had emptied. 'Silly packaging, but hard to come by,' she said and left the kitchen, brandishing the carton.

When the door had shut behind Liz, Trudy said, 'The Worships also have sheep.' She rucked up her nose. 'They are stupid animals.'

'I thought you were a Swiss farmer's daughter.'

'Cows, Colly, not stinking sheep. Majestic cows with straight backs and glossy full udders.'

'I scarcely knew Liz and her husband when I was a child,' admitted Colette.

'You'll soon catch up on that. They are both eager to help out. Bob is practical but... but... in their heads, Riverbend belongs to them. A long time ago, manor houses and the farms and farmland were all one property. Margaret told me. The farmers see themselves as the salt of the earth, while we in the house are just occupants too fancy to be useful in life.'

'The feudal system,' said Colette.

'Don't worry, Colly. If Bob gives you any lip, he'll have me to deal with.' Trudy ushered Colette into the conservatory, offering tea to complement the scrambled eggs with toast.

Right after breakfast, Colette went back to Nonnie's

bedroom where Trudy had already made the bed, its cover so straight and tight it looked like a flower-embellished block of concrete.

The growling sound of the telephone on the desk made her jump with fright. The growl was repeated. Colette had to get a hold of herself; the telephone was just an item which by itself could not harm her.

'Excellent news, darling.' Audrey's voice, when she was excited. 'I have found you a lodger. He is a professional writer – member of the London writers' club I told you about. The secretary called the man a charmer with film-star qualities. I am sorry it is a *he* but perhaps that is what you need right now.'

Colette thanked her mother thinly and put the receiver down.

*

It was about ten in the morning a few days later when a huge, gleaming Mercedes drove up onto the forecourt. Colette, at her desk, concluded that it could only be the writer's – he of the alleged film-star qualities. Colette glued the lashes to her eyelids and put on a flowery calf-length summer dress and her headscarf.

Trudy burst into the room. 'There is a man in front of the house waiting to be let in. I peeked. He is very good-looking and drove here in a fancy car. There is no wedding ring on his finger.'

'All right. Send him up.' Colette sighed.

When the visitor strode in, Colette fiddled with her bangle.

'Gilbert de Villiers,' slid out of his mouth.

She checked her headscarf and almost stuttered, 'Audrey, my mother, found you.'

'More accurately, it was I who found your mother – a charming lady. Charming women bring into the world charming daughters—'

'Tea.' She cut him short.

'Very civilised. I like your house, the generous land that goes with it plus the lovely old trees and, of course, there is the river, the famous Ouse. Audrey was talking about an apartment to rent. At the moment, I share a house with another artist in Chelsea. One booze-up after another. I have deadlines. It is not working out. Would you show me around please?'

'I am not showing you the bedrooms. I don't think I am ready to share with a man, no matter how large. The house, not the man.'

She took him instead to see the caretaker's annexe and apologised for the rudimentary accommodation for someone used to Chelsea.

Gilbert de Villiers seemed primarily interested in the three garages. She had to open their doors. Walking heel to toe, the tip of his tongue out in concentration, he measured their dimensions. 'Perfect,' he declared after the exercise. 'Do you mind?' He took off his salmon-coloured blazer and slung it over his shoulder. The lining was maroon, like the car he had driven up in. The revealed shirt had ironed folds, as if they were still warm from the professional laundry service.

He pressed his lips together while nodding his handsome head. 'It's OK.' More engaged, he said, 'I will rent the garages and the gardener's place. If you want me to pay for electricity, it'll be fine with me. The garages are for my babies.'

'You must know that you are not allowed to turn garages into living space.'

'Ha ha,' he laughed and showed well-cared-for teeth. A back tooth must have had a mishap though; it glinted, capped in gold. This personalised his laughter. 'I own two Mercedes and plan on a third. The pure-breed types need to be sheltered from the elements.'

His offer was generous. She had no intention of owning a car. Mother thought it right to rent to him. Trudy was in awe of him. He would live in Mr Crocket's accommodation and write. That should not bother her. She agreed. They shook hands. She felt the hardness of his signet ring. On the way back to the house, he stroked with his large hand over the stone ball on the plinth. It coated her in shivers. Her head resembled one of those balls.

By the time they had reached the top step, she began to have second thoughts. She turned to him, brusquely. 'Are you married?'

With his constrained smile, the gold tooth did not show. 'I have earned the name of the impossible-to-land bachelor of London.'

Colette nodded earnestly. 'OK.'

'What about you?' he challenged her.

She hesitated. 'There is someone but he does not live here. He is in hospital at the moment.'

'Sorry to hear that.'

Colette reached out to open the door for them but

Trudy, having sat in wait, beat her to it. 'Hello, I am Trudy from Guggisberg,' she announced herself rather loudly. Colette thought that she would have to have words with Trudy about doors.

'Droll,' de Villiers mused.

'She is Swiss and works as housekeeper.'

'Good to hear, with a house of that size.' He beamed at Trudy so generously that she shrank from it. 'Guggisburg,' he said. 'All you will have to do to impress me is make me decent coffee.'

'It's Guggisberg,' she said with indignation, and disappeared into the house like a rodent into its burrow.

*

What are we going to do with this Don Juan in our house? Colette asked herself. *Nobody in Briddleton is going to like a fancy man like that. Oh, and Trudy. They are hardly a match made in heaven.*

And here she came, wiping from her mouth lipstick she had only just applied.

Concerned that Trudy might be reluctant to be given extra work, Collette said quickly, 'I agreed to rent him Crocket's flat. He won't be bothering us.'

'Is that so?'

'He offered to pay for his electricity and I offered breakfast in the rental arrangement. I hope that's all right.'

'Three for scrambles in the morning.' Trudy threw up her arm as if to indicate the start of a flamenco. 'Come and dance with me, handsome man.'

'I am glad you take it that way, although a bit baffled by your behaviour.'

'Margaret would also have been amused by a dandy like that. Our neighbours certainly won't be.'

Davina

For Davina, who had received an A Plus on her six-month florist course, it was the day of the interview with Blooms4You.

'Be yourself,' Colette had advised. That is precisely what Davina had decided not to be.

Since Blooms4You had taken off five years before, it had changed location three times. What had once been no more than a start-up in a disused scouts shed in Lambeth had subsequently spread out in a newly built business park. Since then, the company had recently moved into a location which Max Merton, the CEO, was hugely enthusiastic about. Davina could tell from the way he had sounded on the phone to confirm the interview appointment. The location was in the heart of London, where business space was scarce and expensive. Astley Court was affordable because its aspect was unfavourable, more like a *you-must-be-joking* location for serious business. Surprisingly, it was near St Pancras – unexpected, but of course ideal.

Davina, who had not found Astley Court on any map, took a taxi from the station. It was a quarter to two in the afternoon.

'It's a stone's throw from here,' grumbled the taxi driver. 'You could have walked.'

After a few tight turns, the taxi began to rattle on egg-shaped cobblestones. They found themselves in a spacious courtyard. Her generous tip did not appease the driver who banged the door of his car shut after she got out.

Davina took her bearings. To the east, Astley Court was skirted by an ancient wall built of liver-coloured bricks which, over time, had developed dark spots. Curiously, it was interrupted by a short stretch of stone walling, unevenly built and badly concreted together. In that stretch was a cave. The grotto was in deep shade. There was something magical yet unnerving about this recess. Davina, drawn to it, approached with caution. Inside was a stone bench fixed against the curved uneven wall and, above the bench, a smooth stone medallion with carvings which she could not make out. Further along, the brick wall was interrupted again by steps leading up. There were four of them before a second stone wall blocked any further ascent. One could not but ask oneself where these steps, now cracked and overgrown with grass and mosses, had originally led.

Straight ahead of her was the principal building of Astley Court. A whitewashed rectangular construction which lacked windows on the side facing her. Attached to it on the left-hand side, like an afterthought, was a similarly whitewashed extension, lower in build but with a wide opening, closed now by tall wooden doors on rollers. Most probably during the First World War, it had served as stables for horses to help whatever trade was then installed here.

Suddenly, a train rattled past so close as to make her jump. The tailwind shook cabbage whites out of the bending laburnums growing along the wire fencing. Davina took off her heeled interview shoes and, on tights, went to the fence leading away from the stable building. At her feet was a drop to the train tracks entering and leaving St Pancras station.

By now, the taxi had turned and driven off, and no train was coming in or out, so all that remained were the vague and slightly menacing noises of London.

Davina hobbled across the cobbles towards the tall doors. She stepped over two runnels which connected at a drain hole. A bird with open wings had been forged by a blacksmith into the metal drain cover. It gave away that this place had history.

At this point, one side of the stable doors slid open and a man appeared. His head was up, his neck stretched. Max Merton. She recognised him from a picture in *Today*'s Business Success. She remained hesitant while he, striding with confidence, came up to her.

'This is an unusual location for a flower business,' she said defensively, while slipping her shoes back on, showing him her backside from alternate angles. 'Is it safe?'

'What do you mean by that?'

'The courtyard is wide open to the road. Anyone can drive in, get rid of their old car or dump rubbish. And it is not exactly in the safest part of London, so close to the railway and looking like an overgrown ruin. Most people in London have no idea that this exists.'

'They don't. You must be the two p.m. interview.'

'Wow.' She seemed unable to avoid letting herself down. 'Better tell me all about the job before the ten past two interviewee shows up.'

He remained unfazed. 'This place is special. I am excited about it. I dug around in the archives and found out that, in 1560, it was an orphanage. What they called then a foundling hospital.'

She was looking at his face while he spoke and saw his enthusiasm. 'Perhaps you are right and I should plan for a fence and gate. But then,' he see-sawed his head shortly, 'closing Astley Court off, with flower deliveries coming and going...?'

She backed down. She had not really meant to interfere in the practicalities of his workplace. Why had she started on such a negative note? Especially since his first impression on her was encouraging. Max was tall, a man to look up to. He was dressed casually: beige chinos and a short-sleeved shirt. His hair, the colour of woodland honey, soft and supple, looped from the parting on top of his head like swags of silk either side of his high forehead. His eyes on her, grey like rain, were surprising by their intensity.

He guided her, two fingers behind her elbow, towards the gap in the door he had come out of. She blinked in the neon light. Her *horse stable* was now clearly used as a dispatch room. There were rows of buckets filled with bouquets of flowers. A young male employee was packing them into cardboard boxes.

'This is Winnie.' Max introduced the man.

Winnie shot Davina a short glance. 'Don't say it.'

'*The Pooh*, you mean?' Seeing his expression, she went on, 'Winston Churchill was called Winnie.'

'There will be three more London rounds today,' Max said, before leading Davina into the main building. As the vaulted ceiling was high, neon strip-lights hung from metal chains. Up against the unevenly plastered wall was a stone plaque as one finds in churches. Latin was chiselled into it.

'I can understand why you like these premises. History and flowers go well together,' said Davina, squaring her shoulders and standing straight.

'They don't,' he snapped. 'Flowers are the present, nothing more. Yesterday buds, tomorrow compost.'

Her shoulders sank.

The long room they were in had two tall uncurtained windows on either short side. The colour of the plaster on the wall had faded to pale rose and worn grey. There was a fireplace surround as tall as a man but no hearth. To Davina, it felt as if the room had served as a chapel or something similar.

Blooms4You had only moved in two weeks before and folding tables were set up with buckets underneath. Cellophane and silk-paper rolls stood vertical on them. There were scissors and clippers and several green rubbish bags: a minimum to be able to function at all. She noticed a spiral metal staircase leading up, not to a chancel as could be expected, but with one more turn to reach an upper floor, which was set back and did not extend over the whole surface of the building.

'It had to be an old chapel or ceremony hall,' Davina said to Max, who was watching her looking around.

'Isn't it splendid?'

'If this space together with the packing room is the total of Blooms4You, how do you cope with large orders?'

'You have no faith in me,' he said with calm pride. 'What you could not see hidden behind this building is another, a vast space. The entire wall towards the railway is made of squares of glass, tinted all shades of green, some broken and some with bars on them.'

'Great,' she said. 'How does one get to this ideal place?'

'I'll show you.'

On the long north-facing wall were well-concealed double doors. He pushed them open. She felt a breath of stale air on her face. What she looked into was not unlike a palely lit miniature railway station. The tempered greenish light coming from the collection of windows illuminated an abandoned bucket wagon, its metal wheels on metal rails embedded into the concrete floor.

'Big enough?' asked Max tartly.

'What do you think happened in this room?'

'The orphans must have been made to work here,' Max offered.

'Doing what?'

'I guess they helped out in the workshop which was already here in fifteen hundred. Besides, this site has been used by many other businesses since then, having such good rail connections. From up here, it is possible to throw stuff right down into open wagons.'

'And now it is yours to use,' she said.

'No.'

She held back from asking, *Why not?*

'It will be *ours* if you join Blooms4You.'

They left the rail room to go back into the chapel flower-arranging space.

Max, you are one of a kind, she thought.

'Come up to my office,' he invited her and started to mount the spiral stairs. She climbed after him, trying not to make too much of a clattering noise. Probably, one ought not to wake ghosts of the past in these surroundings.

They stepped off the staircase into a cramped room.

'My office.' He waved his arm grandly.

She entered, pushing past him. There was a round stained-glass window depicting a bird of prey on a stylised tree branch. Max's desk, with twin computer screens on it, filled most of the space. If he rolled his office chair too far back, he would hit one of the two large metal cabinets against the wall, and she asked herself how they had managed to get those up the spiral.

'What's the drawing on the side of the filing cabinet?'

He didn't answer.

In the colourful picture, a stylised girl with a stick body and arms, five fingers spread on each hand, stood in a display of different flowers, all of them with smiling faces turned to the onlooker. In the blue sky, the smiling sun shone. *For Wax* was written at the bottom of the artwork, presumably done by a Year 2 child, the M inverted. The piece of paper showed that it had been pinned up many times and a small corner had been lost.

'A beautiful thank you note from a very young satisfied customer?' she ventured.

'Every flower smiles at you.' He looked away from her, his Adam's apple bobbing up and down. She sensed some tragedy was linked to the picture and felt guilty for having drawn attention to it.

'Nice window,' she said instead, thinking it darkened the room so much that one had to use electricity even on the brightest of days. 'In the window,' she dared ask, 'is that a hawk?'

'It's a kite. In the mid-fifteen-hundreds, apart from the famous ravens, red kites circled over London, dive-bombing and terrorising children, and snatching small babies.'

She remained pensive.

In a second room, which he called the conference room, was a table and eight chairs. At the head of it was another computer – Max's place. Nothing more fitted. She hoped he would not expect her to be experienced in computing. She had learned some basic things from her boyfriend, Simon, but the whole concept put her off. Her thesis, and the book she had written after that, had been typed on a word processor which, at the time, she had thought of as advanced technology.

Max invited her to sit down. The room also had a round window of the same size, with a similar kite. This bird however had an arrow planted in its chest and blood drops ran from it in beautiful, stained-glass ruby red.

The formal interview was more than overdue. Was it in here that the abandoned children were brought to be institutionalised? She imagined dirty mites with sunken, frightened eyes and hungry bellies, who were allocated cots in a grimy building now gone. It had probably been reached by the overgrown steps in the wall.

Davina wanted to work here. She needed the experience of commerce and to get her hands dirty after so many years of study. She was intrigued by Max and liked the location, so close to St Pancras from where it would only take her twenty minutes to her home in West Hampstead.

Tensely, she watched Max read from the CV she had sent him. Inside the building he loved so, his grey eyes had picked up warmth, as he bestowed a short smile on her. She thought him sensitive for a man who had built a company like Blooms4You. She even felt he was hoping to be able to give her the job.

Yesterday, her interview had been in a hyper-modern industrial estate. The interviewer had boasted of the company's links to over one hundred websites, enabling them to distribute all over Europe. The premises were lean, clean, lots of space, lots of light, flower refrigerators all along the wall, cutting and trimming tables for every florist, each at least five feet wide. Cellophane roll, silk-paper roll and ribbons, all fixed to a stand at the end of the work table. Bar stools which swivelled and a human resources person introducing herself as Sylvia, a name with a sharp whistle, who had told Davina that, with a PhD, she was overqualified.

Today, Davina was tapping around in a derelict chapel of a ruined orphanage, tucked away behind St Pancras station, with a man who would have made a good priest rather than an impressive modern business manager.

'Tell me,' he said. 'What are your favourite flowers?'

She hesitated. It was important she gave the answer he was hoping for. 'Roses,' she said. 'Hybrid teas, tall ones.' How could she go wrong with that?

'That's it – roses?' He was not pleased. 'Was there a garden where you grew up?'

She shook her head. 'Not really, not in a semi in Peterborough. But we often went to the park. I like all flowers which give off a pleasing scent.'

Elbows on the table, with both hands he forked the elusive hair away from his forehead, while focusing on her. 'As you must know, in the flower business, customers don't care much for the scent. They rather resent it.'

'Stock,' she picked up. 'Some people hate it. Lilies – many with asthma are allergic to lilies.'

'I see here that you studied plant biology at Royal Holloway. And, most admirably, you based your doctorate on plants growing in Afghanistan, where you spent time researching. I would have thought not easy for a woman.'

She had prepared an answer for this, one which she had used in yesterday's interview. Max's head was bent over her CV again. He did not give her a chance to say anything, as if he did not want to hear a polished answer. Instead, he forged on, 'What made you decide to become a florist?'

'Human contact.'

He did not understand what she meant.

'Say it with flowers. Celebrate someone with flowers. Flowers bringing people together, flowers on tables to make them festive, flowers the consolers at funerals, flowers embellishing a bride. One rose – a heart full of regret, saying sorry.'

He liked this; she sensed it.

'If you are computer-trained, then you are hired.'

'And if I am not?'

'You're still hired. Just testing whether you think you are up-to-date with modern technology and how honest you are. When Blooms4You started, we got customers via flower shops, pamphlets through doors and print advertising. Now we have a website.'

'I know what a website is and can imagine what it can do for a business.'

A silence followed. Both of them looked up at the arrow-speared bird.

'Now that I know more about you as a human being,' he continued, 'let me talk about how our small team functions here in our headquarters. I need you to be joint-head of the product assembly hall with Florence, as well as flower analyst, and inventor of eye-pleasing arrangements suited to the seasons, the occasions. Creations which I will put on our website for customers to be thrilled by.'

'Flower analyst?'

'I've just made up the title. You will tell me which flowers are best for when, what to look out for when buying in bulk, which flowers are intolerant of others, how to keep each type fresh for longer, and what ingredients should be in plant food. Hiring an expert like you will give me a special angle in a business which is cut-throat competitive.'

'Interflora,' she said.

He twitched, almost jumped in the seat. 'That is a word we avoid saying out loud.' He bent his head as if in shame about his spontaneous reaction. Back in control, he said, 'That unmentionable company started in 1928 by walking the streets, pulling wagons full of flowers and shouting their business.'

She suddenly liked him very much.

He forked back his hair. 'Blooms4You already runs on two qualified florists and three trainees, two despatchers, one of whom you have met, one full-time driver, two part-time drivers, and two full-time runners. I am offering to hire you as the third qualified florist, but with extra responsibilities based on your academic achievements. You have limited experience as a florist but a wide knowledge of plants, based on your thesis. I presume you went to Afghanistan and did not copy it all out of books.' Looking down, he kept his smile to himself.

They seemed to have lost concentration on boss interviewing applicant.

'Wasn't it dangerous – a single young woman alone amongst a race which despises us?'

'They are humans the same way we are. If politicians realised this, it would be so much easier.'

'Aren't women considered inferior and have to cover their heads?'

'Tradition, I guess,' she said. Seeing his frown, she went on, 'Women and indeed men have covered their heads since time began, in all walks of life, in all professions and in every country on the globe.'

'When can you start?' He slid a contract across the table.

Davina did not get up. 'Please, before I leave, tell me

what you have found out about the foundling hospital.'

He smiled openly for the first time. She realised that he had spent much time digging around in old papers.

'Baron Boyd Astleyton in fifteen hundred was a dashing aristocrat.'

'Living in Astley Court which then was grandiose?'

'No, no. He was baron of some English borough. He was a womaniser, a playboy of the worst kind, and got a lot of women into trouble. Not just disrespectable women, but ladies of standing. At that time a foundling home was set up in London, called Christ's Hospital, where unwanted newborns were handed in. It was financially supported by the government. There were rules and regulations, and the baby's mother identified. Playboy Astleyton knew a lot of angry women. It is believed that when he found out that two of his offspring had been suffocated by their desperate mothers, he made the decision to set up a private anonymous hospital for orphans.'

'The remains of what we are in now?'

'Yep,' Max confirmed. 'There was a basket into which women could put their newborns during the hours of darkness. Astleyton kept the children and educated them until they were ten years of age. For the next four, they had to work for free to pay off some of the money it had cost to keep them alive.'

'A grim story,' said Davina.

'It gets grimmer. The red kites helped themselves from the baby basket. They attacked small children playing in the courtyard. The baron had the grotto built, so the children could hide from the voracious birds.'

'One more question,' Davina said, getting out of the chair. 'Why is this place called Astley Court and not Astleyton?'

'The baronetcy had two sons and the family split. Playboy Astleyton gave the name of his cousin to the foundling hospital to make sure his own name had nothing to do with unwanted babies in any way ever again.'

Contraception is a blessed thing, Davina concluded, as she walked back to St Pancras after the strangest of interviews.

★

When Davina unlocked the door to the basement flat half an hour later, she kicked some trainers out of the way, dropped her bag on the floor and sank onto the purple sofa, which allowed her to reach down to her hot, sticky feet and prise them out of the high heels. Then she wriggled the tights over her lower body and down the legs. Reaching out to her toes, she pulled the tights off. Only then did Simon appear, coming down from the mezzanine on which was just enough room for his computer desk, a narrow bookshelf and a landline phone. 'You're back. Did you get it?'

'I'll tell you in a minute. First, what are you doing home?' As she said it, she checked the clock on the sideboard.

'Friday afternoon.'

'Of course. On Fridays, you finish early,' she said absent-mindedly, as the voice of Max still sounded in her ears and the impression of the orphanage occupied most of her emotions.

'Did you get the job?' Simon insisted.

'Yes, I got the job. The building is amazing. Nobody, absolutely nobody, knows about that place. These historic lost crannies make London so exciting.'

'How much are they going to pay you?'

She took the contract from her bag and showed it to him.

'You agreed to that without negotiating?'

'I want to work there.'

'And I want to buy a Mercedes Sport. That little salary you have committed yourself to is not going to make that happen.'

'Remember, I've only had a fast-track course in floristry and the only work experience I had was at the hot dog stand at college.'

'I'm off to the pub. Carlos and I have to work on something I've come up with. Look,' Simon said, schmoozing her, 'there is no point in you coming.' He picked up the tights. 'We'll only bore you.'

She snatched them from him.

'Management at work has invested in the latest computer system. DIY ware right down to the smallest screws, all monitored by computer. If one of the items is low on the shelves, the computer goes *bing*. How cool is that?' Simon sprinted back up to the mezzanine and his desk, shouting out, 'Computerisation has only just been born.'

She watched his legs move around his desk. Simon – a boyfriend she had finally managed to keep to herself, but who now drained that first flush of success by being a man. He was wrong for her. They had little in common except for the practicalities of life for single working people in London. When they moved into 27A Calvert Street to cohabit, the main reason was to save money by reducing two rents to one.

A few minutes later, Simon reappeared, rucksack on his back. And then she heard the door shut with a bang. It was such an ordinary thing that saying goodbye was superfluous. Simon would spend the next four or five hours in the Black Lion on Kilburn High Street with Carlos, a colleague from the DIY company.

By this stage in their relationship, she was no longer guilty about feeling relief at his departure. The one thing she yearned to do was tell Colette about the interview.

When the two women were connected by British Telecom, Colette asked Davina, 'Tell me what it looks like where you now are talking from.'

'London, a basement flat. Why is that important?'

'Ever since Kabul, I think that people's surroundings have a major effect on their mental disposition.'

'Colette, are you all right?'

'Sorry. It's just that you are the only one with whom I can talk about Kabul. Kabul has bombshelled my life.'

'We'll talk about it a lot. Promise. Right now, I called to tell you I have been hired by Blooms4You. Yay! The premises of the company are crazy. They are basically a ruin and my boss, Max Merton, is… How should I put it…?'

'You fancy him.'

'Max looks a little like Liam Neeson, has a strange way of expressing himself, and is unique.'

'When are you going to come up to Bedford? I too now have a handsome man living near me.'

'What, you?'

'I said *near* me. Also, I still have this bee in my bonnet about growing jasmine. Could you please send me one to plant?'

Colette

Colette went to Liz next door to borrow her husband for a flower-planting job.

'I'll send Bob round,' the farmer's wife promised, walking through the yard, kicking a chicken out of her way.

Shortly afterwards, Bob appeared. 'What can I do for the lady of the house?'

'I have decided to plant jasmine.'

'What's that?'

'Sweet-smelling flowers.'

'Flowers? You've got room for a vegetable garden, a big one.'

'Jasmine is a climber and I was hoping you could sort of install a wooden grid standing up in the lawn for the plant to clamber up on.'

Bob gave her a look she could not fathom. 'Against the wall of the house, I could fix wires.'

'That would probably also work,' she acquiesced.

'What you have to do is dig a hole where you want the plant to be. It has to be good earth and not rubble.'

'I can do that,' she said, invigorated by a sense of involvement. 'A sunny wall.' She smiled. 'Do we have a shovel?'

'Margaret's shovel ended up with me. She never used it. I'll bring it round one of these days.'

'Now, please. My friend has sent me a young jasmine plant this morning and I want to put it into earth right now.'

'As madam wishes.'

Straight after lunch, with the shovel, Colette started to cut into the lawn at the foot of the south-facing wall. She felt the ridge of the blade despite the thick sole of her outdoor shoe. There was something satisfying in the way the metal sheet cut into the soft soil, driven by the pressure of the foot. It was harder work than she had imagined. The earth she turned up was good and she kept going. Around her, the early September day was foggy grey and silent, apart from the occasional anxious cries of rooks from the wise old conifers.

And then the mood changed with the sound of a car door being slammed and a male voice singing, 'Diddly diddly pum.'

Colette left the shovel planted in the soil. Hunched, she traipsed along the front wall of Riverbend. At the east corner, she dared advance her head to see what turned out to be the big Mercedes parked in front of the garages. The man who had stopped singing was pulling cases from the open boot and carrying them through to his lodgings. When the last piece of luggage was out, he drove the car into the right-hand garage. Colette waited. Light came on in the caretaker's living room. Gilbert de Villiers had moved in. He had not bothered to close the garage doors; he was a careless man. Strong winds would play rough with those doors and then they would need not just a lick of paint but replacing. Colette's income from Nonnie's investments would not reach to making up for vandalism in Riverdale.

She went back to her jasmine and yanked the shovel out of the earth to continue digging.

A sudden whiff of stale tobacco mixed with cheap aftershave reached her. As she turned, both her arms were grabbed and twisted to her back.

'Let go of me!' she shouted and the shovel fell to the ground. Colette's shoulder blades smarted from the unnatural position of her arms. She was forced to stare at the bricks of which Riverbend was built, while her aggressor wound tape around her joined wrists, several times judged on the *crissing* noise of the tape being unrolled. She shouted for help, so loudly her whole body shook from the effort. Where were Trudy, Gilbert, the neighbours? She could not possibly be abducted in broad daylight, yet the man held her tight.

A second man thrust himself between her and the wall. He was shorter than her but solidly built, in a black leather jacket, gloves, and with a woolly cap pulled down low. He turned his face sideways for a second and she saw the scar valley in his beard. *Chin-scar*, the man from the *bureau*, obviously an Afghan terrorist on orders from Kabul. 'I loved him,' she moaned and was knocked down to her knees.

Chin-scar produced a strip of Gorilla Tape which he stuck over her mouth, the attacker behind her holding her head steady by clamping it between his thighs. She felt the tape stuck to her skin from her left ear, over her lips and ending shortly after the right corner of her mouth. Her heart was racing. Her body turned leaden. Paralysed by fear, her long pale legs refused to function when they pulled her up and tried to frogmarch her away. She lost a shoe. Eventually, they grabbed her under the armpits and dragged her into the shadow of the oak tree where the swing hung and their dirty, white car was parked. Trudy must be in the kitchen at the back of the house and Gilbert busy installing himself. The smelly one shoved her into the car and pushed himself in next to her on the back seat. Through the slits of the balaclava, she felt the hatred in his eyes rather than actually seeing them. *Slit-eye* shut the car door.

Beyond anything, Colette feared that she would asphyxiate. She gave a drawn-out moan and Slit-eye slapped her. Her cheek felt pricked with a thousand needles. She sank back into the seat. Chin-scar started the car.

She tossed her head as if that could loosen the Gorilla Tape. Slit-eye reached out and slapped her again. Her brain seemed to ring. The back of her eyes pressed against the eyeballs: her way of crying. She mustn't panic. Agitation would make breathing more difficult. She relied only on her nostrils to get air. As it was, the upper edge of the tape cut sharply into her septum. She moaned faintly. She was at the mercy of these terrorists. They could have shot her, knifed her. But no, they were abducting her to some place where others would torture her. Cardiac arrest would be desirable, she thought, feeling her strained heart.

Chin-scar drove across the front of Riverbend. The tyres crunched on the forecourt gravel. Why did nobody hear it? If only she could climb over the front seat and reach the car horn. Slit-eye next to her, as if he had felt her intention, reached out and thrust her back against the upholstery. *I must remain calm*, she told herself. Panic would induce hysteria and already she was starting to lack oxygen. All she had to concentrate on was breathing evenly, while her nose was still unblocked.

Chin-scar turned right to engage on the descent to the gate. He said something to Slit-eye who pinched her arm. She squealed. They were reassured that she was still conscious. They drove down to the gate. She tilted her head way back. When she felt the seam of the back seat, she started to twist her head left and right, applying pressure. The hijab came off. Slit-eye, seeing her naked head, reeled back with surprise. From his mouth came a string of curses in a foreign language and he took a gun from his trouser belt.

Chin-scar twisted in his seat. Seeing an alien, he lost control of the vehicle. They swerved right. He over-corrected, and the car slewed to the left and rammed into the gate. First they were thrown forward and then back. Slit-eye dropped the gun and Chin-scar, who was not wearing a seatbelt, hit the windscreen. He cried out in pain and blood ran down his face. The car's front bumper was caught on the wrought iron. He engaged reverse, the tyres freewheeling, engine squealing. He increased the revs, while Slit-eye was rummaging around the floor of the vehicle to find his gun. The driver changed tactics. He drove fast forward and immediately back again, which twisted the car sideways, flinging its flank against the gate. The back door next to Colette sprang open.

While Slit-eye's arm was deep under the front passenger seat and his head turned away, she threw herself out of the car. Not able to use her arms and wearing only one shoe, she hobbled back up the drive. Moving her face muscles and blowing air into her cheeks repeatedly, she managed to loosen the shorter side of the tape to open up a small hole. She could now breathe alternately through her nostrils or the gap in the corner of her mouth. Any second, she could be shot or thrown to the ground. She kept going. The pain in her shoulders was becoming unbearable. She forced herself to remember the night of the full moon and Hannan down below, the glittering, the magic.

She was almost at the top of the incline when she heard fast breathing behind her. 'Mum, I love you,' she tried to mumble. A strong hand grabbed her arm. The lack of bad aftershave told her that it was Chin-scar. His hand was over the lapis lazuli bangle, which he pulled off her wrist. She waited shivering with fear. Nothing more happened.

When she dared turn round, she saw Chin-scar back down at the car, wiping the blood off his face with her hijab. Slit-eye had obviously taken the driver's seat. The engine roared and, with a loud metal clang, the car came off the gate and drove away. What Colette did not see was that Chin-scar threw the bangle out of the car window and into the River Ouse.

Was it over? Had she saved herself by showing her naked head? She crossed the forecourt and mounted the stone steps. In front of the door, she was helpless as she could not use her hands or even her teeth to get inside.

Sitting down on the mat, she placed her bound wrists over the metal boot-scraper behind her and seesawed the tape over the blade. Slowly the tape frayed, the pressure loosened and then gave. Her hands were free. A second later, so was her mouth. She opened the door and went into Riverbend, wearing one outdoor shoe. The tall mirror showed her head bald, the grotesqueness of it having probably saved her life that day.

From the door to the kitchen, Trudy shouted, 'Where have you been? Your lodger has arrived.'

'I know,' Colette shouted back, as if nothing untoward had happened at all. She went up to Nonnie's bedroom, dialled the local police number and spoke to a man who introduced himself as Constable Stanley.

She told him what had happened, leaving out her bald head, with the assailants just driving too fast and slamming into the gate. To impress on the policeman the seriousness of the situation, she said, 'I am being targeted by Islamic terrorists. I am on their extermination list. You must have a specialist unit.' Colette's words tumbled out. She finished by declaring, 'I can't live in constant fear. I need protection.'

There was a longish pause before Stanley responded with, 'Let me recapitulate. Whilst gardening, you were interrupted by two men, one of whom you had met before. Then you got into a car which was familiar to you. The driver, who had a scar on his chin, lost control of the vehicle during the drive down from your house. He rammed into the metal gate damaging the front of his car. You were in the back seat. When the car door opened following the crash, you got out and returned to your house. Might I suggest that you have an alarm system installed?'

'I'll consider it,' Colette said and hung up. Looking at her bare arm, she wondered why they had stolen her bracelet. It wasn't that valuable. But for them, it seemed to be. If that was all they were after, Constable Stanley was right in seeing this incident as a blip rather than a full-blown political incident.

Infuriating though it was not to be taken seriously by the police, it helped her to minimalise the impact of the attack and get on with her life.

Davina

At the florists' table in Astley Court *chapel* as Davina, to Max's growing irritation, called the product assembly hall, she went through the job cards left for her by Max, who no doubt had worked till late the previous night.

The first order was: *Coffin cushion, 82-year-old man. Price range C.*

The second: *Bridal bouquet, pillar-shape, off-white dress. Cheapest available.*

The third: *Two table-spreads in The Barley Mow, Woking. Private room, yearly meeting of campervan owners club. 40 place settings. To include pub entrance display. Price range B.*

Thank you for working for me. Max had added a last card, as he did every time.

'You slipped that Barley Mow card into my pile, didn't you?' Davina accused Florence.

'I did not.'

'A display in a pub entrance. How? On what?'

'It's a rural setting. I know the pub. There is already a vintage wheelbarrow in the entrance. I would plan for partridge feathers and wheat stalks.'

'Thanks,' mouthed Davina, because Max was behind them, checking.

'What flowers will you use for the funeral cushion?' he asked Davina.

'I'll go into the railway room and see what needs to be used.'

'Bad answer. The man who died was eighty-two years old. He was born during the First World War. Those who will attend his funeral are equally old. They want to see flowers to which they can relate.'

'Poppies?'

Max walked on.

Florence grinned. 'Surely you have worked out by now that it is Max who does the joking. We say, "Yes, Max".'

'I know this isn't the right moment to ask, but what is the meaning of the child's painting in Max's office?'

After a while, Florence replied, 'There will never be a right moment to ask that question.' She looked up and straight at Davina. 'Max's six-year-old sister, Lucinda, who said, "If you look closely, every flower smiles at you", disappeared from their garden. A few days later, her body was found in the nearby woods.' Tears glazed Florence's eyes. 'When you look closely, flowers *do* smile at you.'

Davina understood the bittersweet reason why Max had started Blooms4You.

That evening, Davina called Colette. 'I spend my working hours creating flower arrangements and none of them are for you.'

'You offered me the jasmine climber, a valuable gift.'

'The downside is that you have to plant it in the garden.'

'Done. I planted it on the day my lodger moved in and something terrible happened.'

'With the lodger?'

'No. I can't tell you over the phone.'

Davina did not reply.

'It is not over yet.'

'We need to talk about this. You and I should meet up again soon.' Another pause, before, 'I believe I could get you a good deal on a subscription. The days will get shorter and darker; flowers would brighten up your house and lift your morale.' Before Colette could say anything, Davina decided, 'I will send you our brochure. Have a look and then we can talk about pricing.'

'I see the Davina businesswoman emerge. You were the one who decided to charge more for the hot dogs that I was selling at university events.'

'Pushing frozen sausages into warmed buns.'

'You will never let me forget that.'

'Nope.'

'Thanks for trying to jolly me up. Something shocking did happen to me. I need you.'

'Oh, Colly. I am so sorry to hear that. Winnie can drive me up next time he delivers in the Cambridge area.'

Colette

In September, the good weather held. Colette checked the jasmine plant daily and it seemed to have taken. She also wrote her journal and was reading books which she found on Nonnie's shelves. It was the nights which were her enemy. Having lost the bangle did not help.

On a sunny day, Winnie drove Davina in the Blooms 4You van up to Bedford. In Nonnie's bedroom, Colette at her desk stared out of the window fixedly, her whole body tense with anticipation. When the van, covered in pictures of flowers, appeared, she finally rested her eyes and loosened her neck, but stayed put. Nonnie's room was warm and personal, the drawing room too impersonally large and awkward.

The door was flung open. Trudy stepped out of the way.

'Freesias, gift from Blooms4You.' Davina held out the bunch with a wide smile, her dark eyes glittering. 'Well, well. You certainly have inherited a gem of a property,' she admired. 'Is that the shocking thing which happened to you?' She laid the flowers on the duvet at the foot of the bed where they mingled with the flowery cover. 'And your pallor has become even more ephemeral, while I am getting rounder, darker and more peasant-like.'

The two women hugged.

'I was right, wasn't I? Kabul is fab,' Davina prompted.

'It was quite something. The fall-out is also quite something but of a different kind.'

Davina frowned. 'But you have to agree that flatbread with nigella seeds and quince jam is better than marmalade on toast.'

'Definitely.'

'And then for me, of course, the exotic plants and flowers.'

'I hope the jasmine I planted against the house will bloom next year.'

'With all the land you inherited, you can plant more than just one jasmine bush.'

'Everyone says that about *my land*, but I don't like to go outside. Three weeks ago, two men were trespassing. They had a car and, just as I had patted down the earth around the jasmine plant, they—'

'Colly, what did they do to you?'

'They tried to kidnap me.'

'Surely not.'

'I only got away because the one driving crashed into the entrance gate.'

'You're telling the truth.' Davina looked at Colette with concern. 'Coming in, I noticed the damaged gate. Have you told the police?'

'They don't believe me. I must not think about it. It is too upsetting. I can't sleep at night.'

'Why do you think someone wanted to abduct you – for a ransom, a prank which went wrong?'

'Probably a prank. Let's forget about it.'

Davina pulled Colette out of Nonnie's bedroom and out of the house.

'Such a nice day and you are wearing an Afghan cotton dress. Bought in Chicken Street, right? I close my eyes and smell the condiments in the market. It left like a taste, a smell, a feeling in me I will never forget, and sort of always will miss.'

'I know what you mean,' admitted Colette. 'Kabul makes you feel like that,' she said barely audibly.

The two women walked across the gravel in front of the house. Davina declared the jasmine bush healthy and then pointed to places in the lawn beyond the driveway which would be suitable for flowerbeds.

'Could that be done perhaps with roses? Freesias are not a possibility, are they?' asked Colette.

'Freesias come from South Africa and are now grown in hothouses on the Isle of Guernsey. As for roses, they need frequent watering, don't like wind, and the mulching underneath is difficult unless you plant primroses, which only bloom in the spring.'

The women turned the east corner of the house.

'What building is that?'

'It used to be stables but is now garages with accommodation for a caretaker. He is gone.'

'Very impressive: a mansion, land right down to the Ouse, garages, staff accommodation. Not to forget those three magnificent conifers over there, which were planted over a hundred years ago. You inherited all this from a grandmother who trusted you to keep it up.'

'I took over a contract with a gardening company to tidy the trees and trim the several miles of hawthorn hedge around the property twice a year. Nonnie had started to negotiate with Bob, the next-door farmer, for his sheep to graze on the land. I have to find out more about that.'

'Sheep? You don't want sheep. They eat roses for pudding and— Look over there,' she interrupted herself. 'A man has just driven a fancy car out of one of your garages. He has stopped and opened the bonnet. He's taking photographs of the motor. Say something.'

'He's my lodger. He rents the caretaker's place.'

'That's the man you mentioned being in your life now.'

'He is the garage lodger and it is a financial arrangement.'

'To start with.'

'To go on with.'

'The man is fabulous-looking. Tell me more about him.'

'His name is Gilbert, Gilbert de Villiers.'

'Wow, now that's a name. Oh oh, he has seen us. His smile. Did you see his smile? The bones in my legs have just melted.'

'It was my mother who suggested he come to rent here. Gilbert writes and was looking for privacy to do so.'

'I bet he is one of those super-famous authors like J.D. Salinger, who spends his life hiding from the public.

Or he needs to protect himself from fans and the Press. Such a dream of a man. So sexy. He has to be famous and rich. Look at the Merc.'

Colette laughed. 'He's got another one of those in the garages. A sporty number.'

'Leaping lizards. His clothes, the camera, his shoes, the schmaltzy name. I'll buy one of his books and then write to him.' Davina stopped to take in air. 'I should control myself. I share a flat in West Hampstead with Simon who, I must say, is nothing like your lodger. How can you not swoon every time you run into Gilbert de something?'

'Our paths barely cross.'

'Ah,' bore the tone of disappointment. 'He is gay. Of course. With such fabulous looks, he has to be gay.'

'I am not interested to know,' said Colette. 'Trudy, my housekeeper, makes it her life's mission to snoop around him and she says that women call him, and that he goes to London and stays overnight at weekends. Not gay, therefore.'

'Nobody comes and visits him here?'

'If you really want to know, you'll have to ask Trudy.'

They watched Gilbert dance around the exposed motor in an effort to get the desired angle for his picture. Eventually, he closed the bonnet. With a handkerchief pulled from his trouser pocket, he wiped down the prints his fingers had left on the maroon car paint. When he gave the women a wave, his hankie still in his hand, it looked as if he was surrendering. Colette tore Davina from the sight.

Under a sky which was a steady blue, the women

went back to the front of the house. A breeze played with the skirt of Colette's dress.

'I should go out and buy modern English clothes, shouldn't I? The last time I went shopping for clothes in England was…' Colette worked in her head, '… a year and a half ago.'

'The Afghan style, with your hijab pulled onto your forehead, sort of suits you. You haven't become Muslim, have you?'

'I fell in love in Kabul.'

'You did? Good for you. Another French language teacher? Someone at an Embassy?'

'An Afghan. One of my students who was in the Taliban army.'

'They are promised virgins after they blow themselves up. You can't possibly—'

'Christians and our civilisation just don't understand.'

It became awkward. Davina looked at her friend suspiciously. 'How did this falling in love end?' she asked.

'I left Kabul.'

'Just like that.'

'Not exactly. He got hurt. Look, Dav, I'll tell you one day. I don't want you to get involved.'

'Were your kidnappers from his people?'

Colette gave a snorty laugh. 'Look, I am not abducted and it's finished.'

'If it were, why would you be sitting in your grandmother's bedroom, afraid to go out?' Davina checked her watch and looked around her as if expecting someone. 'Here comes Winnie. Ten minutes early.'

'Ciao,' she called out of the van window as they left.

★

A few days later, the sun finally rose over the gables of the garages and, on the sideboard in the conservatory, the breakfast buffet had become more sumptuous with the presence of a lodger. Colette was sitting at the table with her tea in one of Nonnie's Royal Doulton cups and matching saucer. Nonnie had believed that drinking from mugs was only for builders. Gilbert came in from the outside using the glass door.

On his left cheek, the folds of the pillowcase had left creases. His strong, barley-blond hair was tousled at the back of his head and he looked sleep-drunk.

'Good morning,' Colette shot at him.

'Huh? Yes, you too.'

He lingered at the sideboard, undecided. Eventually, he picked up the serving spoon and lifted the silver dome off the scrambled eggs, and then moved to the sausages and bacon, but changed his mind again. All he did was pry a piece of distorted toast from the toast rack and join her at the table.

'It is going to be a lovely day,' she said. 'Bob Worship is busy ploughing. I expect ramblers will be making the best of it along the Ouse.'

'Whatever you say. Where is Trudy? I need a coffee.'

Colette rang Nonnie's little bell. She rang it again.

Trudy appeared at the door. 'Santa?'

'A double espresso, darling.' Gilbert sank back in his chair.

'Top priority,' Trudy declared and was gone.

'My friend, Davina, who visited the other day, would

like to know what you are writing.' Colette started a serious conversation.

'Your friend, Davina,' he said, 'undressed me with her eyes. Where's that bloody espresso?'

'You know Trudy has problems with your coffee machine.'

Gilbert got out of the chair and strode off to the kitchen.

Colette, left alone, admired the sun-kissed high grass of her parkland, while from the kitchen she heard, 'How many times have I shown you how to twist the tray into the machine?'

'Shall I tell you a Swiss joke?'

'Not now. You turn the tray clockwise.'

'And the cuckoo comes out?'

'Gently, a little more. You will hear it click. There, that's it.'

'Tell me how long cows have to be milked?' Trudy hollered with laughter. 'Same as short ones.'

From the conservatory, Colette saw a flash of light near the old conifers. She sat up. There was another flash. Perhaps a trespasser's camera. She wished this to be true, even though no camera flash was that strong. Colette felt concern, which turned into alarm when she saw two figures by the trunks of the trees. Something was happening on her land, while from the kitchen came laughter. What was this about? The two figures detached themselves from the trees and dared to run across open land towards the conservatory.

Oh God, both were dressed in black from head to foot. The one in front hauled out a bomb and threw it at the conservatory. Colette fell off the chair and crawled under the table. *I've lived an interesting life.* Her teeth clattered. *I knew love. I am ready to die.* The projectile hit one of the windowpanes. Trembling, she waited for the explosion to finish everything. It did not happen.

Instead, Gilbert asked why she was under the table.

Slowly, she gathered herself enough to stand up straight. A slice of lemon worn out by hot tea was plastered to her shoulder. 'Two men are out there. They are trying to kill me. One threw a bomb, but it wasn't one. They will never give up.'

'Who is *they*?' asked Gilbert.

'The thing they threw hit that window,' Colette pointed.

Immediately, Gilbert went to the conservatory door.

'Don't go outside. They are out there, hiding.'

Undeterred, he inspected the outside of the conservatory, pacing around it. When they were face to face, she inside, he outside, he bent and picked up a lifeless rook. He showed it to her and shrugged.

She joined him outside. 'A rook. He threw a dead rook?'

'These dumb birds fly into glass all the time.'

'I should call the police.'

'They will only laugh at you,' he said, but she was already running up the stairs to Nonnie's room and the telephone.

Constable Stanley, rather irritated, suggested she only call the police if something classified as criminal had happened. He again suggested she get an alarm system, going as far as suggesting a company who installed them.

Probably his brother's, thought Colette. 'I prefer to buy a large guard dog,' she said and hung up.

When she was back in the conservatory, Gilbert was gone and Trudy was clearing the table.

'He likes my jokes,' she said with triumph.

'I hope so,' Colette grumbled and took a clean cup from the dresser against the house wall.

'I'll make you another tea,' offered Trudy. 'Easier than coffee.' But Trudy did not do what she had offered to do. She stood near the sideboard, making a vague dismissing gesture with her hand.

'What?' asked Colette.

Trudy gave a loud sigh. 'Shall I be blunt?'

'By all means, but no cows please.'

'Colly, you have been in Afghanistan. On the political map, it is a war zone. Bob told me. You have come back, but your mind is disturbed. Bob said it was something medical.'

'What else did Bob say?'

'Nothing. But I now say, Colly, you are frightened of things which you think are there and happening. They aren't there and they don't happen.'

Davina

The same September morning sun did not reach Davina and Simon's basement flat in West Hampstead; it just touched the tip of the gone-wild laurel bush in the corner of the narrow space called *garden*. They paid a good rent to the landlord, who never thought of improving the property. The kitchen had been added to the back as a cheap breeze-block job with one single-glazed window. Damp rose through the thin concrete base, puckering the black-and-white vinyl flooring. The bathtub taps were leaking and, with no ventilator, there was mould on the ceiling.

Davina's mother had called the previous evening to say that she and Dad would be in London for a Baptist World Alliance meeting. Could they drop in afterwards to see the flat?

No did not work with Helen.

So, instead of vegging out on Sunday morning, Davina and Simon were stuffing things into over-full drawers, dusting with a wet J-cloth, and hiding the full laundry basket and other ungainly items upstairs.

Davina sprinted to the corner shop to buy a net of lemons, some packets of nibbles, cookies, and a square plastic doily.

She was squeezing the lemons on a manual juicer, as her parents considered fresh lemon juice an honest drink, when there was a 'Hello down there. We're here.'

'Your religious parents have arrived,' Simon called from the mezzanine.

Davina placed glasses on a tray and carried it into the living area, while her parents took rather a long time to descend the outside steps to the front door.

'Welcome to our—'

'Darling, why are you in the cellar of your apartment?' Helen gazed around her, contemplated the floor-to-ceiling bookshelf which separated the sitting area from the dining corner, and bent her head sideways to peek into the kitchen. Nobody said anything for a painful while.

'There'll be more light upstairs in the bedrooms,' said Justin, his lower lip pushed forward, his head nodding.

Davina looked away from the familiar facial expression. 'We're happy here,' she felt compelled to say.

'You turned your back on true happiness years ago,' Helen stated.

'Maybe it was not for me to find it where you thought it ought to be for me.'

'You owe the Baptist church and you know it.'

'I was a young student like many others. They got loans. They had parents helping. They searched for ideologies. How could I have known that the loan from the Baptists would oblige me to study theology, in preparation for work in the Baptist Missionary Society?'

'You knew. The Bible speaks the truth of what we have to tailor our life to, whether you are young, a student, parent or old.'

'The pages of a bible are made of wood. Trees. Biological matter.'

Justin patted her on the back. 'You chose to study natural, growing things on earth, which has led to pages being made and words of wisdom printed on them. I am proud of you.'

'And after all that, you are working as a florist.' Helen paused as if out of breath. 'Compared to your rebellious nature, your dad and I did not shy away from our duty. The four years' missionary work in Africa in that heat and with those insects was a valuable contribution to our church.'

At this moment, Simon came down from the mezzanine. 'Hi,' he said and, probably realising this wasn't good enough, added, 'I had to finish some work on the computer.'

'Computers.' Of course, Helen had an opinion on that subject. 'Those machines are for the rich to get richer. The lot should be destroyed.'

'We can't un-invent things. It will get better and better. Not long now and we will have robots doing our jobs.'

'They already do.'

Simon invited Helen to sit on the purple sofa. Inelegantly, she sank into the soft upholstery with a little panic shriek, her knees coming to rest at the height of her neck. In that position, she saw the cracked ceiling clearly and Davina saw much of her thighs.

Simon went into the kitchen for the nibbles. While he was gone, Helen asked Davina, 'Anything changed between the two of you? I see no ring on your finger.'

Davina poured lemon juice into small tumblers for them.

'Thank you for remembering. We brought you something.' Helen lifted a wrapped gift from a carrier bag. 'It's not so much from Dad and me, but from your guiding Brethren.'

'A cross,' Davina said, once the object appeared, as if she were saying she was cross.

'It is made of Jerusalem tree wood and has been anointed in the church.'

'For peace and happiness in your home,' added Justin.

'It will help keep the devil away.' Helen looked at Davina meaningfully, as Simon returned with a plate of small sandwiches and a bowl of nibbles.

'It is very special,' Davina said, instead of *thank you*. 'We will probably not hang it up. Around us is a multicultural community.' In an effort to change the mood, she continued cheerfully, 'My best friend, Colette – remember my uni friend who is half French? No? Well, she has returned from teaching in Kabul. While there, she fell in love with an Afghan soldier.'

'You mean terrorist,' said Justin.

'What a misguided girl. No good can come from that. At least we were spared that, when you returned from Afghanistan.'

'Because we were already an item before she left,' Simon pointed out.

'Dad, do Islamic extremists have secret gangs in Europe?'

'Sure they do. How else could they have orchestrated the killing in that Paris nightclub?'

'And they might go for individual people they hate?'

'Definitely, but one does not hear about that because it is hard to prove.'

'Can't the British police catch them and put them in prison?'

'You do that, you multiply the problem and so forth. That's exactly what your mother and I tried to resolve by converting heathens to the teaching of John the Baptist.'

'They think *we* are heathens.'

'That is the cross we have to bear.'

'Back to the cross,' smiled Helen. 'Will you now hang it up?'

'Yes, Mum.'

'I had meant to ask, how is your job at Blooms?'

'I'm settling in.'

'Any lovely man, whatever age, crossed your path lately?'

Simon picked up the bowl of nibbles and thrust it at Helen. 'It's called Bombay Mix. Edgy.' He nodded at the woman who would never accept him.

'From your living area window, you look straight out onto rubbish bins and people's legs passing in the road.'

'Not many people pass.'

'The sort of people who live here are the sort who throw their dead cats into the bin,' was Justin's opinion.

Colette

It was the first week in October when a call came from the dog breeder in Glasgow with whom Colette had talked over the phone several times. The four puppies born to her bitch at the end of July were now vaccinated and ready to go. One male which had been promised to someone was available again.

That same afternoon, Colette found Trudy in her kitchen. The housekeeper was ironing. On the board, a shirt lay prostrated, limp sleeves dangling off either side. The iron hissed and skated over terylene.

'That is Gilbert's shirt,' observed Colette. 'Trudy, I don't want you to accept work from him.'

The iron hissed.

'He is a lodger. He doesn't get maid service. Do you hear me?' Colette waited for a reaction. None came. The shirt was turned over. The triangular tip of the iron nudged against the thicker seam of the collar.

'When you are done with this, I would like you to go and tell him that you will not iron any more of his shirts.'

The iron stopped moving on Gilbert's shoulder.

'I will be leaving early tomorrow morning to pick up a guard dog for Riverbend.'

'That's an animal. It will be more work for me.'

'I prefer it to an alarm system and we cannot secure the boundaries of the land.'

'Oops!' Trudy lifted the iron. 'If I burn his shirts, he will send me back to Guggisburg. And it is the wrong place when I come from Guggisberg.'

★

Colette knew that the journey to Glasgow by train via London would take seven hours. One way. Therefore she had decided to get there, stay the night in a B&B and then be fresh when meeting her dog. The first impression the dog would have of her surely was of vital importance. For the return journey with him, she would pay for a large taxi which accepted a dog in a crate, plus dog paraphernalia like bed, bowls and food.

On the important morning, Colette changed clothes twice. Apparently, dogs did not see colours. She first opted for a black dress with white collar and cuffs. Too saintly, too serious. She changed to a pair of dark-blue cord trousers, a loose red top, and a beret. She even stuck pearl studs into her ear lobes. She had never known a dog, never lived with a dog. Her exhilaration was tainted by apprehension.

The train was on time. Edging down the aisle, she chose an empty seat at a table and slid across to the window. The train started to roll. Opposite her sat an older gentleman reading *The Times*. Without looking up, he considerately tucked his legs sideways to give room for hers.

The ploughed fields of Ampthill flitted past. Colette opened the book she had brought with her. It was written by a dog psychologist. *The first impression in a newborn puppy will shape his behaviour for the rest of his life.* Just as she had thought, but it was already too late to do anything about that. In the next chapter, the three-month-old dog needed to expand its vocabulary. By month six, larger canines were expected to understand at least two dozen words. Objects repeatedly flashed before their eyes trained their brains to recognise them. If dog and owner were communicating, the animal would be able to pick up the round toy instead of the square one when asked, every time.

In the chapter on feeding, the vegetarian food option had a lot to be said for it. A vegetarian dog was less likely to chase squirrels and worry cats. Colette shut the book and put it back into her bag.

The train slowed down approaching St Pancras. On either side of the carriage, the view was obstructed by lichen-caked walls. In places, bricks had tumbled away and rubble had followed, leaving holes. The old gentleman folded his newspaper and pulled the spectacles off his nose. They passed a disused building covered in graffiti. Next came a tall mesh fence, which ended at a whitewashed building. Vegetation around it had been hacked away. It looked virginal and out of place. The only features were two tall, narrow windows. Above them fluttered a rectangular banner; *Blooms4You* was printed on a flowery background, the same as the painting on Winnie's van.

The train gave a forlorn hoot. They entered a tunnel.

Colette closed her eyes and leaned back in her seat. 'I will call the dog Hannan,' she said to herself. 'Abdul Hannan.'

Light streamed back into the train compartment. The man stowed his newspaper into a black zip bag.

Gilbert

Back in Riverbend, Gilbert stood in the small shower cubicle, his well-shaped backside squashed against the plastic wall. He was trying to rinse the shampoo out of his hair, but the water pressure was too weak. Irritated, he said to himself, 'There has to be more to my life than this.'

Shaking his wet hair like a dog after a swim, wrapped in a towel and barefoot, he went to the living room, picked up the giraffe-neck-patterned cushion and threw it into a corner, before plunging onto the worn sofa. Feeling the chill of October on his still damp body, he got up again to turn the electric heater to full and pull it close to blow straight at his legs.

He had to endure this primitive accommodation until his financial situation improved. Gilbert had worked out exactly how he could become rich. The problem was that his employers, the Mercedes-Benz people, were not listening. He had explained to the management team that, for many who owned a Mercedes, their car felt like a person or a dream-object with a soul and feelings. Instead of writing promotional blurbs for the company's latest luxury cars, he, Gilbert, could write a novel in which the Mercedes would play the part of the heroine. Had not the Volkswagen Beetle become world-famous? It would be emotional; there would be adventures and dangerous situations. In his head, Gilbert had already concocted a storyline and they could sponsor him. But the stuck-up people did not even let him finish talking. The director intervened. 'Look,' he had said, getting out of his chair, one of the worst *Looks* Gilbert had experienced. They hated the idea and smugly reminded him that he was paid as a professional writer and had to stick to things he was able to handle, write about the specifics in order to sell their cars, get it? Gilbert had left the conference room holding his head high, but his legs were weakened from the put-down.

Cars could be regarded as living creatures. They moved. They were fed and ran on the feed. They digested and expulsed via exhausts. They growled, whined, roared, ticked. They were metal racehorses, princes and princesses of speed and sensuality. Such magnificent creatures deserved to be wooed and written about in a novel to assure them eternal fame.

The shock of the rejection in the boardroom and the hurt it had caused him drove Gilbert to change his life. He decided to leave his shared flat in Chelsea and look for a wholesome country retreat, not too far from London.

The upshot was this humble habitat and an uncomfortable life in a garage building. On the wall facing him was a framed picture of two women washing clothes in a river. *Batik Print, Penang*, it was titled. His landlady, who could not be thirty yet, owned this large property, had lived in Malaysia and Afghanistan. He was still unable to make her out. She dressed in ethnic-style clothes. He had no idea what her hair was like; she kept it hidden.

Trudy had told him that Colette wrote a journal every day. Not long ago, returning from London late one night, he had seen her up by the window, in her headscarf, using the light of a full moon to write. Trudy had emphasised that Colette wrote down everything that happened to her – everything and every day – and she had suffered hardships few people knew about.

Gilbert unlocked his hands from behind his head. It suddenly occurred to him that today Colette would not be able to write her life story because she had gone to Glasgow and would not be back until late tomorrow afternoon.

Gilbert slipped into some clothes and, as an afterthought, puff-sprayed himself with Hugo Boss. He grabbed his rucksack and, swirling with scent, crossed the gap between his lodgings and the main house. In the utility room, the light was on but Trudy was not to be seen. A door was ajar, giving to stairs. Of course, a house of this magnitude had to have a cellar.

As he tested his way down the dark staircase, a single weak bulb hanging from the ceiling revealed Trudy with her back to him. He reached the last step and saw that she had a bottle of wine in her hand. His rubber sole squeaked on the damp flagstone floor. She jerked round, trying to hide the bottle behind her back.

'Well, well, well, Trudy.'

'I have to come down here to clean the bottles. They get dusty.' She defended her presence, speaking rapidly, the Swiss-German accent strong.

'What valuable bottles most require is to rest on their bellies and accumulate dust, not to be swung around by housekeepers.'

'You see, I had to open this bottle because of the flies.' She showed him the half-empty bottle and went on a little breathlessly, 'The flies are attracted to the sugar and go into the bottle because it is open.'

'October in England, flies must be a real problem in wine cellars.' He jollied her.

She rubbed the back of her neck, checking his face to ascertain whether he was serious or not.

'I won't say anything to Miss Colette about your… you know…' He gestured towards the bottle. 'Hand on my heart.'

'She knows about the flies.'

'Perhaps. What I would like you to do is to take me up to Miss Colette's bedroom and show me her journals.'

'She wouldn't like that. Not at all.'

'Let's just go up into the room first and then see how physically fit you still are.'

'Mr Gilbert, really.' She grinned suddenly. 'You're teasing me.' She gave a frightening giggle, rolled one shoulder and then raised her hair above her head, before letting it fall down. Under her pale armpits was a substantial growth of curled greying hair.

They went upstairs to Nonnie's bedroom, Trudy apprehensively keeping at a distance from him, her hair in a mess, her bosom heaving.

'Here we are, just the two of us,' he said and closed the door behind them.

'It needs two to make a calf,' she blurted out and stood there as if she were wondering why she had said that.

'I want you to stand right here. Good. Now lift up one leg. You are allowed to hold out your arms for balance.'

'I am confused,' she admitted. 'Are you trying to flirt with me?'

'No, Trudy. I want to find out how drunk you are.'

'Mr Gilbert,' she gurgled. 'You should be ashamed of yourself, playing with a girl like me.'

'Her journals must be in the main drawer of the desk.' Gilbert's hand was at the little brass ring.

'There are a lot of papers in the top drawer to the side as well,' Trudy gave away.

He pulled the drawer towards him and lifted out a bundle of notebooks and loose sheets.

'You can look but you are not allowed to touch anything,' she said in a sober voice. 'Stop taking papers out of the desk. I will be blamed for letting you do this.'

'All this writing is in a big mess. If she hadn't put dates down, the story could never be put together.'

Trudy went to a bookshelf and pulled out a slim volume, which she brought to Gilbert, who was piling onto the desk everything he had clawed out of the drawers.

'Colly wrote this book. She told me.'

He looked at the book cover. *'The Orphan Boy from the Kampong,'* he read out loud. 'But there is no name of the author.'

'Colly's mother had it published but Colly did not want people to know that she was the one who wrote it.'

'Strange behaviour,' he murmured, while at the same time reading from a page he had opened at random. 'Good writing,' he admired.

Trudy snatched the book back, closed it and replaced it on the shelf. 'She must not know that I showed it to you. Oh no, what are you doing?'

Gilbert was lifting the heap off the desk and transferring it into his rucksack. 'I'll tell you exactly what I am doing. I will take these with me to get them photocopied. Before she returns from Glasgow, the originals will all be back in the drawers the way they were. We are not going to tell her, are we? I'll be back by half three latest tomorrow.'

'What about the photocopies?'

'I will spend time putting this mess into some order for it to be useful if she thought of publishing it.'

'You are doing this to help her, aren't you?'

'Entirely. Don't tell her. It will be a surprise.'

'I don't know about that being a good surprise. You had no right. She will get angry.'

'We make a good team, you and I.' Gilbert grabbed and then shook Trudy's hand which lay limp in his large tanned paw.

Colette

The next day it was dark when the Glasgow taxi arrived at Riverbend. From the glass in the front door, light streamed down the stone steps like a carpet runner. Weaker, it still illuminated the patch of gravel in which the taxi driver had come to a halt.

Trudy, who had been waiting at the drawing room window, came out of the house and down the steps. Colette on the gravel was watching the driver pull a cage from the car. He set it on the ground. Colette paid him with a thick wad, counting out the notes one by one.

He looked satisfied with the tip, hopped back behind his steering wheel and drove off. In the wire cage was a small, curled-up animal.

'How was the journey?' Trudy asked.

'Long. The dog was whimpering all the way.'

Trudy put her hands on her hips before bending down to look into the cage. 'Is that supposed to be the guard dog for Riverbend? He's smaller than a cat and the ugliest animal I've ever seen.'

'He is only eight weeks old. He will grow bigger.'

'I bloody well hope so. And look, this crybaby has no tail. These Scottish people sold you something abnormal.'

'That is his tail.'

'A piece of black string?'

'He is an Afghan.'

'Afghan, like the carpets? What was wrong with a Rottweiler called Brutus?'

'I – er – he is from Afghanistan. I thought that would make me happy. Hush, little puppy,' Colette murmured endearingly to the animal. 'He keeps crying. Maybe he is sick.'

'He doesn't like to be in the cage.' Trudy slid the bolt.

'Don't let him out,' shouted Colette with alarm. 'He will run away. He doesn't know where he is.'

Ignoring Colette, the puppy stepped out of the cage, his elongated face dipped forward, his eyes swivelling furtively. Large fluffy ears hung down like carpets either side of his face. Standing on the gravel, shivering, he started to pee.

'Hannan, darling.' Colette dared to reach out to the long-legged puppy. She stroked over his narrow head, feeling the thin layer of silkiness of his fur over a hard cranium.

'HanHan. Is that his name?'

'No. He is called Abdul Hannan.'

'That's what I said, HanHan. The Abdul sounds too much like Ali Baba and his thieves. I need to have a name for him which makes him cringe, because it will end up with me house-training him. Right now, this sad little chap needs something to eat and drink.' Trudy went back to the kitchen, while Colette carried the puppy to the lowest step, on which she sat, the dog in her lap.

Trudy returned with a piece of cooked chicken.

'He should eat vegetarian,' Colette said.

Trudy put the piece of meat in front of the dog's black, glossy nose. He reacted. His string tail wagged and he sniffed eagerly. Trudy put the meat into her mouth.

'That is cruel,' objected Colette.

'I'm chewing it smaller for him. And then I'll take Pasha Abdul the Great into the kitchen, where he will sleep, eat and make a mess, until I have taught him to do his mess outside the house.'

'I was thinking of taking him to my bedroom, so that he doesn't worry about not being loved.'

'Which bit of the word guard dog did you not understand, Colly? He has to patrol the park at night and tear intruders into body parts.'

Colette wrapped her arms around the puppy. 'He sleeps with me. End of conversation.'

In Nonnie's bedroom, she lifted HanHan onto her bed, cooing to him what a beautiful Afghan boy he was. Turning to her desk, she frowned and then went to push the chair closer in, the way she normally left it. The pen with which she wrote these days had rolled off the desk. Colette went on all fours to fish it out from behind the radiator.

Kabul

In Kabul, Imani the Syrian physiotherapist got Hannan to walk between parallel walking bars. The patient gave a weary smile and advanced his right foot, hands gripping the rails. Imani's 'very good' made him prepare for a second step.

The door opened and Baghish came in. Imani asked him to leave, as visitors were not allowed in treatment rooms.

'I am his brother and an important officer.'

Imani hesitated.

'How are you, bro?' asked Baghish, ignoring the woman. Not waiting for an answer, he encouraged, 'Come on, walk down that plank. Don't be pathetic.'

'He is doing well,' said Imani.

Baghish sneered.

'I can't do this if my brother is watching.' Hannan turned round to get off the walker.

'I'll give the two of you ten minutes to talk and then the brother has to leave.'

Baghish helped his brother off the walker and to some chairs.

Once Hannan, after a groan of pain, was seated,

Baghish's temperament showed. 'I can't believe your romantic streak has brought you this low. You can't be my brother. There was a mix-up in the hospital when you were born. I tell people that you were fighting the Mujahidin in the Babur Gardens when you got the injuries. I don't mention your teacher.'

'Whatever. It's done now and I will have to work to get back to where I was.'

'No. You need to go back to something normal. Mooning after a French woman shows serious mental derailment. Protecting her with your own body is unspeakable. Father wanted to come to the hospital and shoot you in your bed, he was so angry.'

'Shoot me, if you want to,' said Hannan.

'I will do it for Dad if you get together with that bitch again.'

'She is gone out of my life.'

'Oh, boo hoo. She doesn't limp, does she? She walks away scot-free. Well, we have people in England trying to put that right.'

'What are you plotting?'

'Let's talk about something else.' The light dimmed in the room and then went out. Alert, Baghish tensed up.

'The hospital electricity is backed up with a generator. When that happens, operating theatres are supplied first.'

'Mum's cousin, Kamram, came from Iran. He was on business in Kabul. Your booked bride, Shabana, has been matched up with an Iranian Shiite. His family owns a garage and Kamram's Nissan broke down on their return. There goes your chance of a decent marriage.

And – don't say anything. I haven't finished yet – that was decided before they knew that you were a cripple.'

'Brother,' said Hannan, 'I am tired. Very tired. Thank you for coming. Please go.'

Colette

In Riverbend, November showers brought down the leaves. The sky was overcast, the house was dark and joyless, apart from the young dog who discovered his life with enthusiastic energy.

Gilbert stayed locked in his lodgings.

The nights were still torture for Colette. During the day she was aimless, drawn to the windows and ghosting through the house, cringing at her own reflection in the hall mirror, fear following her like a shadow.

Audrey called, mostly late in the afternoon when, Colette knew, her mother had had a few drinks. Colette's reluctance to invite her to Riverbend was excused by the danger of a long drive at this time of year.

Gilbert did not come to breakfast any longer. He could be seen writing at his desk at all hours of the day and night.

On a windswept Wednesday morning, a woman drove up and asked for Gilbert's apartments. She was a sturdy person, with a strong face, hooked nose and wiry grey hair. In her fifties, she could not qualify as Gilbert's lover. Perhaps a relative. She did not stay long, but her visits became regular. Trudy tried to find out what was going on, but failed.

November turned into December. Christmas came. Riverbend's decorations were no more than a Christmas tree which Trudy bought from Bob. At first, she had protested vehemently that he was trying to rob her but, after she and Bob shared a few glasses of red wine in the kitchen, the price seemed acceptable.

The hunt in the attic for the box with the tree baubles was not successful. Trudy, forever resourceful, sprayed cooked noodles from a can of silver paint and hung them on the tree.

The Blooms4You subscription offering was beautifully seasonal: an open-lid wicker basket sprayed gold, filled with sparkling frosted leaves and holly berries amid poinsettia flowers. There were individually wrapped chocolates as well and a personal card from Davina. *Thinking of you especially during the festive season.* After the full stop, Davina had drawn a little heart – the same size as the one Hannan drew, filled in too. It had such a strong effect on Colette that she called HanHan to her side and went for a walk to get her emotions under control. As she trudged along over knobbly grass, HanHan ahead, she thought that the Kabul family did not prepare for Christmas. Had Hannan returned to studying French? Did he remember her, still have feelings for her?

Walking past the three wise conifers, she noticed a red car parked beyond the hawthorn hedge, now more see-through with the leaves lost. There was no reason for anyone to stop there.

'What do you think?' she asked HanHan. The dog wagged his tail and looked up at her, hoping for a treat. Woman and dog went down to the gate, her hand twisted around HanHan's collar. Having full view now, she saw a man standing by the car, a *Burglar Bill* woollen cap pulled low over his forehead. Did he have a scar on his chin? She could not see because the light was failing with four o'clock gone.

With fright, she watched the man reach into his car to the glove compartment, probably where men kept guns. She stepped back, everything about her taut. A last daring peek: he was holding a sponge in his hand and not a gun. He wiped dirt off his windscreen, tossed the sponge back into the car, sat behind the wheel and drove off.

'Good boy,' said Colette with relief down to her dog, who still only hoped to get a treat.

Back in the house, Colette, wrapped in a quilted dressing-gown over her clothes to warm up, decided to invite her mother for Christmas to Riverbend. At first, Audrey played the little game of not realising that it was her daughter who was calling. Once that was out of the way, Audrey played coy. She had met a gentleman; she just didn't want to shout it over the rooftops.

'Mum, do you want to come or not?'

'He plays bridge and has taught me to cheat.' A girlish giggle.

'It would only be Trudy and me.'

They were not at the stage to make plans for Christmas with each other. Perhaps he was Jewish.

'So you don't know him that well.'

'We'll see what happens next.'

'Did anything already happen?'

'Of course not, darling. I am not a loose woman.'

The conversation ended with Colette concluding that her mother would not come to Riverbend for Christmas. She replaced the handset while looking up at the ceiling and rolling her eyes.

To Davina, Colette had merely sent a charity Christmas card: winter was lonely in the countryside, her flowers made all the difference, and they should set a date to see each other again. Somehow, the pen all by itself added that she had lost the Afghan lapis lazuli bracelet and was unhappy about it, perhaps because Davina and she understood each other intimately.

On the day, Colette cooked a plump chicken à l'orange the way the French did with ducks for Christmas. Trudy, having won the cracker gift and wearing the paper crown, seemed morose throughout the meal. When she left the room and returned with photographs of her parents, a cousin, a young man even, much-fingered pictures taken a long time ago, she admitted to being homesick. 'I miss the Alp roses and gentians, the bluest flowers nature ever made.'

Colette noticed a pin stuck to Trudy's grey pullover.

'Guggisberg yodel choir,' Trudy vaunted.

'I will pay for the train if you want to go home for the New Year,' offered Colette. Trudy did not respond. She piled up the used plates and brought them into the kitchen. There was nobody left back there she used to know.

While Trudy laid out coffee and liqueurs in the

conservatory, Colette switched on the small television fixed to the wall. Queen Elizabeth, in pale blue, was sitting at a desk talking to the nation. When her speech was finished and the national anthem played, Trudy declared, 'I don't need to go home again. This Queen lady is as good as was my mother.'

Davina

Christmas in West Hampstead was equally low-key. There was no tree in 27A Calvert Street because Davina's parents, as Baptists, would have found it offensive. Davina had, though, bought a wreath garnished with natural pine cones.

Her parents arrived and the present-giving was also meagre. Davina received a book of naturalesque Victorian drawings of plants – second-hand as some pages had been ripped out. And she gave them a linen tablecloth with four serviettes.

Just as they sat down for the salmon with a dill sauce, the telephone rang on the mezzanine. Simon ran up the steps only to come right down again. 'It's for you.' He sat down and continued to eat.

The caller was Max. 'Sorry to disturb your family Christmas festivities but something big has come up.'

'And Happy Christmas to you,' she said.

'Yeah, yeah. We've got a mega-commission for 14 January – a book launch in the Grand Palace Hotel in Bloomsbury.'

'Oh good,' she said tentatively.

'Pillars, extravagant displays, the works.'

'And you call me today to tell me?'

'It will need careful planning and preparation. There will be Press coverage. I want us to take a look at the Crystal Ballroom in the hotel as soon as possible.'

'This afternoon, I can't. We haven't put the Christmas pudding on fire yet.'

'Very funny. I propose 28 December, right after you get back to work.'

'That I can do.'

Davina rejoined the family. 'That was my boss.'

'What on earth does he want of you today?'

'He booked me to visit a hotel with him.'

'Davina, you and your boss in a hotel—'

'The ballroom, to decorate with flowers.'

For dessert, Davina had bought crème brûlée in ovenproof glass containers, which only needed to be slipped under the grill for five minutes.

'Dav is in love with Max,' Simon trumpeted, before the brown sugar had started to bubble.

Davina handed out the pudding. 'Ridiculous. I work with Max. Actually, I work for Max. He is dynamic and works during holidays.'

'His wife must be long-suffering,' said Helen.

Without thinking, Davina blurted out, 'Oh, Max doesn't have a wife.'

★

On 28 December Davina and Max were in a taxi going to the Grand Palace Hotel.

'This is a big order,' he said happily. 'A big brouhaha

will be made of this event and Blooms4You can ride on the back of all the free publicity. We can push this to six grand if you give of your best,' he mulled on. 'I need you to be on top form for this.'

'Who is the author?'

'We might have to have our columns repainted.'

'Jeffrey Archer, Salman Rushdie?'

'A new talent apparently, a newly discovered sensation. Around three hundred will be invited. I forgot his name. Never mind, the flower budget is between four and six thousand.'

'Pounds?'

'Of course pounds.'

'We only have two weeks to prepare,' she said, 'and that is with New Year in the way.'

'New Year is slow. Did you ever receive a flower arrangement for New Year?'

They arrived in front of the hotel. The deputy manager led them to the ballroom. They stood at the open double doors, overwhelmed by the impact and size of the room in front of them. It would be a challenge to *flower up* this vast space. The walls were bronze-coloured, hard to complement and almost impossible to embellish.

'All that caramel gunk on the walls.' Max looked around him. 'The chandelier light explosion on the ceiling is taking over everything else. Reminds me of the alien airship finally landing in *Close Encounters*.' He sang the five notes which were key in the film.

'Again, you are not helpful,' she complained mockingly.

'I'm not responsible for the flowers, am I? You are.'

Talking measuredly, she proposed to go light, to overcome the chandelier with white gladioli and peach roses, and marry it all together with bronze leaves.

'Be light and marry,' he said, trusting her judgement.

'I am thinking of two plaster pillars either side of the large podium, with flowers on them like a firework bouquet. Away from the light projection on the screen of course.'

'Good,' is all Max said.

'That's not enough. I propose a two-tiered flower fountain near the entrance. I did one for my final florist's exam. Flower-fall rather than water, with fruits, especially grapes, woven into it. I got an A plus.'

'And such a fountain could be found where?'

'In my parents' loft.'

'And your parents live in Dubai…'

'My boyfriend, Simon, can pick it up from Peterborough and drive it to Astley Court.'

Boyfriend was all Max heard. 'We got ourselves a boyfriend. Simon not only *says,* he also *does.*'

Davina stayed calm, despite Max pushing his annoying being to the limit.

'What else?' Max got back to business.

'We have money to spend. Along the gunky wall, we could put baskets filled with flowers. One and a half metres apart. Still staying in the white, peach and bronze foliage. Solidago, craspedia, marguerites could be added perhaps.'

'That wall will be pushed open for refreshments after the presentation,' said the deputy manager.

'Does anyone know what the book to be launched is about?' Davina insisted.

'I have absolutely no idea and don't care,' came from Max, rubbing his hand against the bronze wall.

'I am afraid I am not at liberty to say, Miss,' contributed the deputy manager. 'All will be revealed at the launch.'

'Are we done?' asked Max, suddenly bored.

Davina and her boss returned to Astley Court.

Colette

It was 14 January when Gilbert reappeared for breakfast in the conservatory. Colette was very much aware of the date. Almost exactly one year ago, she had walked to the French Institute in Kabul to give her first lesson. She let the joyously strong memory sweep over her. The way Hannan's eyes had challenged hers, the impact on her was still vivid.

Gilbert pulled his chair away from the table to join her at breakfast. She expected him to start to nibble at a dry toast, crunching annoyingly, but instead he asked for tea from Trudy and not in jest. So unlikely for him, Colette took a better look. He had washed his hair and blow-dried it with a brush, giving it a soft lift. His aftershave was so overdone it was pungent and he was wearing mascara. She was sure of it.

'Stop gawking at me,' he snarled, more like his normal self. 'Today is a most important day,' he said, sipping tea.

'Why?'

'I want you to join me in London. I'll drive and you take the train. It is important to me that you are there for the event.'

'What are you talking about?'

'When you get to the Grand Palace Hotel in Bloomsbury at half past one, go to the Crystal Ballroom and wait with the others until I arrive. Don't talk to the Press.'

'Gilbert,' she said resolutely, as if she were in charge of a class, 'you're not making any sense.'

'At two p.m. today, my novel will be launched in the Grand Palace. There will be two hundred guests, plus the Press.'

'You've written a novel?'

'You think I'm too limited to do that?'

'Now, well, I guess anyone can write a novel – anyone who has a lot to say and has experienced many things. You have been writing furiously, according to Trudy, for weeks now.'

'Indeed, I have.'

'I once wrote a novella about a boy in Malaysia and it was published privately.'

'I know,' slipped out.

'You don't. What is the novel about, for your publishers to give you a launch in a five-star London hotel?'

'That's why I want you to be there. You deserve to be there.'

'I thought your sole interest lay in Mercedes cars.'

'The novel is not about cars. That idea did not work.'

'I wouldn't fit in at such a fancy event. The only literary thing I do is write a journal.'

'You must come, please. You need to take the twelve-fifteen train to be there on time.'

'That's in less than four hours. What would I wear? What should I look like?'

'The woman with whom I share a mansion in Briddleton.'

'I'm only comfortable if I can cover my head.'

'Perhaps one of your berets, although a hijab could work.'

'How do you know the word *hijab*?'

'I read it somewhere,' he said and got up from the table. 'When I make my grand entrance in the Crystal Ballroom, you had better be there.'

'Can I come?' asked Trudy. 'I still have my dirndl.'

'No, but you can make sure Colette gets on the twelve-fifteen train from Bedford station.'

*

'What is a launch?' asked Trudy, once Gilbert had gone.

'Audrey suggested he came to live here because he is a writer. I never quite believed that he was, with the fancy cars and his suave behaviour, but obviously I was wrong. A launch is an event to celebrate the publishing of a book, normally only an important one.'

'Ah,' said Trudy. And Colette was glad her housekeeper did not say more.

'You'd better get that train. He wants you to be there.'

'Probably because I have underestimated him.'

*

In her beige coat and a black beret, Colette travelled to London on the twelve-fifteen.

'Have fun,' had been Trudy's parting words. 'A change from sitting at your desk will do you good.'

Would it? Such an unpredictable undertaking. And what's more, an event to glorify her lodger – a vain and uncompromising man who carried his manhood like a trophy on a red velvet cushion in front of him. People would clap; surely that is what they did at a launch. She would have to smile and then buy a book, which he would soil by scribbling his fancy name in it – a name he might well have invented. For weeks, he had been typing in his room as if possessed. Prolific writing did not necessarily prove he had artistic imagination. So what was this about? And why was he so insistent on her being part of it? The bottom line was, she did not trust him. From the first moment he had moved in and then not bothered to close the garage doors, she had decided that he was untrustworthy.

The sudden dark of the tunnel interrupted her thoughts. Soon enough, they emerged. So close to her destination now, a disturbing thought hit her: Gilbert had borrowed her as his story's main character. The way he sometimes observed her with cold, calculating eyes. The little comments he dared make about her Afghan-style clothes and her hidden hair. He had stolen her identity to use it in his novel. Knowing him, he would have cast her in a role involving a lot of sex. Colette felt nauseous when she stepped from the train onto the platform in St Pancras.

The Launch

In the Crystal Ballroom, the thousand bulbs in the five-metre-wide Baccarat chandelier glittered like a celestial firmament, their brilliance highlighting the extravagant floral displays. Over 250 people, a large gaggle of them from the media, had gathered, their conversation muted like the bronze colour on the walls. Of the chosen guests in possession of an embossed invitation, the women did not wear low-cut dresses or tarty four-inch heels, and the men were in waistcoats, hickory stripes, braces and bow ties. This elite class of intellectuals mingled with those in sharp suits, who were intent on turning their know-how into money. It was a promotional event of the highest order, the christening of a major novel. Press releases in the hands of the guests described it as a masterpiece, written by a man in his early forties from the point of view of a woman – a love story crossing the divide between Christianity and Islam, and it would make a lot of money for many.

The Gold Panther publishing house had opted for five hundred thousand copies to be released in bookstores all over the country. Negotiations were ongoing for foreign editions and translation rights. It could be estimated that the author would make twenty million pounds. The publicity for the launch was critical to the sums of money which would be made by many of those present: not just the publishers, but also the media, marketing industry, and film production companies, apart of course from bookshops. A successful launch could achieve all of that and many would benefit.

Directly under the chandelier, a Hollywood agent was rubbing his eyes and stifling a yawn, as it was six in the morning for him. He was in conversation with Gilbert's literary agent, a tall, angular woman with wiry, grey hair in her fifties, who wore a long-sleeved dress of titian-red velvet. Her lips were pressed together when not speaking, as if to safeguard her opinions, most likely strong ones when displeased. The American tried to remember what her name was.

She scratched shortly with four fingers in the unruly hair. 'Of course, we will need to retain control of the film script. Too much quality gets brushed under the carpet when a masterpiece is brought down to camera level.'

Suddenly he remembered her name. Fielding, Brenda Fielding. 'You seem to be given a lot of authority in dealing with the author's rights.' He sounded more self-assured now that he had her name.

'American film-making generally lacks the important ingredient called empathy. Something Gilbert's book is mostly about. Take, for instance, the scene where the couple came close to kissing.'

The American zoned out as she went on talking. He disengaged himself from this velvet and hairy inconvenience, and went to network with a group of lawyers.

Close to them, a journalist from the *Evening Standard* was trying to engage Colette in conversation. She had just arrived and was still looking around the room with astonishment. Who had the money to pay for so many beautiful flower arrangements? There was a cascading of them right at the entrance. And who were all these people assembled? She felt increasingly uncomfortable in her Kabul Chicken Street dress.

'Actually, I am de Villiers' landlady,' she found herself saying.

'Good of you to bowl up today,' the journalist said and her hand went up to the black beret which she wore pulled right down over the ears. Her blue eyes gave him a startled expression, when he continued, 'I've heard all about you. We all have. The mysterious French woman who lives with de Villiers.'

She wrung her hands and stepped back. 'I'm not living with Gilbert. He is renting a flat in Riverbend, my house, that's all.'

'Thank you for clarifying that for our readers. You live together in a house in the bend of a river, a twenty-something attractive French woman and an Adonis, sharing bedrooms, bathrooms.'

'Only the breakfast room.'

'Breakfast normally comes after a night's sleep. Just tell me one thing—'

'Definitely not.' She squirmed. 'And never again.' Colette eased herself away from the journalist, but she was only out of the frying pan and into the fire.

'One shot if I may.' The photographer's flash made her jump. Too late; he had *mayed*. Colette was furious. She threaded her way to the Ladies next to the cloakroom where she had handed in her coat in return for a numbered token.

The Ladies resembled a boudoir from the time of Madame Pompadour. At one of the make-up tables sat a woman fiddling with her hair. 'The hairdresser got it wrong again. The top layer shouldn't stick up like that.' She slapped the comb down on the tabletop. 'It's hopeless.'

Colette splashed cold water over her flushed face.

The woman twisted back in her upholstered, bergère-style chair, eager to communicate. 'I can't wait to read de Villiers' book. He's obviously gone where angels fear to tread.'

Colette pumped Elizabeth Arden soap from the dispenser and washed her hands.

'Love between a guerrilla terrorist and a naïve French teacher – unimaginable.'

At this moment, another woman emerged from a stall. Having been privy to the conversation, she added to it with, 'Quite a sexy situation, I would have thought, but then with the beastly terrorist being Muslim, I wonder how de Villiers managed to write about that.'

While the women found pleasure in talking some more, Colette went back out into the ballroom, where a lot more people had gathered by the flower fountain. The clusters of intensive conversation seemed to have intensified. Camera flashes popped here and there.

Colette had just learned that Gilbert had not just

based one of his characters on her, but had used her whole love story. All of a sudden, she felt claustrophobic. *How could he have known?* hammered in her head. Who had he talked to? How could something so intimate be made public? Women in loos talked about it – her, the naïve French teacher. She had to leave. She had to run away. She had to hide somewhere. Anything rather than stay here and listen to her love being slaughtered.

At the very back of the ballroom, she found a door, just a normal door. *Emergency Exit* was above it.

*

'Press only.' An arm barricaded the back entrance to the Grand Palace.

Prepared for it, Davina flashed a card. 'Blooms4You. Flower contract for the event. I'm here to make sure everything is still in place.' She was let in.

She had made an effort on her appearance. As a qualified florist in charge of an assembly hall, she ordinarily wore jeans, tops, tops on tops, and trainers or Swedish clogs.

She was now striding down the corridor and intermittent tall mirrors on the wall reflected her in a flowery, debutante dress and heeled shoes, the chestnut hair not in its customary ponytail but twirled up and held in place by a toothed hairclip. Passing the last mirror, she pulled out her tongue at the reflection and, punished for doing so, tripped over a fold in the carpet.

When she had set out this afternoon, Max had looked her up and down appreciatively. 'Ouch!' she had spoilt it by complaining. 'My poor little toes. I'm doing this for you, you know.'

'Grin and bear it. We're talking here about a major showpiece. We might even make it into tomorrow's newspapers, reaching three million Britons.' He gave her his *concentrated-with-responsibility* expression, before pushing her into the taxi. 'Make sure everything goes honkey donkey.' Max had his own way of speaking and, in the five months she had been working for him, she had learned this language and, unaware, even made it her own at times.

A woman came walking down the corridor towards her, someone in such an agitated state she was moving in untidy zigzags. The person wore a black beret, the type with the silly little tail sticking up, and as she approached, she turned into Colette – Colette who spluttered, 'I can't breathe in there.'

When she recognised Davina, she stopped in her tracks. 'What are *you* doing here?'

'The flowers. Blooms4You. We were commissioned to do them.'

'From what I saw, they are fantastic, the flower fountain especially. But these horrid Press people and the others started to pester me the minute I arrived. They believe that I am a harlot living with Gilbert.'

'What does Gilbert have to do with this book launch?' asked Davina.

'He is *IT*. He is the one to be launched.'

'Are you sure about that?'

'Go into the ballroom; Gilbert is on a screen the size of Trafalgar Square. And that brings me to another thing which is driving me insane.' Davina stepped back to let Colette fully express her fury. 'Apparently, the book's called *Behind the Veil*, and I've just learned that it is all about me and my life in Kabul.'

'You? How well does Gilbert know you?'

'He doesn't know anything about me really. And we have nothing in common. They call it an extraordinary love story.'

'There you are. Smile, Colette. It can't be about you.'

'Women in the loo described it as being about an innocent French teacher and an Afghan warrior.'

'And you lose your head over dumb and shallow prittle prattle?'

'Dav, I don't know. I'm talking nonsense. No…' Colette made a move as if her hand could brush the thought away from her head, '…I'm not. You know when you just know about something and you have been duped and kept in the dark. That's how it feels and this makes me sick and angry.'

'Let's go into the ballroom together and find out what this is all about.'

Colette checked her watch. 'According to the plan, Gilbert ought to be arriving in about five minutes.'

The two women hurried down the corridor, holding onto each other.

The event was about to begin. The chandelier faded to a mere glow. On the wall behind the presentation table, between towering flower arrangements on reconstructed-stone pillars, de Villiers' enormous headshot was replaced by abstract shapes amalgamating into each other tantalisingly.

The tinkling sound of a cimbalom hushed the conversations. Those who knew themselves to be VIPs started to seek their seats in the front rows and install themselves for others to guess who they were. The polished shoes on their crossed legs whipped in anticipation; designer handbags were cradled on laps. If not recognisable, it was clear that they were famous authors, publishing house directors, film and finance wizards – in short, the rainmakers.

A very thin man, not exactly deformed but twisted, his head bent to his shoulder, stepped onto the wide podium and started to add gypsy violin music to the cimbalom tinkling. Colette, standing towards the back in front of the cordoned-off Press, thought the music was cleverly chosen to give the event a certain *je ne sais quoi*.

*

What was Gilbert supposed to do when, dressed in his best, he athletically sprinted up to the entrance of the Grand Palace and a fat pigeon shat on him from the rim of the portico roof?

Did he smile bravely at the sign of good luck and laugh it off once he was inside?

Did he make a dash for the lavatory to wipe off the mess, as best he could, with toilet paper, wash the stained area in the sink, and hold it under the air-drier?

Did he whisper to the porter at the entrance to the Crystal Ballroom about a delay, while he popped round to Joseph's to purchase another Ted Baker jacket?

Gilbert de Villiers chose none of those options. He strode through the entrance in his Gucci shoes and Ralph's socks, past a display stand sporting his enlarged photograph. With a well-practised ability to detect top quality menswear, he spotted a cashmere jacket on a tall, middle-aged, English-looking gentleman. As a hawk falls onto bumbling prey, he approached and tapped the man on the shoulder. 'The price tag of your jacket is still dangling down your back. Thirty-seven pounds for a cashmere lookalike?'

Hurriedly, the man took off the jacket. 'It cost me two hundred and ninety quid.' He checked the back for the price tag and then the inside lining.

Before he could check the sleeves, Gilbert had snatched the jacket from him. 'You deserve better than this junk.' He gave the man the mobile he had fished out of the jacket pocket and the glasses case from the breast pocket. 'Aldi Special, was it?'

Confused and intimidated, the man tried to take his jacket back. 'What is wrong with you, asshole?' he hissed.

Gilbert put the jacket on, pulled at the sleeves which were an inch too short and, chin up, walked away. The protestations of the man went unnoticed in the comings and goings of the hotel lobby.

Gilbert headed for the ballroom via the reception desk. Bending nonchalantly over the polished mahogany within reach of the concierge's discreet ear, he confided, 'That man over there in shirtsleeves shouting seems to have mental issues.'

'Thank you, Sir, for reporting it.'

Gilbert inclined his handsome head and bestowed

the hotel employee with a *helpfulness is my middle name* smile.

At the inlaid double doors with gold handles, Gilbert raised his head, settled his shoulders, and grandly pushed both doors inward.

★

With a bang, the double doors were flung open just as the violin bow frenetically skipped over the G string. Gilbert de Villiers burst into the room like a jack out of a box. After a brief startled silence, he was greeted with sedate applause which befitted a writer and not a stage performer.

He went to stand behind the presentation table, in front of the lower part of the screen. With the gesture of a conductor silencing his orchestra, he forced the exuberant violinist to give his taut gut one last slice. Gilbert, having picked up his notes which had lain in front of him, started to introduce himself. A short glance down, and he let the paper go; it sailed across the table. Brenda Fielding stared up at him with concern. In a *sauce mornay* voice, he spoke of why he had become a writer. In the artificial light, his barley-coloured hair looked bleached. From time to time, his signet ring caught the light. He mentioned a first book he had written which was now out of print; it had been about Malaysia.

He expressed himself with animation, as if he were a physical animal rather than a thinking man. Davina was mesmerised by the little jerking of the head in an upward twist, which made the longer strands of hair fly, like the head-tossing of a palomino mustang. He whisked the straying hair back up with another brisk toss of the head, allowing him to give the audience a short dark-eyed look. His pink, marzipan lips formulated words, revealing regular teeth, the white of bathroom enamel.

'It is confusing,' Davina whispered to Colette. 'Don't people expect an author to be an intellectual – a grey man with glasses? Instead, the gorgeous man I saw photographing his car at your house turns out to be the very one who has written a novel people call deeply moving. You live with him and did not know.'

'For the umpteenth time, I do not live with Gilbert de Villiers and I wrote this book.'

On the mega-screen, Gilbert was seen walking through a summer meadow towards the banks of a river, a landscape Colette recognised.

'Plagiarism, you know. I'll chuck him out of Riverbend.'

Davina put her hand on Colette's arm.

Ceremoniously, a copy of the book was brought to the table. Brenda did not open it. She stood up and gave a condensed description of the novel. Her hand on the book, as if she swore to tell the truth, she talked about emotional development, spontaneity and instinct. A love story handled with sensitivity amidst the prejudices of Islam versus Christianity. Her voice in a crescendo of excitement, she talked about an insight into a woman's psyche the depth of which has never before been achieved by a man. Subtly, step-by-step, the reader becomes emotionally involved, by a glance, a fleeting touching of hands. The impossibility of the situation becomes growingly evident. When it comes to a violent head, the hidden passion is revealed. *Behind the Veil* by Gilbert de Villiers, published by Golden Panther.

There was a theatrical silence planned into her presentation. Brenda looked around her to measure the effect of her speech. Gilbert gazed up at her with a flirty wink.

The tinkling sound of the cimbalom started up. The fiddler, lifting his instrument, jolted the flower column which started to sway but then stabilised, as did Davina's breathing.

The double doors opened and two girls looking like secondary-school hookers pushed a trolley stacked with hardback books to the presentation table, all immature thin arms and peach-skinned legs, slender in miniskirts and high heels, long silk strands of hair tucked behind ears repeatedly with nervous fingers.

'London bunnies,' whispered the photographer right behind Davina. 'Tarts, Gilbert's.'

Gilbert, Davina noticed, gave the girls a little finger-puppet froggy-mouth wave with his hand. They reacted with shy, kittenish glances, mixed with reverence. Suddenly, they gave the strange sound of a giggle, but a wagging of his finger 'no' changed the childish expressions on their made-up faces. They took each other's hand and stood there awkwardly and out of place.

Brenda announced that the trolley would pass along the front row with signed copies – gifts for the guests who could show their VIP invitation. Afterwards, Gilbert would be available to sign copies for guests who wished to buy them.

Gilbert pulled a book towards him and turned the pages. The audience hushed.

Davina felt a hand on her shoulder.

'Max?'

'How is it going?'

'The fiddler is the only danger. Pssst. Gilbert is about to read from his work.'

On the screen, Gilbert was now seen reclining in a mature summer meadow in rolled-up shirt sleeves, a grass stalk between his teeth. In the far corner, Colette saw her Afghan hound running and leaving the picture.

The next day, I went back to where it had happened. And the wind blew silently over the dried grasses. Your body was no longer on the ground. I bent to where your blood had tinted the earth of your land. A tender young plant grew on the barren sand, and I knew for the first time exactly what it means to fall enamoured with the foreign country for which you were sacrificed. I will make you proud by living my life with purpose, fed by the hidden treasure of love in my soul, and the zeal of selflessness and sincerity which fill me. I have to leave for there is nothing left to keep me back. One day I will return and put my hand again on the soil of your country. One day, I will see you before me and it might well be in my last hour.

The image on the screen changed to the cover of the book. The violinist started with a Hungarian dance. It was announced that Gilbert would not be taking questions. Addled, the audience got up in slow motion.

'I'm out of here,' said Max without checking his voice.

To the side of the room, a wall was slid away to reveal cocktails and finger food laid out adjacently. The spell was broken.

The lighting changed. Colette held onto Davina.

'So, this is not about you, Colette, is it? Are you all right?'

'What you do not know is that it *is* my story.'

Colette fled from the Crystal Ballroom.

Blooms4You had exactly fifteen minutes to put all flower displays into their van, until the parking time which Davina had been given by the council ran out. Two runners stood ready for action discreetly at the back door, while Gilbert signed books.

'Go,' Max ordered and the runners rolled in their carts.

At the van behind the hotel, Davina held the vehicle's back doors open while the flower arrangements were carelessly piled into it. Her mobile dinged. It was Simon and he whined, 'Are you going to be home soon?'

'Look,' she said to him. 'We're packing up.'

The second plaster column was shoved in and hit the first, which broke.

'If you're not back by seven, Carlos and I are going to grab a bite.'

'Whatever.'

Davina was wedged between Winnie and one of the runners on the front seat, with the other kneeling between the flower arrangements and breathing down her neck. As they drove out onto Russell Square, she saw a police car arrive. Two officers opened the red cordon around the parked Mercedes in front of the hotel. Winnie did not drive on, curious as to what would happen next. Under the portico appeared the Hollywood agent and

Brenda Fielding, who had thrown a brown shawl over her titian dress. Both were helped into the back of the Mercedes saloon. Next, Gilbert appeared and right behind him the girls, long legs scampering after him, the sinuous arm of one of them tugging at Gilbert's sleeve in an effort to hold him back. Gilbert shook her off, ignored their presence, stooped and slipped behind the steering wheel. The doorman closed the car door sedately.

The Blooms4You van finally turned into Woburn Place and back to base.

Gilbert

'That went well,' said Brenda. 'Very well. I made a reservation for us in Gordon Ramsay's. It's one of the best restaurants in town,' she explained to the American.

Gilbert pulled a face, which the ones on the back seat could not see. A drawn-out gourmet meal with salivating waiters and staring co-diners was undesirable right now. Brenda liked to eat there, because of the atmosphere and Ramsay's salmon and raspberry soufflé, while the American would besiege him with plans for more public appearances to hype up his image, prior to selling him in Hollywood. They were still in the car and the American was already putting on pressure. 'I've read your novel. It is film-friendly material.'

Gilbert checked his face in the rear-view mirror. He quite fancied becoming a film star. He could take a few acting lessons; the physique to please he already owned.

The American continued with, 'Of course, for the role of the hero, we'll need to find a Semitic-looking actor.'

That is when Gilbert realised his mistake, which made him even more averse to a gourmet meal at

Ramsay's. All he felt like was a hamburger with chips and a beer.

Installed at the best table and waited on with great diligence, he did not enjoy the food. Before a choice of dessert was made, he broke a rose head from the table display and pushed it into the lapel buttonhole of a jacket which was not his.

Brenda knew what he was up to. She had got to know him in the mad four months when she had guided his speedy writing to meet the crazy deadline she and the publishers had insisted on.

The meal came to an end. They stepped out and the American flagged down a taxi to go and see Tower Bridge.

'Back to Bedford for you?' Brenda looked at Gilbert with narrowed eyes.

'I want to celebrate my way,' Gilbert said petulantly.

'Very well.'

'I deserve it.'

'Fine.' She got into the taxi next to the American and they sped off.

Gilbert stood on the pavement in Royal Hospital Road. *Fine* was not good enough. 'Why couldn't the old goat have said I did a splendid job at the launch?'

'Are you talking to me?'

'No, you stupid tramp. Go away.'

Leaving his car safely parked, Gilbert walked up Tite Street. At the familiar cottage-blue door, he knocked the head of a brass dog against the painted wood. At first, there was no answer and the dog got headbutted again. Then, a familiar squeal confirmed to him that one was at home. In that case, a great probability existed that there would be two of them. He smiled to himself and brushed his warm hand over his golden-barley hair.

'Trick or treat?' he asked at the door.

He was let in with, 'Treat!' and Lottie called back over her shoulder, 'Buntsy, the star is here.'

Noises were heard as he was led down the corridor. In this house, he was used to the unexpected. Before moving to Riverbend, he had rented a place not far away, a flat he had shared with another man. His relationship with the girls had begun with partying fun but, to promote his new-found celebrity, he was now paying each of the girls a hundred pounds a month to assist him with his image amongst the younger demographic. It was too late to do anything to improve their intelligence, but they were in total awe of him and they tapped into London's exclusive, intimate circles, which a writer sitting at a desk alone could never achieve.

Both London bunnies came from upper-middle-class parents in the Cotswolds. Pink ponies had turned into real ponies. Their boarding schools had awarded gold stars to those students who managed to get to the first lesson of the day on time, despite the pressure in the bathroom in front of a mirror.

These creatures were bliss when one was worn from too much reality. Equally, they were hell when one had a serious task to perform.

Gilbert patted along the wall. 'Why is it so dark in your hallway?'

'The bulb in the lamp is broken. We don't know how to rewire it. Mummy has asked an electrician to come and help.'

'Really.'

'Come, I'll guide you.' Lottie pulled him upstairs behind her and into the main bedroom.

Buntsy appeared. 'Sit.' They pushed him onto the duvet and Lottie pulled the rose from his lapel. She brushed the flower over his lips up to his nose which tickled.

'Eat it,' she suddenly said, pushing the bloom into his mouth.

'No, thank you. I've just had a large meal at Gordon Ramsay's.'

'Gordon,' they both repeated. 'Gordon. An ugly name.'

'Maybe, but a damn good restaurant.'

'What did you eat?' She played with the rose, rolling it over her own lips, not realising how sexy this was.

'I ate rabbit stew.'

'Bunnies. How could you?'

'He is joking, Lottie.'

'Were you with boring big-nose Brenda who fancies you and that American who was at the launch?'

'The one who said he had brought maple syrup from America and offered us money to go upstairs with him to a hotel room. Gross,' added Buntsy.

'Brenda was there but left after the salad starter. On a diet.'

That lie satisfied them.

'Now you have all that food inside this stomach. Let's see.'

They undertook to undress him. Buntsy pulled the shirt out of his trousers. 'Big belly.'

This game had taken a turn he did not desire but did not know how to steer it in another direction.

'Look. Boing, boing.' She prodded his belly, which he saw did bulge out a little, seen from his position lying on the back. He would definitely cut back on food, check his weight and go for a jog every morning before anything else.

'Why don't you go to the bathroom and get rid of some of the food?'

Gracious, they were basic. 'OK,' he agreed and rolled off the bed.

When he returned from the loo, he had taken his trousers off and was now only in his Calvin Klein boxers, his belly pulled in flat, his stance straight. 'Better?' he beamed.

'Ah, much better,' they agreed.

Lottie wrinkled her nose. 'But now you must be smelly and need a bath.'

'You're out to torture me tonight,' he said and thought that things were going in a better direction.

'Your bath time, Mister. We'll bathe you. Buntsy knows how to.'

'My parents used to have a Newfoundland dog and I always helped bathe him.'

Wrong direction.

The bathwater was not warm enough. He let them wet his hair. They shampooed it and applied themselves. Lottie clenched her teeth in concentration. He suffered having his hair conditioned and then spiked up with gel. Peals of laughter. Both girls were now in their undies, pretty bras, a lace whisper over young-girl breasts, tiny string panties. They panted from the effort of manual labour. He was led back to the bed nude and laid prostrate, before they towelled him dry. When finally one of them got close to his special place, as they called it, things went his way.

They shared him equally. They were not competitive. There were some clumsy manoeuvres when climbing over each other, but then they weighed little and their limbs were slender. Their long hair got caught here and there, or slid over his face. They offered each other the finale so politely that he nearly came, exposed, on his own. Their warm elf-like bodies had the sheen of alabaster and the noises they made were those of kittens in a litter basket.

Colette

In Riverbend, Colette had spent most of the night tossing and turning, so much so that the dog had given up and jumped from the bed. She was now sitting at the conservatory table, bony elbows on the pinewood. If it started to rain hard that would be a relief; if hurricane-force winds whistled around the house, that would do as well, but neither happened. Her land looked uninspired, dull and so uncaring, when she hated her lodger with such passion. Fires ought to flare up here and there. Flocks of shrieking birds should darken the sky. The three wise trees should stand like giant, burning torches testifying to the injustice done to her.

Trudy walked in carrying tea on a tray, wearing thickly knitted socks instead of shoes.

Trudy returned to the kitchen and Colette nibbled at the corner of a slice of toast, and then realised that is what Gilbert did. She dropped the toast. At that moment, Gilbert came in. Despair overwhelmed her and she felt as if she were suffocating, because he was sharing the space with her.

Lifting up her head, she pressed out, 'You have a nerve.'

'I'm late because, on my way back from London this morning, I went to get newspapers.'

'That's not what I mean.'

'Let's find out what the Press thought of *Behind the Veil*.'

She watched him like a cat as he chose *The Times* from the pile. He unfolded it, turned pages. 'Are you ready?'

'Am I ready? What does any of this have to do with me?' She pounced too early.

He lowered the pages he had held up. 'Everything,' he said. 'It has everything to do with you. That is why I am so grateful to you.'

'You are a monster. You stole from me the only love I ever had and ever will have. You turned a beautiful relationship into a vulgar commercial exploitation. You put on paper things you could not have known. You made it up, but it is based entirely on my inner thoughts and my seven months' stay there. You had no right to dirty something unique and beautiful. There is no decency in you. You sold my soul to the highest bidder.'

'Listen to this, I am quoting from the literary critic: *The novel is one of its genre, doubtless a masterpiece and the effect of it is still sinking in.* Bla bla bla.'

She watched him get up and reach up to the small television. The news was on. Gilbert had timed it.

The female presenter sat at a table with a Joan-of-Arc haircut. The caption ribbon at the bottom of the screen read, Latest News: *Gilbert de Villiers – Behind the Veil*. Gilbert grinned. Only important news was flashed on the breaking news ribbon.

According to the presenter, Gilbert de Villiers was a contemporary genius – the man who is *not* from Mars, the man who joined women on Venus. He did not shy away from empathy and labial desire, the whole story set against the crude reality of the abyss between the Muslim and Christian worlds. 'We have asked Dr Vera Bulova from the Council of Psychology and Behaviour to join us.'

A short and unimpressive-looking woman appeared. Her thinning red hair seemed plastered to her head, which she moved left and right in a nervous way as if she distrusted the instructions of the film crew. She sat down opposite the news reader, who fired away, 'What are your thoughts about *Behind the Veil*? It has only been available for twenty-four hours, but I assume you have read it.'

Almost timidly, Dr Bulova answered, 'Hasn't every woman?'

'You think it is primarily a novel for women.'

'I was at the launch and had the privilege to observe the author in flesh and blood. In the shadow of his perfect presentation was an inferior jacket. The sleeves were too short.'

'An interesting perception. What does that give away?'

'The psychic components of a human mind are not there to give away clues. His jacket was superimposed.'

'Ye… yes. Now to the content of his writing; he does not just understand women in the sense of interpreting what they say. He really feels them.'

'Let me stop you right there. I don't think he wrote the book.'

'Erm, I'm afraid you lost me. Who wrote the book then?'

'His alter ego.'

'That's a relief. You had me worried there.'

'Bloody useless women,' Gilbert spoke out, jumped up and turned the television off.

'How did you get at my journals? How?' Colette glowered at him.

He squirmed a little, picked up a dollop of jam from his plate and put it into his mouth. Only then did he dare look up and back at her.

'You stole my life. You are a criminal. You destroyed me. While *Monsieur* is a newborn star in Britain.'

'Internationally, actually.'

'Eeeek!' she screamed, grabbed her breakfast knife and stabbed it into the butter.

'I'll give you some money for Riverbend. I will pay for a swimming pool.' Seeing her expression, he added, 'A pool house with jacuzzi and gym, and, and a library.'

'It was my life, my love, and you came here to take advantage of me.'

'Your mother—'

'Leave my mother out of this. I will pray the angels destroy you. I will implore heavenly creatures to torture you with illness. You should already have a weak heart with all the coffee you drink.'

'Have you finished?'

'I will never stop being furious with you.'

'It certainly brought pink to your pale cheeks. You write well. Your journal entries are poetic and involving. Come on – a genuine love between a Taliban soldier and an innocent schoolteacher. Far-fetched, that's why they love it. Read it in the Press, watch it on TV news. You would not have done anything with your writing. It would have died unknown in a drawer of your desk. Your first effort on the Malaysian orphan was published incognito. I picked it up as mine. It cried out for an author.'

Something clicked in her. 'That's why you have been writing all day every day in the caretaker's room. You copied my diary entries. And when Brenda Fielding came, it was to discuss the publishing of *my* writing.'

He spread out his arms. 'There will be a book tour. Eleven cities in Europe where the author will have to bare himself. My agent tells me that the Turks expect me to perform a dervish whirl.'

'I couldn't do any of that.'

'That's why I'll do it for you.'

'How did you get access to all my papers? Out with it.'

'I borrowed the papers and had them photocopied.'

She screamed again and banged the table with her fist.

'The end of the story is all invented and written by me. The Afghan warrior walks through a city in the rain, and they meet and live happily ever after. That, I believe ought to be the culmination. Don't you?'

'I will not give you the satisfaction of seeing more of my despair. Go pack your bags and take those bloody big cars with you.'

'Why don't you sleep over this?'

'I can't sleep. And I can't cry. And—'

'Gilbert is right.' Trudy had tiptoed in. 'You are overreacting, Colly. Gilbert meant to help you. Your story is clearly so *schtunky* the world should know about it.'

'What is *schtunky*?' Colette, sidetracked, asked irritatedly.

'Trudy is right,' said Gilbert, 'The story is beautifully *schtunky*. It needed to be told.'

'You traitor,' Colette turned to Trudy. 'You are in this with him. You gave him my writing when I was out. Let me think – during my trip to pick up the dog from Glasgow. Abdul Hannan.' She had softened her voice before bending forward and putting her forehead on the table.

Nobody moved; nothing was said. When Colette's head came back up, she touched her nose and then put her finger into her mouth. The only kiss Hannan had given her.

'You do that all wrong.' Gilbert bothered to go round the table with the jam jar. 'Finger into jam and then into mouth. The way I do. Leave out the nose.'

This brought a hint of a smile to Colette's face.

Trudy cunningly used this tiny opportunity to change Colette's mind. 'Let Gilbert stay, please. He did this for you. I would love to have a swimming pool; I could learn to swim. I always wanted to learn to swim.' She drew wide arm movements into the air. From behind her appeared the dog. He sat down next to her and sniffed the woolly socks.

Colette stood up rapidly, causing her chair to fall backwards. 'Trudy,' she stated. 'You know no boundaries.

You eavesdrop on conversations which do not concern you. You allow lodgers into my bedroom. I don't understand why Nonnie didn't train you better.'

'Woof, woof,' went Trudy and retreated into her kitchen, taking HanHan with her.

Davina

Davina buttoned her blouse.

'Why did you change clothes?' asked Simon.

'I am coming to the pub tonight.'

He glanced at her. 'Why?'

She pulled the blouse down over her hips to hang straight. 'I need to get my mind off that book launch last night. My friend, Colette, panicked, Max was difficult and one of the plaster columns got broken.'

'Carlos has already copped a squat there.'

'And you two need to talk about start-ups. Look, I'm going there on my own. All I need is a large G&T and something else to think about. Maybe the JJs will be there.'

'You don't really know how to drink. Your Baptist parents aren't exactly pub experts.'

'See you there.' Davina put on her coat.

'Sure. I'll catch up with you.'

From Kilburn High Street, she stepped into the warmth of the Black Lion pub. Unwinding the boa-like scarf from her neck, she noticed Carlos perched on a barstool with a beer in front of him.

'Where is Simon?' Carlos asked, watching her legs

as she passed him, heading to a group of armchairs near the fireplace.

'He'll be along in a minute.'

Carlos rolled himself off the stool, which was immediately claimed by another customer, picked up his beer and joined her pushing through the standing crowd. They sat down on faux-leather seats. Now he looked at her bosom as she wriggled out of the coat and draped it over the seat. Holding her woolly hat by its bobble, she pulled it off and heard the crackling of static in her rising hair, reluctant to detach from the wool conductor.

Carlos stared at the long chestnut web settling down. 'Funny,' he said. 'Do that again.'

They did not converse as they had nothing to say to each other. She watched the flames play in the deep-set fireplace. The Black Lion pub had a most intricately carved baroque ceiling. In fact, the whole building was Grade II listed.

Carlos did not offer to fetch Davina a drink at the bar. She knew that he thought he would get it wrong; women were not his forte. Carlos and Simon worked in a DIY store, the former in screws and nails, the latter at the paint-mixing desk. They could hope to advance to manager level but it would take years. 'A dead-end job', Simon called it when he was sober, and 'a crap job' when he returned from the pub after a day of being told by his supervisor he would never amount to anything. The solution was to prove the supervisor wrong.

Simon could now be seen approaching. 'Dav, you haven't got your G&T.' And he turned back.

'It's busy,' she shouted over the din to cover for Carlos.

Simon was clearly better with women; she was proof of that, wasn't she? Carlos and Simon took out their Apple Powerbooks and seemed to pick up where they had left it last time. Normally at this point, Davina zoned out while they stared into the tinted glass, as ancient humans must have stared into glassy ponds hoping to find answers, but this evening she watched Simon, with his short-cropped ginger hair, large blue eyes, and broad heavy features, mouth slack in concentration.

Looking for company, Davina acknowledged the couple sitting next to them, a man and woman called John and Jane – the JJs who were regulars.

'It's getting colder,' Davina started a conversation with Jane. She responded, saying that she hated the cold and enjoyed warming up in front of such a gigantic fireplace. At home, wherever that was, John, her husband, was unwilling to make a fire because it was messy work.

Carlos tapped his laptop with irritation. 'That's the best estimate of how long it will take.'

John picked up the tongs and moved a log back onto the pile in the flames.

'I can't wait that long,' Simon snarled at Carlos.

'Can't wait for what?' Davina challenged Simon.

'Success,' he said with a hiss.

Nothing to do with her. She knew that both men dreamed of making it big, which apparently was supposed to be available to everyone sooner or later. The way out of their impasse was with a trendy, new start-up. For this, they had to use talent and ideas; they had to come up with something brilliant, something fast-moving, some niche thing which had been lacking so far but which everybody would find they needed. Assuming they had the talent, all they needed were good ideas; in fact, just one bloody good idea would do the trick. They were out there, the ideas which could take off. That was so excitingly frustrating about it.

Simon had urged Davina to run some of his ideas by Max, in the hope of getting useful tips from the annoying man who had already made it. 'Beer ideas,' Max had dismissed them.

Simon and Carlos's first project had been: *They poop We scoop*. Customers would receive a tray and sacks of pet litter, a bin with a lid, and string-pull plastic bags. The bag with soiled litter went into the bin, which would be taken away by the poop-and-scoop employees and replaced. Success was certain as the collections would be on a subscription basis, with a continuous sale of new products a further bonus. It never took off, despite the fact that Simon's mother who owned three cats was willing to invest some of her savings in it, if she could be the first customer.

And then came a new idea which they pulled down from the sky like a balloon on a string: flat-pack coffins made of sturdy cardboard. Funeral costs reduced by more than fifty per cent and the body decomposed within three years.

And there were other ideas along those lines. Davina told them that they were hopeless dreamers, but they objected, 'All we're doing is throwing shit against the wall to see what sticks.'

Davina continued to watch the two men talking animatedly. They would probably not succeed in setting up a viable business. She and Simon were eonic years away from owning a home and starting a family. They hesitated to invest in an expensive microwave oven, not knowing whether it would be worth it in the long run. Why did they not advance in life? Was Simon not as bright as she had assumed? Davina immediately kicked that thought out of her mind. She had already invested four years in him. Behind every successful man, there was a patient and loving woman: one of the wisdoms of her mother's Baptist pastor.

'Is Kilburn High Street getting rougher or is it me?' Jane stretched her open hands towards the fire. She had not taken her woollen jacket off, only undone the one giant button holding it together in the front.

'It was rough to start with,' said Davina, and Simon put a second gin and tonic in front of her. With a 'thanks', she looked up at him.

'What kind of gin did you ask for?' Jane wanted to know.

'I don't know about gin. If it's see-through and gives me a lift, then that's the one for me.'

'Some sort of gin-snobbism is slowly growing, though,' insisted Jane.

'The world is going nuts, I know,' assented Davina. 'I hear they have invented a cordless phone, which can also take photographs.'

'As long as it doesn't transmit the pictures.'

'That will be the next step,' contributed John, Jane's architect husband. 'I hope it will soon be available. Imagine how that could help me in my job.'

Davina turned her attention away from the JJs.

'Tomorrow is Saturday,' she said, raising her glass. 'Cheers everyone.' The JJs turned theirs seats to join the others in a circle of five.

'Gilbert de Villiers,' started Simon as if he was tossing down a gauntlet.

'His name is pronounced the French way, *SHILLBARE*,' enunciated Jane.

'Sounds like shit bear.'

'Men are so crass.'

Simon insisted. 'Gilbert de Villiers,' he pronounced in an exaggerated French accent. 'He's all over the telly and Davina was at the book launch.'

'No!' Jane's eyes were wide open.

'We got the flower contract for the event. That's why.'

Jane became all wriggly. 'He is a sensation. I read in the *Standard* that his novel is going to make him double-figure millions and that a film will be made. Imagine, a dangerous terrorist and an innocent French teacher falling for each other in his Islamic country.'

'Twenty million smackers for just one book,' put in Simon. 'Davina could have got me into the launch if I had only known.'

'I saw him on the breakfast show this morning,' Jane enthused. 'Did you see it, Davina? I so wish I had been at the launch. A perfect man, enchantingly mannered, dashingly handsome, almost too charming for his own good, *and* he is a famous writer. It's hard to imagine him sitting for hours on end alone writing a novel about how a woman feels.'

'Give me a break,' said Simon. '*Behind the Veil*, the

hottest love story ever according to the newspapers. How much did he pay someone to say that?'

'I would have thought Shakespeare had bagsied that role with *Romeo and Juliet*,' said John, who seldom joined in.

'What about *Love Story*? Nuns went nuts about it.'

Everyone ignored Carlos.

'One lousy chicks' book written by a bloke and twenty million just for starters. Royalties to rain onto lover boy for the rest of his life.' Simon was heating up. 'A book is just made up of words,' he went on, 'words we learned when we were three, strung together in sentences since we were five.'

'But those words have to be the right ones,' observed Davina. 'And in the right order.'

'That's where a thesaurus comes in. My store manager said during the Monday morning meeting that computers will become so clever, they can do half of the work we do now and faster. We are approaching the millennium, guys.'

'And leaving the dark ages behind us,' finished Davina with a snigger. 'But I doubt that computers will be able to write a novel. They are machines and don't have imagination.'

'George Lucas wrote *Star Wars*. How much time did he spend in space? A computer could have done just as well,' Simon defended himself.

'There are techniques in writing,' Jane observed.

'You can learn that from a book,' John joined in again.

Jane suddenly laughed shrilly. 'Ironic, isn't it?'

'Writing is one thing. What about someone picking it up, publishing it and publicising it?' Carlos observed.

'Some writers shy away from publicity,' Jane said.

'You're right,' picked up Davina. 'Gilbert is one of them. He is living in a small place in the house of a friend of mine. I've been there and seen him polishing his Mercedes in front of the garage.'

Simon sat bolt upright now. 'Dav, you saw it and didn't tell me? You know how I love Mercs.'

'The gossip columns are arguing about whether a Colette Fountain is his housekeeper or his lover,' commented Jane.

'Who is Colette Fountain?' asked John.

'Neither,' said Davina.

'The Press tends to think lover, but I opt for housekeeper. Mrs Danvers as in Manderley.' Jane made a grimace.

'A bloke like Gilbert can have any chick he wants,' was Carlos's opinion.

'At the launch, a photographer told me Gilbert ran two London bunnies. And he plans to get another Mercedes.' Davina stoked Simon's fire, just for fun.

'Lucky bastard. I tell you, it can't be that difficult to write a successful novel and pocket all that dough. I'd settle for ten million. Actually, just one of the Mercs would be enough for me.'

'I'm sure it would.' Davina played him along still.

John concentrated on his wife. 'Jane, I tried to buy you this book on the way here but W.H. Smith have run out.'

'That is so sweet of you.' Jane bent out of her seat sideways to plant a kiss on her husband's cheek.

'Gilbert read a passage of his writing,' said Davina.

'Is it really superb?' asked Jane.

'It came across as a powerful tear-jerker, but then there was the gypsy music, the lighting, not to forget our Blooms4You flower displays.'

'Guys, can we drop the subject please? I am getting bored hearing about de Villiers, de Villiers. I had a hard day with a supporting wall which had been moved without my consent. Let me get us another round. The same for everyone?'

'Oh, there's Max.' Davina pointed her chin towards the crowded bar.

Simon got up at once and made his way towards Max. Davina felt uncomfortable about the two of them meeting; Simon had drunk two beers and could easily become obstreperous, but he returned to the group bringing Max along. Another armchair was dragged to join the circle. Max was drinking something in a long tall glass. It had a slice of orange in it.

'Now you, Max, make about a million a year with Blooms4You, right?' Simon plunged in, to Davina's annoyance.

'Two point five million last year,' corrected Max. 'Net.'

'Right,' Simon said slowly, as if having difficulty swallowing the figure. 'But this bloke de Villiers is making twenty million from a book about two inches thick. I reckon four weeks' typing. Give us the secret of starting up a company which does as well as that book-writing. You went for flowers and that stuck.'

'I didn't start by imagining that it would succeed and

make me rich. I was prepared for hard work, relentless sweat and tears. You and Carlos are scared that, when your dream becomes reality, it will be unmanageable for you. Guessing with crossed fingers, if they are not on a beer glass; still dreaming rather than actively seeking cash funding or expertise. The stakes in your tentative start-ups were never high enough. Go out there with exaggerated optimism. Take risks. Sell the idea you are entirely believing in. Communicate that belief. But then, it would help if the ideas were not rubbish to start with, and some of yours…'

'So you bullshitted.'

Max shrugged.

'But what do you, a bloke, know about irises, violets, that sort of stuff?'

'I don't. I hired a woman who does.'

For a moment, Simon was puzzled as it sounded like the AA man and then he realised that Max had meant Davina and felt uncomfortable.

Max gave Davina a short sideways glance, got up and left them without another word. Carlos picked up the glass Max had left behind and sniffed its contents. Then he tipped it to his lips. 'Dr Pepper,' he said, 'with orange.'

'Coming back to this Gilbert,' Simon started again. 'He's got it all worked out. None of that sweat and tears. I know it. I connect with Gilbert. He drives Mercs – the only car worth driving in both our opinions.'

'Enough is enough. What are your plans for this week?' Jane asked Davina.

Simon looked at Davina.

'I won't have much time off work for a month.'

Jane cocked an eyebrow.

'Fourteenth of February,' said Davina. 'Valentine's Day.'

'And Davina very, very busy,' added Simon.

Hannan

In Kabul, the ambulance steered through the streets of the city. When it was blocked at the Massoud Circle, the driver put on the siren which permitted it to wriggle through. In front of Commander Qader's house, it came to a stop. The shrill noise ended and it felt as if it had never been there.

The paramedic helped Hannan on crutches out of the vehicle and into the house. He left the moment a woman appeared, identified as the patient's mother. Mona stood tall and proud in her modest floor-length housedress. 'Hannan,' she said, keeping her voice gentle. He noticed though that she had added a glitter-woven hijab, gold trimming hanging way down her back, and realised that his mother had been told of his return home and had made a special effort. He went to her and leaned the crutches against his body, so that he could bow and kiss her hand.

'They're in the dining room,' she said, and added, 'Be brave.'

Qader and Baghish were sitting at the oval table with Hannan's training officer. Hannan worked himself into the room, having to go sideways through the door and banging a crutch against the doorjamb. He regained his balance to proceed towards the table and the chair Qader had pulled out for him. The sitting down was a slow and awkward manoeuvre. There was a silence during which they stared at him, as if holding their breath.

The training officer broke the silence. 'Qader, as you can see for yourself, that is not good enough for us.'

'The doctor in the hospital prided himself on how well Abdul Hannan has progressed.' Qader sounded bitter rather than angry.

Hannan avoided looking at his father. Instead, he executed the sitting down in reverse and clomped unsteadily out of the room.

Mona, who had come in through the kitchen door with tea, watched the scene, tears in her eyes. 'Go to him,' she said to Baghish.

Baghish disappeared and the door closed.

'Please be lenient.' She put the tray on the table. 'He's only just out of hospital.'

'I am a commander and a man,' Qader started. 'I am born to fulfil a mission in those capacities. I am also supposed to be in charge of my family. *Lenient!* Look at the mess which happened to us, because I did not exercise my power as a man.'

'Hannan was born premature during the night of a new moon.'

'In what way is that relevant?'

'Such babies are chosen to be different.'

'By whom?'

She hesitated. 'Allah.'

'More like overprotective mothers.'

The brothers came back into the room, Baghish carrying one of the crutches, Hannan leaning on him.

'Sit down,' ordered Qader, 'and make it snappy. Your mother thinks I am not kind enough, nor patient. Faced with this catastrophic son, I think I have been admirably level-headed.'

'I would say so,' commented the training officer. 'Perhaps I can find an office job for your son.'

'That is decent of you,' said Hannan. 'But I will still be busy with physiotherapy every day for at least three more months.'

'Office jobs can wait. Anyone with half a brain can perform them.' Qader took command.

The officer thanked him for his hospitality and Mona for including him in the family. It was time for him to take his leave.

Qader escorted the man out of the house. In the fresh air, the officer rather unwisely said, 'Our army had such high expectations for your son.'

'So did I,' groaned Qader. 'While I have a chance to talk to you in private, tell me why the abduction of Fontaine failed. You had assured me that the cell in England had clear instructions, but the woman was not brought in to be dealt with as we had agreed.'

The officer nodded in a thoughtful continuous motion. 'The two mules reported back that the tracking beacon failed; they could not get a signal, so could not locate her. The operation could not be executed.'

'Lousy work,' commented Qader. 'Cheap excuses. They are going soft in England. The best we can do now is to change tactics and go for the kill.'

The two men parted without a further word or gesture. Qader returned to his dining room at a sprint, probably because he could still sprint. Back in the bosom of his family, he heard Hannan say, 'When I am able to walk unaided and feel stronger, I want to go abroad.'

'Of course,' said Mona. 'You will need a break from the traumatic experience. I will contact my cousin in Iran. They will be happy to have you.'

'I want to go to Europe.'

'In Iran, you will see Shabana again.'

'Remember, Mum,' intervened Baghish. 'Shabana is already in the bed of an Iranian.'

'Oh.' Mona exhaled.

Qader bashed the tabletop with his spread hand. The effect of it was minimal compared to the pain he inflicted on himself. It did not help his mood.

'It's all the doing of that French Institute and the loose women they hire to poison our sons' thinking. Verb-learning is a codeword for undermining our spiritual values.'

'Well, I bet my elder brother is planning to go to France.' Baghish leaned towards his brother, leering. 'The Moulin Rouge, I presume. The Rockettes.'

'They are in New York.'

'I would not mind going to Europe and seeing some of the things they have,' joined in Mona. 'In England, they live in lovely old houses.'

'She means *Upstairs, Downstairs*,' laughed Baghish.

'Enough!' roared Qader.

Obediently they shut up and left the table.

Many things remained unsaid in that dining room in Kabul on that day.

Simon

And late that Friday night, Davina and Simon walked home after drinking in the Black Lion. She stopped to look up at the night sky. Those stars were also visible from Kabul. Colette had found love in that city, something which had escaped her through university and later.

'Are you coming?' urged Simon. 'I'm freezing.'

How had Gilbert de Villiers written a book about the innermost loneliness of her friend, when he was the sort of man who only went for superficial floozies?

Once Davina and Simon were back in their basement flat, he insisted on having another drink before turning in. 'I need to think,' he declared, pouring whisky into a tumbler.

She took her mug of tea to the sofa, worrying about him becoming drunk and argumentative.

'It is of the greatest importance—' Simon was interrupted by a row of sneezes, 'that I find the right title. It has to be catchy and racy at the same time.'

'A title for what?'

'My novel, of course. I'm starting right now to work on a bestseller. My pen name I have already decided on.'

'Simon le Cornichon,' she suggested, annoyed with him and another of his futile ideas.

'Pierre de la Tourette.'

Davina cackled. 'Where did you get Tourette from?'

'The French cheese wrapper in the fridge. It's not carved in stone yet. The P and the T are towards the end of the alphabet. I ought to find a name and a title for the book beginning with A or B.'

She rolled her eyes.

'*Aaron Abbot*. I would be at the start of every list. A book title starting with A will be placed at the beginning of the shelf in the bookshop, where readers will reach out first. It's called consumer psychology.'

She shook her head at him. 'Shouldn't the content of the novel dictate the title?'

'A, Alpha,' he gulped from the whisky. '*Alpha bitch*. That's not bad. What do you think?'

'You'll write about dogs?'

'I'll write as Gilbert did, from the point of view of a woman.'

'You can write about me. I am a woman.'

'Your thoughts are not sexy enough. Gilbert knows a lot of the right women. He and I have to talk.'

She laughed. 'And how are you going to arrange that? He's way out of your league.'

'You don't know the first thing about writers. They bond.'

'Millions in Britain admire Gilbert and want to meet him.'

'With me, it's different. We already share the same love.'

'Mercedes cars,' she guessed. 'Of the admiring millions, tens of thousands drive Mercedes.'

'You are just jealous. I will be a writer, walking in the footsteps of Gilbert, being nurtured by him. You probably want to have sex with him, but I was there first.' With a theatrical gesture, both hands spread, he said, 'Gilbert belongs to me.'

'Is that so?'

'I will of course have to read Gilbert's book.'

'To copy it.'

'Why are you so mean to me all of a sudden? Ha!' He beamed. '*All of a Sudden, Arrogant Arabella Arrives.*'

'I am tired and want to go to bed. I have to work tomorrow.'

'Do we have a dictionary?'

'If it's not on the room-divider shelves, then I don't know.'

He got up and scanned along the books. 'I need a dictionary right now.'

'We are going to bed.'

'Not before you give me a sexy title starting with A.'

'The most obvious is a rude word for backside. And in *Gilbert de Villiers*, there isn't an initial A or B.'

Simon pondered over that. 'He cheated. He has connections because he comes from a French *de* family. You know, chateau with servants...' And his voice became wobbly with emotion. '... and a stable of Mercs.'

Once they were settled in the bed in the upstairs front room, she bunched her hair with a rubber band so it did not tangle while she slept. Simon next to her twitched and turned. At one point, she heard his naked feet tap across the bare floor going to the door but ignored it for the sake of sleep.

Lacking a decent English dictionary, Simon found a school pocket French-English dictionary. Coming back up with it, he cradled it tight against him lying back in bed again. If he woke Davina and she found out it was because he was still insisting on finding the right A words, she would get very angry.

Someone in the road shouted and a woman shrieked, followed by the noise of a motorcycle roaring off. Simon lay stiff with fear that this would wake Davina. It didn't. The bedroom window giving onto Calvert Street had latticed shutters rather than curtains. Outside were streetlights. A mere upward touch of his finger and the horizontal lattices let in more light. It was enough to read the small print of the miniature dictionary. *Abaissement, abandon, abasourdir.* He was in the French section. He turned pages. Before he had found the words which inspired him, he fell asleep and didn't even realise it started with an A.

*

In the DIY canteen, Carlos returned to the table with a full plate. 'So, haven't come up with a title yet?'

'Dav thinks the book should be written first and then a title would come to mind naturally.'

'Look, we're bright enough to figure out a title for our novel.'

'It'll be mostly my novel, because I will be writing it.' Simon sat up in his chair.

'Yea, but you can't write, and we agreed that I will do the grammar checking and the research.'

'Sixty forty.'

'OK,' said Carlos. 'From twenty million, I'll get… Still, a lot.'

'But you have to prove you deserve that money. Start by coming up with a catchy title. Just off your head, spontaneous. Come on.'

'Give us a clue. What will the story be about?'

'Dav thinks it is about a sensitive woman and a hero. But the way I get Gilbert, it has to be birds gagging for sex and men driving off in Mercs.'

'*The Bleeding Thumb on the Altar*,' Carlos splurged out.

'That would be crime, wouldn't it? We need a woman's perspective.'

'*Lipstick, Dipstick and His Dick*.'

Simon nodded, his lips pursed. 'That's got a good ring to it. But *dick* is probably against some sex language rules.'

'*Behind the Veil*,' Carlos said pensively. 'Have you actually read it?'

'I don't need to. I've got Gilbert right in here.' Simon tapped his chest.

From the neighbouring table, the HR woman said, 'I can't listen to this any longer. That's the dumbest conversation I've ever overheard.'

'Then eat your salad and don't listen.'

'It's too good to miss. A novel – you two are going to write a successful novel?'

'Rude bitch,' escaped Carlos.

'Say that again,' said Simon.

'She heard it the first time.'

'No, I mean for the title. What about *Rude Bitches?* No, we need an A. *Arrogant Bitches*.'

The woman burst out laughing.

Colette

In Riverbend, Colette sat at Nonnie's desk with a new clothbound diary. She had started to record how she felt about her story having been stolen and published by her lodger. After all, it was still part of what linked Hannan to her, in some disturbing roundabout way. There were a few short moments when she felt good about the story being out there and read by so many, but her inbuilt shyness and insecurity did not let such moments linger.

Her contemplation was disturbed by the bang of the door and the appearance of Trudy.

'I once brought down a runaway bull by jumping into his face and forcing his horns to the ground,' Trudy bragged.

'You've told me that story before.' Colette waited to find out what Trudy had really come to say.

'There are again hordes of people in front of the house, wanting to get in to meet or at least see your fancy, famous Gilbert. HanHan is useless at chasing them away. The dog appears and they throw themselves over each other to stroke him or photograph themselves with him. One mother put her toddler on the dog shouting *giddy-up*.' Trudy hopped onto the made bed. 'You, Colly, are legally responsible for any damage done to these people,' she pronounced her legs dangling.

'For a rodeo queen, you seem well informed about legal responsibilities.'

'Bob warned me. Haven't you noticed the goings-on from up here, sitting right against the window?'

'When I write, I pull the curtains against the glare.'

'They park their cars down the lane and duck under the chain which Bob fixed across the gap in the gate last week. The notice says *Private*, as if that deterred them.'

'I thought the novelty would wear off.'

'Nope, it's getting worse. Because some of them drive a long way and can't see Gilbert, they get angry. Two of them tried to push one of the stone cannonballs off the balustrade. I used my broom. It's not a good enough weapon. What I need is a rifle. In Switzerland, I would have one, if I had joined the army and not come to England to be an au pair.'

'We have to get help from the local police with this.' Colette gave in. 'I'll call Constable Stanley. Again.'

Simon

The next day, Simon, still searching for a title for his novel, decided to go to the British Library. That is what writers did.

He approached the building, head down, because he had to cross a tiled expanse. His late Irish grandmother had drilled into him the dire consequences of stepping on the grouting between slates.

At the glass door, Simon took a deep breath as if he was about to dive: inside, there were millions of books and, one day, one of his would be amongst them. He wiped his trainers on the mat and found himself in a glassed-in space. There was nothing special about that apart from him being seen from all sides. He progressed through another door into a larger foyer. On one of the walls hung framed quotes from authors, scientists – those who had written books and become famous. Simon could never bother about clever sayings or philosophical thoughts, but here now he had to live up to expectations.

The most original authors are not so because they advance what is new, but because they put what they have to say as if it had never been said before. Goethe.

The difference between the almost right word and the right word is really a large matter. Mark Twain.

Simon hoped that this was grossly exaggerated. No wise words from Gilbert de Villiers were framed. Simon smiled in recognition of the truth about that; Gilbert had not found the right saying. In the place he lived, called Riverbend in Bedford, there had to be piles of crumpled papers, discarded drafts, pages covered in his writing which he considered not up to scratch.

Another frame caught Simon's attention. *Always scrunch up your first draft. It is bound to be rubbish.* Simon beamed. He had thought of the scrunching up all by himself. What could be considered rubbish in Gilbert's writing would mean at least one million's worth for a start-up author like himself.

He steered towards reception and was asked to fill in a form. Which book did he want to use as reference? The zoology section was temporarily closed.

'I just want to look at books and their titles, like in a row on a shelf.'

She did not understand.

He aggrandised himself. 'I am a writer. I want to look at the best English language dictionary in this building because I need the right A-word for a title.'

She shook her head. 'I can't help you with that request.'

'In all of this, you don't have a dictionary?'

She blinked. 'We don't.'

'Aardvark,' he shouted at her angrily, before leaving the building.

Colette

With a bunch of Blooms4You daffodils, Colette brooded in the barely heated drawing room, the chador from Kabul wrapped around her. It was a room she had avoided since moving in. The portrait of the French *grandmaman* she did not remember looked down at her. Why hadn't Mum returned to Riverbend to collect the painting or the silver? It weighed on Colette that the mother-daughter relationship had taken a blow with the death of Nonnie and the estate going to Colette. She would have to find a way back to her mother.

At that moment, someone shrieked in front of the house. The sense of danger took her straight back to the Babur Gardens – recently, she had been reliving those dreadful memories all too frequently and, every time, it tore into her consciousness with the same effect of dread.

Colette approached the window with trepidation. Liz was running, her hair undone, her progress hampered by gumboots. She shrieked again and Colette saw a group of Gilbert fans chasing her. Bob arrived, yelling, his arms up. The intruders slowed and stopped.

This frenzy was happening because of Gilbert's

successful novel. She had to insist that he move out; it was getting out of hand. At the drum table, she pulled at the knob. The drawer was still a fake.

Of course, the disturbance was also a result of the love between her and Hannan. She had never thought of it that way. Their love was celebrated. Their love was reaching thousands of people. These running intruders did not come for the author – they came for the story which had touched them, although they did not realise that. Hannan probably did not know anything about all this. She would write to the moon tonight. It was only two days short of being full.

Simon

'This is getting ridiculous.' Davina put the book down.

Simon was pacing in their living area.

'You are stalking Gilbert de Villiers.'

'I am working at making contact with him. Writers do that.'

'Mentally challenged people do such things.'

'You were the one who told me that Gilbert was renting in Riverbend because Colette's mother had found him in the London writers' club.'

'Something like that.'

Simon resumed his pacing. 'That has to be Gilbert's second home. All I have to do is rock up there. After all, I will be a writer myself. There, you see, it's not a bad idea. No stalking anywhere. I'll take the day off and go to the club tomorrow.'

'You'll lose a day of your holiday entitlement.'

'It's worth it.'

The next day, a Thursday mid-morning, it started to snow as Simon entered a featureless London street. No 13 was on the side he was not walking along, all the better to find the house easily. And there it was, *Thirteen* etched into a brass plaque. Simon felt his breathing accelerate, the tension building up. He looked at the three shallow steps up to the black lacquered door, steps on which Gilbert had put his famous feet. Known writers probably came for pre-lunch drinks and after-dinner ports. Simon checked his cheap watch. It was definitely pre-lunchtime and now a tall man with a greying beard strode up those steps. He wore a dark felt hat, ranger style. Exciting, but it was not Gilbert.

It snowed harder, or rather the flakes became more furry. They fell on the pavement in front of Simon and sat there for a short while before melting into the wet asphalt. 'I've just observed this,' Simon said to himself. 'A writer notices such details. A writer is a superior being. Well, Gilbert is anyway.'

Simon dared to cross the road and put his foot on the first step. He lifted the other leg and went all the way up. *I am separated only by a door from the welcoming lair of novelists.* He rang the brass bell because a notice said he should. The bell made a deep purring noise.

'Members only,' a woman said to him. No, it was a recording. And then she said, 'Password, please.'

'Shit.' He had not anticipated being unable to get inside. The door buzzed and slowly opened.

Simon slid through the gap and found himself in a vestibule. It was panelled and paintings hung on the walls. There was a recess in which members had hung their winter coats on available hangers. Simon pulled off his fleece, rolled it and shyly tucked it into a corner. He pushed the door which stood ajar and – *Bingo!* – he was in the writers' magic world – he, little Simon, who had clipped a clothes peg to a cat's tail and insisted the screeching and hopping animal had done it to itself.

He padded into the room and nobody held him back. There was a bar to one side at which several men and a woman sat drinking. The rest of the room was furnished with heavy leather chairs, some of them occupied. Smoke came from one, but that was because the occupant was smoking a cigar. It was clear even before Simon ventured further into this sanctuary that Gilbert was not amongst them. After all the trouble, losing a holiday day and coming here, Simon was unlucky again, but then he *had* stepped on tile grouting in front of the British Library. Damn it.

A man pushed himself out of an eared chair and looked at Simon with pale weak eyes. 'Can I help you?' His tongue licked over his fleshy pink lips. In his breast pocket was tucked a hankie. His podgy be-ringed fingers reached out to touch Simon, as one would approach an apparition to make sure it was not a ghost. Simon moved back till his spine reached the now-closed door behind him.

'I am looking for Gilbert de Villiers,' he defended his presence.

'He is looking for de Villiers,' the member shouted into the room. 'Pet of his, are you?' The glistening lips formulated, 'It's Thursday. *Shit* Thursday. His lordship de Villiers only graces us with his presence on Saturday evening, when it is *Ablaze* Saturday.'

'Ablaze.' Simon lit up. 'That's it. *Ablaze*. Thank you so much.'

Davina

It was nine-thirty in the evening when Davina, Florence and two trainee florists had finally finished preparing the many different baskets filled with Oasis foam bricks, which Max had calculated they would need for Valentine's Day, now less than three days away. Davina trundled down the steps in St Pancras station and caught the train to West Hampstead. Available seats were not a problem but her exhaustion was. She sank into the first seat in a group of four and forced her feet out of her shoes. She brushed back the strands of hair which had escaped from the ponytail, with hands which were raw and pink from constant exposure to water. She had never worn a ring even though there was one in her jewellery box. Simon had given her the white-gold band with a diamond, a tiny diamond looking lost, after she said no to an engagement. 'I've bought it now,' he had said rather philosophically and she had joked, 'Let's make it a friendship ring.'

'I know it's too modest for someone like you,' he had muttered.

'Well,' she had given a deep sigh, 'I didn't really expect anything from someone like you.' As a last thing said on the subject of engagement, it remained hanging in the air, indestructible.

In one of the seats opposite Davina sat a serious-looking man resembling John Major and next to him a woman unconnected to him. The woman had ink-black Cleopatra hair including the fringe. She was rummaging around in one of those leather-lookalike bags with chains and extra straps and doggies hanging from a zip pull. One by one, she extracted tools for make-up.

And then, Davina saw *him* making his way up the train compartment. Instantly, she gave up speculating about Cleopatra's life.

Gilbert de Villiers' eyes and concentration were already on Davina, who sat there curling her toes in embarrassment. The train left. Gilbert did not choose one of the available seats near him – no, he came closer to her, with perfect equilibrium despite the shuddering of the carriage.

'Don't I know you?' he uttered the much used and abused line.

She looked away.

Gilbert remembered. 'The woman who came to Riverbend and looked at the garden with Colette.'

'The woman who did the flowers for your launch.'

'Of course.'

Did he know about Blooms4You or not?

'The gladioli were splendid and so were the carnations.'

'There were no carnations.'

The train stopped in Kentish Town; John Major alighted and Gilbert's hand reached out to grasp the handle of the seat which John Major had liberated.

Davina panicked that Gilbert would take that very seat opposite her. He didn't.

'Where are you going?' he asked instead. At the sound of his soft voice, Cleopatra snapped shut the compact to look at him.

'Home,' said Davina.

'Where's home?'

'Next station. West Hampstead.'

'You need to put on shoes.'

She gave him a fangy smile and squeezed her feet back into the pumps.

'It's going to snow and you look tired.'

The train slowed.

'Excuse me.' She pushed past him.

'It is also chill and dark. I'll escort you home.'

Cleopatra said, 'I get off at Cricklewood and that's next.'

Gilbert ignored her.

Davina pressed the button by the folding doors and then again.

'Let me.' Gilbert used his thumb and, of course, the door unfolded. She stepped out of the carriage. He was right behind her. The train glided away. They were the only passengers on the platform. She did not move, did not go to the steps to climb up to street level. She did not know what to do or how to feel. Her heart beat violently; he was after all an Adonis, as well as a plagiarist.

'Let's have a coffee,' was said chillingly close to her neck. Perhaps it was the night breeze which had caressed her nape and not his breath.

'It is past ten at night,' she remonstrated.

'I need to talk to you.' A flat hand came against the middle of her back. She was defenceless. Together, they climbed the stairs. The hand was still there when he guided her across the empty street to the Crazy Bean coffee shop, open twenty-four hours, which she had passed so many times without ever contemplating going in.

He chose a table right at the back. They sat down. 'You can take your shoes off again,' he said. 'I won't mind. Tough day at work, I take it. I guess a florist has to be on her feet all the time. That's what you are, aren't you – a florist?'

She should now say, *I have a doctorate in plant science*, but this wasn't the moment.

He ordered two capuccini from the waiter. She frowned for two reasons: first, he had not asked her what she wanted and, second, the coffee was called a cappuccino.

'The final *o* becomes *i* in Italian.' He read her face.

She nodded. Whatever. He was a famous writer; he had to know about language.

'A sandwich? Hot dog? A slice from the cakes over there in the chill cabinet? You can have anything you like. You need to keep up your strength.'

'I'm not twelve.'

The coffee arrived in small cups.

'Cheer up, sweetie.' He seemed to dig his eyes into hers.

Sweetie? She blinked several times. What type of man called women *sweeties*? But then, no man had ever called her that and he was four times better looking than she was, and there was no female competition around. Therefore she was it and he had meant to *sweetie* her.

'I don't often ask women to share coffee with me.'

Davina cringed. 'Especially not at this hour.' She felt she had to fill in to humour him or herself.

'I am a night owl,' he went on, seemingly pleased with himself.

'No kidding.'

'Coming Sunday is Valentine's Day, right?' Gilbert challenged her. 'I would like to put in an order for three dozen of your best red roses. Is it acceptable if I pay by cheque?'

He was unlikely to cheat her. Everybody in Britain knew who he was and where he lived.

'What are your best roses?'

'Baccara, long-stemmed, velvet red, flown in from Kenyan hothouses.'

'Make it four dozen, with some, you know, fuzzy things around them.'

'Gypsophila. They look like tiny white fur-balls.' Davina took a deep breath. 'That would cost a hundred and eighty-seven pounds and I don't know whether my boss will accept—'

'I understand,' he said.

She dipped her head and waited for another *sweetie* but he had run out of them.

'Hole in the wall,' he said instead, got up and athletically sprinted through the coffee shop and out of the door.

She scooped milk foam off the top in her cup and enjoyed the taste of sprinkled cacao powder.

Gilbert was already back with, 'It's freezing out there.'

His nose was red. She thought he would probably not like it if he saw it, while he counted out the notes, and slapped an extra twenty pound note on top. 'Your tip.'

'You don't tip in the flower business.'

'At night, you do. For twenty quid, you can buy some plasters for your feet and lanolin hand cream.'

He was observant with women.

'I need to go home,' she said and tucked the spoon back against the cup on the saucer. 'My boyfriend will be wondering what happened to me. His name is Simon and he is dying to meet you.'

'Many are dying to meet me and nobody is dead yet.'

She gave him a shy, little grin. His charm smile back had the effect of the heat whoosh when you open an oven door.

By the time Davina reached 27A Calvert Street, an icy wind was frosting anything metal. Once inside, she gave a last shiver.

'It's about time.' Simon in pyjamas appeared on the stairs to the mezzanine. 'You have to ask for overtime from your boss or a pay rise.'

'I'm tired. I could have been home earlier, but I met Gilbert de Villiers on the train.'

'Yea, yea, yea. Why would he take the train when he owns two Mercedes?'

'He got off with me and invited me to a coffee in the Crazy Bean.'

'Gilbert? Gilbert de Villiers?'

'The very one.' She took her coat off.

'I don't believe you.'

'We were talking and having a good time. He has a great sense of humour.'

'Stop being such a cow.'

'He ordered flowers for his Mrs Danvers in Manderley – four dozen of the most expensive red roses for Valentine's Day.'

To her horror, she heard the sound of weeping and it came from Simon.

'Don't be silly,' was the best she could come up with under duress. 'I told Gilbert you wanted to meet him and he thought it was a good idea.'

Simon snuffled like a child who has not yet learned how to blow its nose. Pulling himself together, he said, 'I burned the two ready-meal spaghetti bolognaise, but yours is still edible if you avoid the plastic rim which has melted.'

Colette

Hoarfrost covered the land in Bedfordshire. Led by his nose, HanHan hoovered over the icy surface, seeking smells which were hidden beneath. In the kitchen, Colette was talking to Trudy about the surplus of eggs from the neighbour. Sudden animated barking brought the women into the hall and outside into the cold. A Bedford taxi was parked right in front of the stone steps. At the sight of it, Colette gave a shuddering gasp – the terrorists had found a new way to get at her. The dog raced up the steps, to lean his weight against her leg to protect her.

Out of the taxi came first the driver. He wore a pale blue turban. Colette tensed but quickly realised that he was a Sikh, not a Muslim. He looked up with a wide smile at the woman with the dog by her side, before opening the rear door. Audrey appeared, a black-fur circular ear-warmer framing her face, a carpetbag in her hand.

Colette reacted to the appearance of her mother with a string of coughs. When they subsided and she took the tissue away from her mouth, there was a man standing next to Mum, a man years younger than her, in faded jeans and an unzipped leather jacket over a rollneck pullover. Colette realised that she was not ready to face her mother with one of her unsuitable conquests. A quarrel between mother and daughter would be so vulgar, especially in front of a stranger. The taxi drove off which intensified Colette's dismay; the means to get rid of them as soon as possible was fast disappearing.

'Surprise,' announced Audrey. The man probably in his early forties took her elbow to help her up the steps.

Once inside Riverbend, Audrey directed the man to the drawing room. Colette mooched along behind them. Trudy, back to the kitchen door, observed the procession. 'Psst,' she pressed through pursed lips. 'Who is that man with your mother?'

Colette shrugged her shoulders. 'Her latest beau.'

'Looks more like owner and puppy. I'll make some tea.'

'Don't. They must not be encouraged to linger. And if you hear my scream of frustration, come and save me.'

Trudy advised, 'Never look into the eyes of the bull when he charges.'

'No. I'll grab his horns and wrench him to the ground.'

'You'll be fine.' Trudy's head movement indicated embarrassment about her bull-taming.

In the drawing room, Audrey pretended the place was hers. She pointed to the painting of her French mother-in-law, talking about the impressionist period in Paris and the brushwork. She explained that the silver tea service on the drum table was a unique set of Davenport silver, invaluable. Only then did she pretend to notice Colette standing by the door like a schoolgirl at Catholic boarding school, called in to be reprimanded by Mother Superior.

'Come in and sit down,' ordered the mother who was not superior. 'He is the surprise,' she smiled saucily at the younger man. 'Thomas, this is my daughter I told you about on the way here.'

'Pleased to make your acquaintance,' Thomas said stiffly.

Colette waited for the continuation of revelations.

'Thomas has been married before, shortly, very shortly – some student infatuation. He is in fact Doctor Thomas Reece, a doctor of chemistry. And I...' Audrey lifted the fur ring off her head, '... I believe that the chemistry between the two of you is destined to work. Amusing, isn't it?'

From that moment, Thomas and Colette did not dare even look at each other.

Audrey blundered on. 'I told Thomas all about you, the lodger who is a writer I was able to organise for you, the advice I am giving you on managing your grandmother's house.' She lowered her voice and leaned closer to Colette. 'I haven't told him about your... you know...'

From this, Thomas picked up the words *lodger* and *writer*. 'You have a writer living here?' he asked, looking at the painting of the mother-in-law rather than Colette.

Audrey twitched in panic. 'Oh, it is not what you think. He is a little man who wanted to hide away somewhere so he could think about what to write.

Colette tells me Giles is living in the garage building, too shy to come to the house.'

'Giles? Gilbert de Villiers, Mum.'

'At my age, one forgets the names of people one has nothing to do with.'

'Gilbert de Villiers?' Thomas perked up. 'He is living in your garage?'

'Not in the garage but—'

'That is incredible.'

'Why is that incredible?' Audrey's expression showed the first signs of doubt about the chemistry between the young couple.

'He is the most famous contemporary author. Haven't you heard of *Behind the Veil*?' Thomas turned to Colette. 'How do you cope with the Press, the fans?'

'It's becoming a problem,' Colette admitted.

'Is it possible to see him?' he asked hopefully.

'Not a good idea,' joined in Audrey. 'I brought you here to appreciate my daughter and not to salivate after her male lodger whom she stuck into the garage, unable to live under the same roof with him. Could you call for a taxi, darling? We need to go to the station. Our cars are in Brent Cross where we bumped into each other in the new Marks and Sparks delicatessen.'

Audrey got out of her seat. 'My daughter will soon be thirty and is in desperate need of a husband. There is always something not right with the men she meets. It is an excuse not to get involved. And now you tell me that the little shy solitary writer is a sensation.' Audrey twisted back to her daughter. 'Just tell me one thing, Colette. If everyone admires this Gilbert de…'

'Villiers,' filled in Thomas eagerly.

'Why don't you? You, the lucky one who can have him all to herself.'

'I detest him,' Colette said and the echo of the word seemed to haunt the room for a while.

'What more can I do to help her?'

'Nothing would be best,' put in Thomas. 'Matchmaking went out of fashion with *The Fiddler on the Roof.*'

Audrey rose on tiptoe to lift the French portrait off the wall. At the drum table, she moved the silver tea service into her carpet bag, piece by piece, sliding the tray in last.

The taxi took ages to arrive. The three of them sheltered under the porch from the sleet.

'The taxi is late because of the weather. Britain is badly equipped for snow conditions,' said Thomas into the silence. 'It doesn't sleet or snow often enough to justify the expense of sanding and salting equipment.'

'True,' admitted Colette, picking up contact with Thomas for the first time. She thought that he looked rather nice and the sound of his voice was pleasant.

Audrey remembered the silver candelabra and went back to fetch it.

'Your mother is quite a force when it comes to convincing someone they have to meet her amazing daughter.'

'I apologise for her.' Colette cringed.

'Don't. I have three pet snakes, one of which is a red-tailed boa. Women never stay long in my apartment. You and I have the commitment problem in common at least.'

'A real boa?'

'Here is the taxi. Two more minutes, Colette, I will be gone and you can breathe again.'

'I did enjoy your company,' she said quickly.

'I can tell. You have someone in your life whom you love. Someone impossible for you. You remind me of de Villiers' novel.'

The taxi took Audrey and the snake-lover away. Colette was able to breathe normally again.

Valentine's Day, 1999

Five a.m. – it was the Day of Lovers and the new moon cut a cookie slice into the black sky. In the Blooms4You flower-arranging chapel under dangling neon striplights, three extra florists and four extra drivers had arrived. Florence helped the women to plastic aprons. In Astley Court stood an enlarged fleet of vans. Davina pulled her canvas tabard over her head.

'Today, Cupid is going to be a pain in the neck,' Florence, who had done this before, announced to no one in particular.

'Inaccurate,' came on cue from Max up the stairs. 'Cupid is love, and today any man or woman can express their love with our roses, daisies and pink balloons.' Max disappeared.

'From the horse's mouth,' laughed Florence.

Davina pushed the clippers into the pocket of her apron to have them handy whatever this tough day should bring. Tough, as she was an outsider. Simon did not love her, nor she him. Sex between them, never passionate or needy, had dried up and the worst was that neither regretted it. And there, all along the wall, were the large square buckets filled with one thousand four hundred tall red roses, all just about to open, many to conquer hearts. She knew their number because last October she had accompanied Max to the flower auction in Amsterdam for the experience. The professional aspect of this trip interested her and she felt proud when Max asked for her advice, but the part she had felt nervous about was him and her abroad, possibly a night in a hotel.

With other bidders, they had trailed along tables displaying roses one stem at a time in narrow glass flasks. Max had listened to what she had to say after examining the leaves and the crown of the rose. He told her the company would take out a loan to purchase more than one thousand roses for next Valentine's Day, based on the figures he had needed last year. It was a gamble; roses are living matter, they get diseases like leaf rust. Insuring them would be financially unviable. One February had been so brutal, the lorries got stuck in snowdrifts, the electricity ran out, and the flowers froze.

Once the Amsterdam auction was over, he had her flown back to London that evening, while he stayed on for two more days.

Davina started to line up baskets in front of her. Max appeared on the iron stairs again. He looked as if he were still bed-warm, his shirt hanging over jeans torn at the knees from wear. In action, he looked attractive.

'Look, we're facing a bloody awful day. Things will go wrong; mistakes will be made. Let's just accept that now as a fact, and ignore it. Everyone hands on. No breaks, and – er – the first-aid box is at the back near the john.'

The florists moved to tables set up with spools of ribbon, boxes of bows, and block upon block of Oasis. In the despatch room, folded boxes were piled high. Miles of cellophane paper had been ordered, crates of champagne bottles and mountains of chocolate boxes. An army of teddy bears, holding *I love you* heart cushions, stood in ranks, in front of an equal number of red heart balloons on sticks.

Extra runners were to help coordinate between the upstairs office, the packing and despatch rooms, and to load the vans.

Priority was given to the orders which would go by lorry at seven o'clock to the airport. Next up would be the seven-thirty departures for the distribution centres in Slough, Milton Keynes and Peterborough. After that, they could concentrate on Greater London deliveries which the vans would handle, coming and going.

'I didn't sleep a wink,' said Florence. 'My brain is singing. I will have to work on automatic.'

'Last year, was it bad?' Davina asked nervously.

'Bad?' Florence squeaked. 'It was disastrous. Max lost his temper, big time.'

'Now that is bad. I can't imagine him that way.'

'We'll see.' Florence left it at that, as work started.

From the office, a runner brought down the first list of orders. T meant a teddy, B a balloon, *Lux* needed a bottle of champagne, and C a narrow box of chocolates.

The florists started to hand-tie cut flowers, and complete baskets with the washed and trimmed stems. They bunched faster, tied quicker, rolled into cellophane and taped, ready to hand over to the runners who put them into boxes in the despatch room, where Winnie checked each order.

The first enormous lorry backed into Astley Court; it was already half-filled with packages from other companies. The runners loaded it up. A second lorry beeped to park next to its twin. Orders were piled in. Max, his hands on his hips, watched the monsters drive off.

Winnie came running. 'We're missing four love baskets for Paris.'

'Hold it!' shouted Max, waving both his arms as he ran after the lorry.

Winnie went back to the chapel room and explained the problem.

Davina checked her list and shook her head.

'There must be a mistake,' pointed out Florence.

'Romantic Paris,' said Winnie. 'They must have flower shops coming out of their ears. Why do they order things from us?'

'If Interflora had taken that attitude—' Florence put her hand over her mouth. 'I'd better shut up.'

Davina was already sticking flowers into the missing four baskets.

'Ready?' shouted Max from outside.

Winnie and a runner snatched the baskets and ran to the lorry. The runner dropped the champagne.

'Nitwit!' shouted Max. 'Don't just stand there with pissed trousers. Get another one.'

Florence looked at Davina. 'You see what I mean, Max is starting to crack up.'

As morning grew and bouquets were wound,

messaged, cardboarded and addressed, the pace increased. Two buckets had already been knocked over, sloshing the floor. One behind another, all six vans left for their second round.

'Already nine o'clock and six boxes returned *owner not found.*'

'Max hates that,' explained Florence, 'for obvious reasons. Winnie is checking the addresses and they will be delivered a second time. After that, they stay behind.'

The day progressed: tie, sachet with plant food, re-tie, extras if ordered, roll into cellophane, clip correct message to cellophane, last wrap around the stems. Picked up from the work tables by runners, packaged in the despatch room, runner to the van with the right number. Winnie ticking on his list.

'No way,' said Florence. 'I've got here an order for four dozen Baccara roses. Now that's a lover. I could do with one like that.'

'Give it to me. I know where that goes to.' Davina slid off her stool, snatched the order card and disappeared into the rail room where the roses were kept in the cool.

'Put four dozen of those in that bucket,' she ordered a runner, while she stretched her spine, stiff arms up.

'How many?' he asked.

'Forty-eight stems,' she specified. 'What is four times twelve?'

'I dunno.'

Davina returned to her table.

Florence observed, 'That many roses won't fit into any of the boxes.'

'I know that.' To a runner, Davina said, 'Bring me

one of those empty pails. It is very important that the roses arrive in pristine condition. You understand?'

'You're the boss,' he said and went to fetch a pail, slipping on the slimy floor. 'It's nothing.' He brushed it away.

Florence looked at Davina. 'He twisted his ankle, I believe.'

'When he breaks his leg, I will go and fetch Max.'

'You're acting weird. What is it with you and that mega rose order?'

'They are for a friend of mine.'

'Up in Bedfordshire?'

'Yes, up in Bedfordshire.'

At eleven, Max shouted down for Davina to come up.

'Drop everything,' advised Florence. 'He needs you. I'll finish that basket for you.'

'You're a good colleague.'

'I don't want Max to go berserk, that's all.'

Once upstairs, Davina was asked to help with writing message cards. The temp was getting behind.

'Too busy downstairs. I can't—'

'You can,' Max insisted.

At the conference room table, Davina picked a card from a printer's box. It had tulips and forget-me-nots, Victorian-style.

Max handed her a print-out of orders. 'Nice calligraphy,' he asked of her. 'And here, my fountain pen. Don't twist the nib.'

Davina started to write on the card, copying from the printed list.

To my little Froggy. Be mine. Your Groggy.

'Do I really have to write this?'

'Don't think. Write.'

An alarm started to ring downstairs, followed by shouting. With all that water, they could not possibly be on fire. She ignored it and wrote on.

Remember the runaway kite in Devon. Guess who.

'Damn it.' Max returned after investigating. 'Five more undelivered boxes. The alarm was nothing; one of the idiot runners thought it was a light switch.'

'There is a message here which I refuse to write.' Davina said. '*I want to be a tampax inside you. Guess who.* It can't be, not again.'

'If you are in doubt, do as royalty does.'

Max did his midday speech from the chancel. 'Individual-sized pizzas will be delivered from *Little Sicily*. There is no choice. Margherita it is, and a can of coke for each. You have fifteen minutes to eat and drink, and use the restroom. After that, we will have to work twice as hard to meet our target. *Why?* you may ask. I'll tell you. Those who believe they deserve to be loved find it demeaning to have to wait till the afternoon to be wooed. Late-afternoon deliveries are only favoured by divorce lawyers.'

'No time to pee,' a runner complained. 'You could have hired more runners.'

'There weren't any more morons available.'

★

In Riverbend, it was a quarter to twelve when HanHan barked and a van drove up.

'Are you the lady of the house?' The man in overalls held a metal bucket in which was a huge bouquet of deep red roses. It was so heavy that he had to balance himself with his left arm stretched out. 'Ms Fontaine? Colette?'

A frightened nod from Colette.

'For you.'

And at the back of the hall, Gilbert skulked for no other reason than to watch her reaction to the roses which he had bought for her.

'I can't leave you the pail. It belongs to Blooms4You.' He transferred the roses into her arms and poured out the water from the bucket on his way back to the van.

'You like?' Gilbert tilted his head to the charm angle.

'Too much.'

'It is Valentine's Day.'

'Too ostentatious. The act of a guilty man who tries to be cute. It doesn't work. What you have done is criminal. I have a mind to sue you.'

'Let's not go there again. Let's talk about Eros and love.'

'All I wanted was to lead a serene, quiet life and enjoy Riverbend, which my Nonnie left me.'

'You are not a private person the way you think you are. You are the typical left-on-the-shelf virgin who makes it a virtue to protect her sainthood. You shrink from my masculinity, you hide your head under berets, scarves, ridiculous shower caps even. As for your choice of clothes, Bedouin beggar-women do better than that.'

'Thanks to what you have done to me, there are uninvited visitors to get rid of every day, there are bags of mail and dozens of telephone messages left. All that turbulence for Monsieur Gilbert de Villiers' magnificent novel.'

Trudy, who had heard the raised voices, appeared and did a double-take. 'Giddy goat!' Both her hands flopped onto her head. 'A bloodbath of roses bundled in your arms, Colly.'

'One can count on Trudy to say the wrong thing,' came from Gilbert while, undeterred, Trudy approached the roses and with her lips moving counted the heads. 'Forty-seven.'

'Wrong,' Gilbert snarled at her. 'Forty-eight. Roses come in dozens.'

'They are from you to her.'

'You don't need to state the obvious.'

'I'd better take the flowers before Colly drops them. We'll need our large fish-pan for that vulgar lot. Love has really punched the air.'

Relieved of the bunch, Colette tried to squeeze past the two argumentative people she shared her house with, but Gilbert took this opportunity to wedge her into a corner. Was he really shallow enough to make a forceful pass at her as payment for the expensive roses? She felt him touch the shoulder of her dress, running his fingers slowly along the Afghan embroidery of the V-neck.

'Real lovers don't need a saint, do they? They don't even need flowers.' His face was close to hers.

Hairs on the back of her neck would have bristled.

'Unwrap your damn head for once and step down from your pedestal. Let a man bonk you. The guy in Kabul obviously couldn't because he was shot. I am still very alive. Come on, loosen up.' Both hands were now back on her shoulders and Gilbert started to rock her body. Of course he knew about the Babur shooting; her life was in his novel.

'*Spay bachai*,' she shouted out, finding instant relief in the Afghan phrase meaning *son of a bitch*, one of the few lines Laura had taught her. Gilbert had not only exploited her love story; now, he was stooping so low as to belittle that love.

'A tough Taliban guerrilla. That's what turns you on, Miss Colette, isn't it? An individual whose aim is to destroy our civilisation.' He let go of her shoulders. 'You fall for an enemy who offers you a few pink roses after class. I offer you four dozen roses of a much better quality.'

She lost all fighting spirit.

Gilbert let go of her at this moment. 'You're no longer useful to me.'

In the tall mirror, Colette saw Trudy carry the roses to the kitchen door.

Gilbert shouted, 'Hold it,' just as Trudy was about to push the door with her backside. With a few steps, he was next to her. Pulling one rose from the bunch, he clicked his heels and bowed, before offering her the flower. Having no hand free, she opened her mouth and he lay the stem between her lips. 'For you, fair lady. Now, there are forty-seven and you were right all along.'

She couldn't respond, not with a green bit between her teeth. Instead, she giggled like a shy primary schoolgirl.

Colette saw it all in the mirror.

Simon

For Simon, Valentine's Day in 27A Calvert Street was just like any other Sunday in February, except that Davina had left before he woke and she wouldn't be back until the stars were out. Simon had the whole day to himself. Recklessly, he jumped onto the purple sofa and frisbee'd the cushions across the room.

'Gilbert, ooh là là.' Simon, lolling on the sofa, pronounced it the French way. 'I'm not going to ride around on trains in the hope of meeting you. And as for *Ablaze* Saturday in your club, forget it. You are not successful because of yourself; it is your writing – just words.'

Someone knocked on the door. It was an upstairs neighbour, complaining about the bins. She suggested he police the situation because, from the basement, he could see what was going on. He told her to piss off. If he were a famous writer, such dreary women wouldn't dare ask him to do things. If he were a famous writer, he would have money and not live like a rat in a basement flat.

New energy took hold of him. He saluted the bins in front of the window. 'You're the solution to my problem. Thank you.'

He changed into a brand-new polo shirt, chinos which sat gently on his hips, and a blouson jacket. He dunked a comb into olive oil and slicked back his short ginger hair. 'David Bowie,' he said to himself in the shaving mirror.

The train journey to Bedford was easy. Nobody noticed him. Not yet.

At the station, Simon asked around. Obviously nobody in Bedford knew where Riverbend was. He was forced to pay for a taxi and sat tense on the back seat, watching the meter ticking. Eventually, the driver pointed to a large mansion surrounded by greenery. Simon asked to be let out just after the wrought-iron gates, of which there was only one.

The sun came out. His Irish grandmother would have interpreted it as a good omen. Up there was the place where de Villiers lived, ate, slept and wrote bestsellers. Simon felt excitedly unnerved.

The hedge around the property was made of something prickly. Hawthorn – yes, that's what it was. Loads of it and about the height of a man. There were parts where it had thinned but not enough to crawl through. It had to be the gate, but there were bound to be security cameras and it was important he was not seen.

As he walked back to the gate, a flower-covered van came out. He tried to look like a rambler; he even started to swing his arms. The missing half of the gate lay on the ground inside and the still-standing one was badly bent at the bottom. Checking no car was in sight, he rolled his body around the gatepost the way he had seen it done in films. He was inside the property. Before him was a tarmacked drive at an incline. Of the mansion, only the roof and several sets of chimneys could be seen.

As he strode up, more of the house revealed itself. That's how the rich live. That's what he would get if he succeeded. By now almost all of the building was visible, therefore anyone could see all of him too. It was too dangerous. He stepped off the drive and into the bordering bushes. From there, he chose to walk diagonally over coarse, wet grass heading toward the garages on the east side of the building, where Davina had told him Gilbert did his writing.

The day would come when Simon could walk right up the steps to the entrance where Gilbert would be waiting to greet him. Now, working himself through the tough grass wearing the wrong shoes for it, the noise of a car engine made him spin round. A car roared down the drive, lifting a dust cloud. It had to be a twin-exhaust beauty. A glimpse of the driver showed him Gilbert's face. More dust, and the red Mercedes Maybach 57 and Gilbert were down at the gate, through it and gone.

Simon forged onward and upward, till he came to the gap between the main house and the garages. Nobody seemed to have seen him. He headed to the garage door which Gilbert, leaving in a hurry, had left ajar; luck was on Simon's side. He slipped into the garage and stood in the emptied space. Next to it though was parked a Mercedes C280 Sport convertible. Simon sighed with pleasure at the mere sight of the silver beauty. There was no time to look at it properly; at any time, he could be caught. There was an internal door. He tried the handle and it opened. He crept past a single bedroom. There was a narrow Ikea cupboard and an unmade bed. The next door revealed Gilbert's living room-cum-study. It had an odd shape with panoramic windows. Simon entered, stooping below the windowsills. On the back of the office chair in front of the word processor and printer was a pullover, soft to the touch and smelling of expensive aftershave. A two-seater sofa with a giraffe-neck print cushion was pushed against the wall.

And then Simon saw what he had come for: the wastepaper basket under the desk. He pulled it towards him and thought his heart would stop beating. The basket was full to the brim with scrunched-up paper.

On his knees, he picked out one of the pages and flattened it against his body. There was typing on it. He read a sentence at random. *You push her harder and she starts to growl sensually.* Wow! Even for a first draft, there was no way that was rubbish. *Growl sensually.* How sexy. He flattened more pages and, not having brought anything to carry things in, he stuffed them under his polo shirt.

Simon peeked out of the windows. Nobody was around. Nobody had seen him. Why not take more pages, seeing he had come all the way and paid for a taxi? The next bundle of papers did not fit under his top. He stuffed them into his trousers, where the pages crumpled up again. Enough, or he would not be able to walk any longer.

He took a last glimpse: *Never rub, always use caressing moves.* Heigh-ho, he had to have that page.

He left the way he had come, scuttled over the pebbles walking awkwardly, legs apart, and only slowed down when he felt grass under his feet. He was now far enough from the house not to be shot at. He was stuffing the last page into his trousers, when the most horrible sight materialised behind him. It was speeding towards him, mane flying and narrow jaw open – a grotesque beast.

Simon started to run, but soon hot breath was upon him and the animal threw itself at him. He lost his balance and ended up on the ground, both hands slapped over his face for protection. Two front paws were placed on his paper-covered chest, the animal's mouth approached and a string of saliva dripped from the fleshy lips, behind which was an impressive collection of teeth. *Play dead*; that was always the advice in safari documentaries. Simon lay flat, arms out. The weird animal, with an anteater's face and a curtained body, climbed onto him and sat down.

'Get off me,' Simon hissed at the creature, which just eyed him steadily. By rolling himself sideways, he managed to get out from under the animal and lope towards the periphery of the property. A glance back showed him that the hairy creature stood tall and still, letting him go. A few more strides and Simon would have made the hedge.

But no, the animal lolloped up to him, tassels swinging, long sinuous legs working. The beast knocked him over and sat on him again. The crumpled paper cut into the skin of Simon's sensitive genital area. It dawned on him that the ferocious exotic creature might actually have been tamed, annoyingly so.

'Get off me.' He slapped the head and the animal

seemed to look at him with hurt surprise. Simon managed to inch himself out from under and crawled away. He reached out and his hands were torn by the hawthorn as he tried to get through the hedge. And then – he was bitten in the buttocks! It only felt like a nip because the pages had moved around in his underwear. Another bite, more painful this time, and Simon got up from all fours and, eyes closed, dived through the hawthorn hedge.

★

Up in Nonnie's bedroom, Colette had been daydreaming until, gazing out into the garden, the horror of her nightmares materialised in the shape of a man running diagonally across the lawn. Chin-scar or Slit-eye, she couldn't be sure. She folded her hands in a prayer pose and whispered, 'Hannan, please ask your father to stop them hurting me. Hannan, you can hear me. I know inside me that you are alive. Please put a stop to this. All I did was fall in love with you. All you did was choose to learn French. It was fate, beautiful fate.'

Her Afghan hound appeared, chasing the man who moved unnaturally, as if handicapped. Colette got out of her chair and pushed aside the gauze curtain to see better. Her dog caught up with little effort, knocked the terrorist to the ground and was investigating his prey. She thought of Slit-eye and his gun. HanHan might get shot. Colette gripped the gauze so hard, some of the curtain hooks snapped off.

Outside, the scene changed. The terrorist had got

away and HanHan seemed unharmed. At the hedge, HanHan finally got the message and bit the man as he dived through the hawthorn.

Up at the rail, the curtain hung in two ungainly loops. Colette dialled Constable Stanley.

Finally back in the bathroom of 27A Calvert Street, Simon washed and put plasters on his cuts. And after all that, only a few of the stolen pages had survived the adventure and they were in bad shape. With Sellotape, he pieced together the torn text and, on the ironing board, tried to iron out the moisture from the wet grass. The Sellotape melted and stuck to the underside of the iron.

'Valentine's Day is over,' Davina declared in a loud voice, when she arrived hours later and carelessly kicked her shoes off. 'So much love, faked and otherwise, so many hearts, so many teddy bears, so many froggies and moochies, and guess whos. Tomorrow some normality will return.' Calming down, she asked, 'Did anything come for me today?'

'Like what?'

'It is Valentine's Day for me as well.'

'Nobody sent anything,' he said. A look showed him that she was vexed.

Davina

Monday, the day after Valentine's madness, Davina arrived at work at eight o'clock. To her surprise, the premises were neat and tidy, apart from the boxes which yesterday had not found their way to the heart of a loved one. It was one of the things Max had predicted would go wrong.

'Don't just stand there looking stunned.' Max appeared out of the toilet. 'I had the place cleaned as a thank you for all the hard work you and your colleagues did yesterday.'

'Thank *you*,' she said.

'Let's go upstairs.'

She followed her boss. In his office, he sat at his desk typing with his back to her. She marvelled at the two muscular bands sweeping up his neck to disappear under his hair, marking his nape with a wide W of hair growth. She smiled almost affectionately at the collar of his un-ironed shirt, a chaffed collar tip sticking up. Max, she knew, was careful with money; he paid himself a minimal salary, preferring to put the profits back into the company and salaries for others. He was a strange man with a strong aura of self, unapproachable for some. She took a deep breath. He heard her do it.

'Wait! Don't talk.'

After more bashing of the keyboard, causing figures to skate on the screen, he abruptly stopped and swivelled to face her. 'We made £376,000 in the UK delivering 690 orders, and 12,000 Euros in France delivering 160 orders. We have to improve France and work on their distribution centres. Other countries we have not yet considered; so far, the profit margins are too slim.'

She resisted picking up the stray hair which lay in a curl on his shoulder.

'A start-up only keeps flying, if it is regularly pruned down to the last penny.'

'Didn't you do better than last Valentine's?'

'We need to do *a lot* better,' he said with self-fabricated strictness.

'I understand.' She tried to furrow her brow, but failed. A full smile slipped out before she had a chance to repress it, while he sat twisted to look up at her over his shoulder.

'What are we going to do with the undelivered roses? We can't sell them, pretending they are pristine,' she mused.

'Why not give them away?'

'To whom?' she was surprised.

'Deserving early Monday morning citizens.' He got out of his chair. The rising sun of this new day came through the stained-glass window, casting multi-coloured tints onto the walls. Max switched off the ceiling light.

Shortly after that, they opened the undelivered boxes, removed the messages and delivery details, and shoved them into the back of the van closest to the building.

'Hop in,' he invited her onto the passenger seat.

'Talk to me, Max. Don't make me do something uncomfortable.'

The vehicle rattled over the paving and out of the compound into Camley Street.

Driving in a van gave a sensation of superiority over the surrounding traffic. Other van drivers acknowledged them as mates, forming an O with their finger and thumbs as if it were a secret language. In commuter traffic, they advanced down the Old Marylebone Road, turned left into Edgware Road and ended up in the Marble Arch circle where, unexpectedly, Max drove up onto the pavement and parked on the edge of Speaker's Corner in Hyde Park. He pushed the stick into neutral and shut down the motor.

She slowly turned her head towards him. 'Have you gone insane?'

'Get out of the vehicle,' was his response.

'Definitely crazy.'

Max opened the rear doors and pulled twelve red roses out of a box. Holding them high, he strode confidently over to a woman, who instantly backed off in horror, then scuttled away until she found herself at a safe distance.

'Well done, Max.'

'You do women; I do men.'

'Let's practise on a man together.'

Armed with a new bouquet, Davina scanned the park. An older gentleman sat on a bench. He had a soft face, gentle white hair caressing the top of his head, and jowls that pulled down the skin beneath his eyes.

'That one.'

They approached him. She held out the roses with a red bow. 'A gift for you,' she said.

'You're newly-weds, aren't you? I can see it from the way you are together. If that's the bridal bouquet to throw, I'm unlikely to be the next to marry, you know. I have just been diagnosed with Parkinson's.'

'My turn,' said Max, and presented the next bouquet to a middle-aged woman being pushed in a wheelchair by a young man, who asked, 'What charity are you from?'

'A free Monday morning gift.'

'You're not allowed to do that without being approved by the Association for the Mobility-Impaired.'

A girl in a grey school coat caught their attention. The child had to run to keep up with her mother, who marched along talking animatedly into a portable phone the size of a shoe. When Davina bent down and handed the child a romantic posy, the mother's phone came off her ear. 'I'll call the cops,' she said. 'Perverting children.'

'They are beautiful,' admired the child.

'This lady and I are florists. We decided to make people happy by giving them flowers today.'

'Thank you,' the girl said, flushed with pleasure. Her mother was on the phone again and they walked on, the girl carrying the bunch like a trophy.

'We've still got nineteen to give away. At this rate, we'll never make it. Let's go for unlikely prey.'

Max singled out a tall black man in a camelhair coat. He looked well-groomed, had gold-rimmed glasses on his nose, and *get out of my way* tattooed invisibly on his forehead.

'A gift for you.' Davina played as innocent as possible. The man reached into his coat pocket and handed out a £5 note, before walking on. He did not take the flowers.

'We've got to crack this. Me next.' Davina was getting into the spirit of the task. She chose an elderly woman in a fake-fur coat, pulling a pug on a diamanté leash behind her.

Max shook his head for *no*, Davina hers vigorously for *yes*.

'For your dog.' Davina offered the roses.

'Hercules, how lovely.' The pet was lifted off the pavement to have his inbred nose pushed into red petals. 'For you, lovely flowers.' She turned to Davina. 'He loves flowers, you know.'

From Marble Arch, two police officers walked over to them. They took their ease, wide smirks on their faces as they approached easy villains.

'Your van, your flowers, right? Do you have a licence?'

'We're not selling flowers; we are giving them away.'

'Sure.'

'One for you.' Max applied charm as he held out a 24-stem bundle to the policewoman. She hesitated, her face close to the velvet curls of perfect pedigree roses. Her uniformed colleague pointed over to the pug woman walking away carrying similar roses, turning back and waving.

'See,' said Max. 'Giving is more rewarding than receiving.'

The policewoman's hand curled around the stems of the bouquet. The deal was done.

'But we want you two out of here in twenty minutes.'

'Yes, sir.' Max gave half a salute.

'A police bribe, a pug and a schoolgirl.' Max looked up at the bland February sky. 'Pathetic, isn't it? What shall we do? Humanity has lost its innocence so much that it mistrusts gifts.' He suddenly sprinted to the trunk of the Reform Tree under which a public speaker had left a crate. Max set it up in a visible place and stood on it.

'Keep handing me bunches,' he ordered Davina. 'Ladies and Gentlemen of this Monday morning, the Government has decided to hand out flowers to people whose family name starts with the letter R or S. Anyone with a name starting with these letters, come up here to get your flowers.' People stopped in their tracks, approached with curiosity to see why a man was waving around expensive flowers. 'You Richardson, Robertson, Redfern, Saunders, Smith, don't be shy. This is your day.' Quite a group gathered, but nobody came forward.

Max stepped down and they sat on a bench. 'I have another idea.'

'The police will be back, you know that.'

Like a man on a mission, Max got onto the box again. 'Ten quid for a bunch worth seventy-five, off the back of a van, till the cops come.'

In no time, they had sold all the roses. It was astonishing to see people disperse at such speed, cleverly concealing the flowers under clothing, in carrier bags, dots of red here and there. Max slammed shut the van doors and climbed into the driver's seat. They took off.

'That is one of the most exciting things I have ever

done.' Davina was counting the money on her lap. 'We've made just over two hundred pounds.'

'Perfect,' he said. 'Lunch.' He drove to the Grand Palace Hotel and asked the concierge to park the van for him.

They strode inside and were directed to the bar. Two barmen watched the tall good-looking man in jeans and an unspeakable shirt pull out a bucket chair for his attractive companion with a swinging ponytail, Swedish clogs and no trace of make-up.

Max ordered Moet et Chandon on ice, and she felt physically uncomfortable from head to toe but emotionally thrilled to bits. Original oil paintings graced the walls above bees-waxed antiques in an atmosphere so rarefied that the guests talked in whispers.

The bubbly arrived in a silver bucket and was expertly opened. It was champagne on an empty stomach; she had not had time to eat yesterday evening or that morning. She sipped at the coupe glass, having to suck over the edge to get to the liquid. It went straight to her head. How deliciously exotic to be here alone with Max, the elusive man, the much-respected man, but also the avoided one – avoided by the kind of people who felt ill-at-ease in his presence, with his short sentences and frequently weird way of speaking, and the unspoken sadness and mystery of his lost sister.

She was one of another kind: the curious-about-him type. She had a second sip at the glass. Perhaps also the irresistibly-drawn-to-the-mystery-man type. And now they were here together, alone, sipping champagne, and she noticed that he was the most attractive man in the room, her boss of whom she knew hardly anything personal. Was this not an opportunity to learn more about him, in this fancy hotel? There were rows of rooms upstairs. Of course, she had been alone with him in Amsterdam, but he had given away nothing of himself and put her into a taxi to the airport while he stayed on.

Davina nose-dived into her champagne glass again. 'You work so many hours including the weekends, your girlfriend can't see much of you.' She thought that was an innocent start to open him up.

'I can't see any girlfriend either.'

'Have you not got one?' She had to keep digging. 'Have you been close to a woman lately?'

'Yes,' he said simply.

'What happened?'

'The usual.'

'Maximilian,' she exclaimed, as if a Roman emperor had just materialised. 'May I call you that today because you deserve to be admired?' She emitted a salvo of laughter, not discreetly.

'You'd better have something to eat,' Max decided. He hailed the waiter. 'We need canapés.'

'I'd like blinis,' she exclaimed. 'Lots of them.'

'Bring us Gruyère straws and two dozen salmon blinis.' Max sent the waiter away.

'Where did you meet this woman?' Davina resumed her pestering.

'Holland, the flower auction.'

'Aha! So you whisked her off her feet there and then, after having sent me home,' she declared, waving her glass around.

'Sit down,' he ordered. 'You're annoying the other guests.'

'What is her name?'

'Helga.'

'Effing Helga in a windmill.'

'Please don't shout, and sit down.'

'How long did you stay on?'

'A couple of days.'

'Sneaky, sneaky. At least I am learning something about you.' Davina felt launched. The room rotated elliptically but her focus remained on him.

The tray with the food arrived together with a second bottle of champagne.

Davina watched the waiter force the swollen cork out of the bottle neck. 'It's like being constipated, isn't it?' The waiter took the bottle to the bar where he continued to work on the cork. 'So now, tell me more about making love to Helga in Amsterdam,' she insisted shamelessly.

He grimaced in pain.

She saw it not very clearly. 'You met up with her again. Or of course she comes to London.' Davina realised that she had some problems controlling her lips forming the letters S and L.

'I see her when I go to Amsterdam. That's it. Eat some food. And sit down, for God's sake.'

'Two days of porn sex.' Davina swung her glass towards him and hit his shoulder onto which it spilled. "Ere's to the lovers of Amsterdam!'

She knew she was flying now and that, tucked away inside, there would be a price to pay for her letting go.

'Life is snort,' she declared more sedately and sank back into her seat.

Colette

'It's spooky.'

'What is?' asked Colette, coming into Riverbend's kitchen.

Trudy at the AGA rattled a pan with onions, but it was Bob who had spoken. He was sitting at the kitchen table, his fingers massaging his weather-beaten nose.

'What are you talking about?'

The hand came off the nose. 'In February, the ewes are three months pregnant, for lambing at five in April. A critical time and now several of my ewes have miscarried. The moon spooked them.'

'That is exactly what happens to our goats and cows in Switzerland. Magnetic moonlight interferes with their pregnant bodies.'

'You're talking about full moons, Trudy. I am talking about a lunar eclipse which happened a week ago and was visible in Bedford. It is a disturbance of the natural order, which they pick up on.'

Colette clutched her face. Was it possible that she had caused this by sending letters to the moon for Hannan? Could passionate emotions cause Trudy's *magnetic interference*? The luminous disk in the sky was cast into shadow. Farm animals could pick it up. What about humans?

Kabul

Qader had one of his most trusted military adjutants drive him to the French Institute. It was Saturday, the first day of a new working week.

When the Commander, in full uniform, alighted from the car in front of the building, the guard lurking at the corner had a jumping fit, before gaining control of himself. Qader did not even acknowledge him but strode straight into the building, while the guard pulled his turban off to massage his hot and hairy scalp.

In the large entrance hall, Laura alert, her feet on polished mountain-stone tiles, dared face the important visitor. 'Salam alaikum,' she pronounced.

Qader hesitated, as if he had not planned what to say or do once he was inside the offensive premises. 'Show me the place where you teach our sons French.'

'The class has started.'

'Then interrupt it.'

In the classroom where Colette had taught Hannan, there was a young man standing at the blackboard. He objected to the unwelcome intrusion by throwing the stick of chalk onto the teacher's table.

'Is this the room in which my son sat?'

'There.' Laura pointed to the desk right in front. 'He sat there.'

'Is that all that happens in here?'

'Sorry, I don't understand you.'

'The students sit at these tables and the teacher is in front teaching.'

'Well, yes.'

'There is no mingling, dancing.'

'No. There is recess and everyone goes outside into the outside-in for fifteen minutes.'

This confused Qader.

'I'll show you.'

In the garden, he looked around. 'One of those old Kabul houses,' he said, looking up at the woodwork.

'Beautiful,' she said, and as a reward got a near-smile from the fat lips of the Commander.

'Tell me…'

She was prepared.

'… how come my son, Hannan, and his teacher got so close?'

'She was, of course, not like me, who comes from the Limousin. She was far more fancy, and half-English as well as being French. She thought everyone ought to like her and frankly she flirted with your son, which was inadmissible.'

'What is flirting?'

'Oh, smiling at him – er – letting him write on the blackboard – er – saying nice things to him – er…'

'My son would sneer at this. Something else happened.'

'They were attracted to each other from the start.

They looked at each other starry-eyed. In recess, they sat together on that bench over there. Going up the stairs, they made sure they walked close to each other.'

'In a way, you were responsible. Aren't you in charge of this place?'

With a courageous intake of breath, Laura replied, 'They were in love with each other. It could not be undone.'

Qader looked at Laura, in a tight skirt and loose blouse showing under the chador. 'He risked his life for her. My elder son risked his life for a little nobody teacher. My son is still in a clinic, learning how to walk. This has nothing to do with love whatsoever. There is enough hate on my side to annihilate that outrageous woman. It can be undone; it will be undone.'

Colette

In the middle of March, early morning in front of Riverbend, Colette stood stooped, looking at the tentative tendrils of jasmine which had started to scale the wire grid fixed to the house by Bob. 'Come on, you jasminlings, show courage. By summer, I want you to fill the air with the scent of happy memories for me. The sun will be warming the wall for you.' Not today though; it was heavily overcast. All of a sudden, it started to rain, rain which rapidly increased in intensity. Colette fled back into the house and its conservatory.

Gilbert had returned to breakfasts as if nothing had happened, so he and Colette now sat silently under the prattling rain, so heavy that the conservatory roof looked like hand-blown glass and distorted all that could be seen through it. The two of them did not talk, because it was easier that way, both knowing that eventually they would have to confront each other. Next to her plate lay an open book about flowers which Liz Worship had lent her.

The door opened and Trudy came in. 'I am depressed,' she declared and sank onto a chair. The rain still prattled dully. 'I miss Margaret.'

'We all do,' said Colette.

'It is so depressing when it rains, and Margaret is in her grave.'

Gilbert looked at Trudy, his face saying, *Stop talking*.

'On 21 April is Margaret's birthday.'

'That is the same as the Queen's birthday,' Colette remembered.

'Yes,' said Trudy. 'Exactly the same day. When Margaret was younger, she always celebrated her birthday in Riverbend with a garden party. Balloons, bunting, strawberries, sugar and cream. On her seventieth, there were even fireworks which Bob Worship set up and lit for us. The youngsters went swimming in the river, not minding the cold water.'

'It's all coming back now. The year I jumped into the river wearing only underwear, that year Uncle Tom and auntie had come from America with their three sons, and Travis fell into the stinging nettles.'

'His lah-di-dah American mother wouldn't let me put a vinegar wrap on him.'

Colette closed the flower book. 'Do you know what? On the twenty-first, in five weeks' time, Nonnie would have been ninety years old – ninety years!'

'We will have to celebrate her that day.'

'Trudy, you are right. We'll give a garden party in Riverbend and invite all those who still remember her.'

'Ninety years – that deserves fireworks to turn the sky fizzy.'

'I have work to do.' Gilbert got up and went to the glass door as if he had not heard a thing that had been said.

'Hey, you. You will help us on the day,' Trudy shouted after him.

'How can I know what I will be doing so far ahead?'

'I can tell you exactly what you'll be doing.' Trudy pointed her finger into the air. 'Already on the twentieth, you will help Bob Worship put up the tent. And on the day, you will set up trestle tables, fix decorations, and run back and forth from the kitchen to the tent, carrying things.'

'No way.'

'What else are muscles for? Don't think I can't see your push-ups from my window.'

'This has nothing to do with me. I never even met Margaret.' Gilbert's hand was on the handle of the door.

As in Grandmother's Footsteps, Trudy crept up behind him, head stretched forward. 'You sit in her house,' one step closer, 'you enjoy her park,' another step, 'you eat from her plates, you use her maid to iron your shirts.' She was right up behind him. 'Margaret would have said that you were a weakling. Just as well she did not have to meet you.'

Gilbert fled; a furtive glance back showed him two laughing women.

Colette returned to her desk upstairs, eager to start planning for Nonnie's party. A guest list had to come first. Her pen wrote the name of Davina at the top. After that she remained motionless. As it often did, her mind brought up shards of memory as if she was looking into a slowly rotating kaleidoscope. Spritely sparrows twittered while wriggling their small feather-covered bellies in sand in the Babur Gardens. The leaves, which Davina had touched and studied, rustled by soldiers hiding in them. The dry sound of a shot. A twist of the tube and a shift of the colours. The gentle way Davina had lain the freesias on the bedcover on her first visit to Riverbend. Hannan's face lying on the blood-coloured grit, his eyes closed. Another twist. The petal coming off the pink rose on the teacher's table in the darkened room. The burning of her muscles as she ran down the steps in panic. And back to Davina and her uninhibited laugh, ponytail swinging, the 'ciao' she had shouted out of the van after a visit.

HanHan, closeted with Colette in the room, became impatient. She underlined Davina's name and almost unwillingly put the name of Simon next to it, before she went to open the door for the dog to go and do what he liked. Next on the list of invitees, Colette wrote the names of her neighbours Bob and Liz, Peter the vicar and his wife Victoria, Constable Stanley and his wife, the Pakistani couple who had manned the village post office for so many years now, and an Italian upholsterer who had moved out of Bedford and to whom Nonnie had taken a liking. Colette decided to add to the list the newly qualified vet who had been so excited about having an Afghan hound as her patient.

And there was Audrey, her mother, of course, and why not Davina's parents, Helen and Justin, whom she remembered from college, when parents bonded bringing and picking up their sons and daughters?

Trudy would offer to prepare the food for the party, if it were simple. The celebration of Nonnie was to be a joyful event, a party she would have cherished. The thought made Colette feel so good, she lifted the receiver to call Davina at work.

Davina announced herself amid background noises. 'Colette,' she said with pleasure in her voice.

Colette, even though sensing that Davina was under some pressure, nevertheless told her friend about the ninety-year-old grandmother party. Davina approved of the idea, the tent, the party, even the extension of invitation to her parents, but right now she was asked by her boss to attend a first work appraisal.

'Tell him from me that you are an outstandingly talented, committed and competent employee.'

'It doesn't work like that.' Davina laughed and Colette knew exactly what Davina looked like at that moment.

'Must go. Love you.' Davina hung up.

Love you. Colette kept the receiver cradled against her. Nobody ever said that to her except for Nonnie.

'I love you too, beautiful Davina,' she said into the dead phone and put the receiver back.

Colette, as a teenager, had never had the possibility of a friendship with another girl; hair was too much of an all-consuming interest at that age, so Colette had learned to protect herself. At university, she had been lucky to find Davina, a friend to whom she could entrust her secret. Oh, she would hold onto Davina and love her back. Davina could be included in her feelings for Kabul and even be trusted with Hannan. Colette could walk chin up. *Davina is my friend and she loves me.*

Davina

In London, Davina was up in the Astley Court conference room with Max for her appraisal.

'I can't say how sorry I am about my behaviour in the Grand Palace Hotel.'

'You were as drunk as a sailor.'

'Only because I am not used to drinking. That should confirm to you that I am a restrained drinker of alcohol, which must be seen as desirable in an employee.'

'The way you knocked the Moet back showed clearly that you were a pro. And I believe you proposed to me.'

'Oh damn, I can't win.' She deflated. 'With you, it's impossible.'

'It's not a race, Davina. I am the boss and you are my minion.' When he saw her shocked face, he added, 'People get drunk, get loud, and lose their inhibitions. Don't let it bother you. I was flattered by the proposal.'

This for him was the end of the episode. She relaxed with some regret. Anything personal between them in the future would now be marred by her uncontrolled behaviour.

Max being Max, the review had to be done in a unique way. 'You will have two tasks. A: come up with a novel idea for selling Blooms4You flowers. And B: give a verbal appraisal of me, your boss.'

'Can I do B before A?'

'No. If you can't come up with a project original enough to arouse my interest, the appraisal of your boss might change a lot.'

Davina looked at the arrow-speared bird of prey in the stained-glass window. Max looked at her.

'We sell glass vases and we make baskets of all shapes,' she started tentatively. 'What about using more ceramics? Old-fashioned jugs, sugar pots, antiques. Something to keep once the flowers have wilted.'

'And where would we find hundreds of antique pots the right size?'

'We ask a ceramic factory to make us *antiques*, copied from pictures of Royal Doulton, Spode, lovers' cups with two handles, Sèvre, the French style.'

'Too costly,' he objected.

'Not if it is done in China.'

'Done in China, it will have a Chinese style about it.'

'The factories in Shenzhen can do any style, believe me. My Dad has a Royal Doulton shaving pot Dickensian-style. The stamp on it says *Made in China*. He tried to scrape it off but it's under glaze.'

Davina saw that Max was considering her idea rather favourably, the way with both hands he forked back his hair-curtains, his eyes still on her. The curtains closed. 'Now appraise me.'

Davina sat up, cleared her throat. 'You are a good boss because you show that you work alongside us and as hard as us. That way we, your employees, naturally want to share your dedication to the job.'

'OK,' he said.

'You want more?'

He made a movement of his head and shoulders indicative of dismissal.

'You are also kind and generous. I won't mention the strange way you express yourself sometimes.' She stumbled over a chair leg on the way out of the room.

When he could not hear it any longer, she whispered to herself, 'Sometimes, you unobtainable men are even adorable.'

Kabul

In Kabul, spring had not made a mark on the land. The temperature was in single figures and snow still capped the Hindu Kush.

Commander Qader, wrapped in a handwoven shawl, was on the roof terrace of his house. He hadn't put a foot out there since the Russian withdrawal. Reaching out to the metal rod of the satellite dish concreted into the floor, he started to shake it violently. 'You're not going to outmanoeuvre me. You are not going to spread insult, shame and humiliation on Islam and my people all over the world.' He applied such angry force that the receiver in the middle of the dish detached and landed, clattering next to his feet.

His rage was disturbed by the roar of two fighter planes soaring through the sky, their bodies way ahead of the sound they produced. Qader let go of the metal rod to give them the thumbs-up. The army was practising.

Head back, his hands in fists, he talked to the clouds way above him. 'I'll make sure the pink swine perishes, if it's the last thing I do.'

'Father,' said Baghish, who had come onto the terrace, 'who are you going to kill?' Not waiting for an answer he went on, 'What happened to the satellite dish? I was watching Formula 1 and puff – it went black. Why is the downconverter on the floor?'

'Who, what, why – chatter like a woman.'

'Did something happen?' Baghish tempered his voice for fear of provoking an outbreak of rage. He and the rest of the household had heard Qader's tantrum. Probably the neighbours as well.

'It's about the French teacher bitch who abused Hannan's trust and got him shot.'

'My brother survived and is getting better.'

'Yes, but his reputation will never recover and nor will ours. Some shit has written a book, telling the whole world what happened between the two of them.'

'What is written in the book?'

'It is a detailed account of me.'

'You?'

'Our family. Hannan's romance with the bloody teacher. Hannan drawing her little hearts. You're in it, the idiot of the family. He writes that we are not able to offer our guests decent lamb stew. It mocks Islam, the Koran; we are the greatest joke in the world right now.'

'Why don't we go inside? You need to sit down, Dad.'

'That reminds me.' Qader marched back into his den, grabbed the upholstered armchair and, walking backward, dragged it across the floor, one of its legs catching on the carpet. He yanked it through the glass door, breaking one of the panes doing so. Outside, he lifted the chair, as if he were suddenly years younger and of superhuman strength. At the terrace rim, he pushed his head and shoulders underneath the seat.

'No, Dad,' shouted Baghish. 'There are people down there. You'll kill them.'

'Ha!'

The chair balanced on the rim. Baghish caught one of its legs but his father's kick forced him to let go. The chair tilted.

'Don't do that. It's madness.'

The chair fell off the rim. Qader dusted his hands.

Baghish ran back inside the house and did not see Qader fall to the ground, laughing, laughing tears.

The Birthday Party

On 21 April, the sun shone with warmth. Spring was established. In Riverbend, the jasmine plant had clambered up the wall, cluster buds promising flowers and sweet scent.

The folded party tent and its poles had been brought down from the loft the previous day. Bob, with the help of Liz, Trudy and Colette, had erected the frame and managed to pull and lift the heavy canvas into position, with no help from Gilbert who had absented himself for the day.

On the morning, Colette strung bunting along the scallops of the tent, while Trudy and Bob set up the trestle tables, and the benches which Bob said he had 'found' somewhere.

Trudy blew up a few balloons with the number *90* on them, despite Colette's objection that it was not a children's party.

'If they sell balloons with ninety on them, they must have clients for it.' Trudy had a point. 'Margaret is not here to see it, is she?'

Bob had prepared a cassette of big band swing and the music enlivened the air as guests started to arrive in their mid-season finery. Colette thought with pain that Margaret, her Nonnie, was no longer here to enjoy the moment. Among the first were Davina and Simon. Davina, familiar with the house and garden, immediately set off to check on the jasmine, and Simon asked when he could be introduced to Gilbert.

'Excuse me,' Colette brushed Simon aside. 'The vicar has just arrived.'

Walking across the lawn, Canon Peter and wife came towards them. 'I couldn't have missed this remembrance event for Margaret. She was a fine woman.'

And then appeared Audrey, dressed in a lavender two-piece, having paid for a taxi so that she could enjoy a drink. 'Vicar!' she exclaimed. 'Here we meet again.'

Peter pulled up the corners of his lips.

'A nice sermon you gave my mother. People walked away from the grave thinking Margaret had lived the life of a saint.'

Colette guided Davina in front of Audrey. 'Mum, you do remember Davina from Royal Holloway?'

'The young woman with the religious parents.'

The vicar showed sudden interest in Davina, and just as Davina launched into a comparison between the Baptists and the Church of England, a sheep brushed passed them.

'If I had known there would be animal entertainment, I would have brought my old carrots.' By Audrey's standards, this was a joke.

Jogging behind the ram, Liz passed them with, 'Sorry about that.'

'Shall we help you catch him?' offered Colette.

Liz stopped and brushed hair away from her face. 'No. I brought him as a playmate for HanHan.'

'Ridiculous. Pedigree dogs don't play with farm animals,' Audrey said.

The tall blonde woman joining them disagreed quite forcefully. 'They are about the same height and recognise each other as equals at some level of awareness. It is good if they interact, good for both of their mental development.'

'What gobbledegook,' escaped Audrey. 'The ram has horns. The dog doesn't and could get hurt.'

'The animals know that.'

'Who are you?' Audrey's tone of voice rose with the *you*.

'I am Dr Venika, veterinary surgeon in the Briddleston vet clinic. HanHan and the sheep are my patients.'

From the tape player came *In the Mood*. 'The bar is open,' shouted Bob. Trudy, behind the kitchen table, banged a ladle against a metal bucket filled with ice. 'Come and get it.' Colette gave a loud sigh and was asked what was troubling her by people she recognised as Davina's parents, Helen and Justin. Helen wore a canvas dress, almost a sackcloth cover, with little attention given to female curves. It hung stiff and unforgiving. Justin wore a corduroy jacket, several pins stuck into the lapel. He picked spectacles from the jacket pocket and threaded the thin temples over his ears to inspect Colette, whom he seemed never to have met.

'We drove all this way right after service. Davina told us that our attendance here mattered to her. We are here as parents, privately. We do not appreciate a priest and will not converse with him. Let that be known. So it is not to be interpreted as being rude.'

'Thank you for coming. There is not just clergy here; there are sheep too. You don't have to engage.'

Davina pinched Colette's arm. 'Ten out of ten – for humouring my parents.'

'They are guests. It is my duty as hostess to make them feel at ease.'

'For them, booze is not the answer. Force them onto the vicar and then say something religious which is outrageous. They would love you for it.'

Trudy carried in a large dish of potato and sausage salad. Behind her Liz came in with Mowbray pork pies and rosemary roasted chicken thighs. Most guests chose to sit at the tables close to the food. More guests had arrived from Briddleton, the noise level had risen, and at the makeshift drinks bar, Trudy was now in her element. Instructed only to fill the glasses half full of whatever the guests chose, she had objected. 'Why don't we use smaller glasses?

Colette explained that it looked better that way but still cost less and did not make them drunk.

'Aha!' Trudy had triumphed in gained wisdom and from then on poured so sparingly the guests walked away looking put out.

Simon came up to Colette. 'Is everyone here?' he asked.

Colette looked over the lawn and saw the Pakistani couple making their way to the tent, a child of about ten between them. Not far behind them walked a man using a cane – the Italian upholsterer with snow-white hair and an endearing face and a surprisingly young-looking wife behind him. She leaned his way and stroked his arm with tenderness. Colette understood why Nonnie had liked these people.

'Where the fuck is he?' Simon lost his temper.

Colette, with a jerk of her head, focused on Davina's boyfriend. 'You're waiting for Gilbert, aren't you?'

'That's the only reason I came.'

Colette thought how unrefined Simon seemed.

'Did he say he would be here?'

Colette shrugged, feeling sorry for Davina who had to live with him.

'Can I go over there into the garage building and knock on his door?'

'How do you…?'

'He leaves the garage open.'

'How do…?'

'We blokes do that.'

From the bar, shrieking laughter.

'That's him over there, isn't it?' Simon shot off.

'Fill it up, woman,' ordered Gilbert, carefully placing his Panama hat on the bar.

'I was told to go halfway only,' objected Trudy.

'A woman of your stature should only ever go all the way.'

'An appalling remark,' said Max, who had ignored the parking signs and left his car right in front of Riverbend, to get into the party tent from the side.

'Who is this sanctimonious git?' Gilbert asked of Trudy, who shrugged and then filled his glass until it spilled over.

'Max Merton, owner and director of Blooms4You.' A hand was proffered. 'I saw you at your book launch, arrived just before you read some of your stuff.'

Gilbert ignored the hand and said, 'Why are you, Max, at this provincial garden fête when you should be in London selling your flower *stuff*?'

'I wanted to see the house Davina was so impressed by. Miss Fontaine is a customer of ours.'

Gilbert took a sip of wine and his face creased into a grimace of distaste.

'A lot of land belongs to Riverbend,' Max continued. 'With the river nearby, it is fertile and as yet uncultivated.'

Gilbert put his glass on the bar next to his hat. 'You want to buy Riverbend,' he suggested. 'Not stupid. The owner is a young idealistic hippy woman.'

'I said nothing of the sort. All I did was comment on the land surrounding the house.'

'I wasn't born yesterday.' Gilbert adjusted his crotch by shaking his trousers holding onto the belt. Max walked away into the crowd. A Lindy Hop tune played; a child in a tunic dress imitated dancing by swaying.

For Simon, who had lain in wait, this was his moment. He pounced and, finding himself alone at the bar with Gilbert, had first to tame his wild heart. Finally, Gilbert noticed his presence and asked, 'You want some red wine?'

Simon's dream was realised. 'Um, er, no.'

'Wise decision.'

And a dead end for Simon. Why hadn't he accepted? 'I'm not interested in wine,' he tried to repair the damage. 'You don't go to the writers' club on *Shit* Thursday and you own a smashing silver Mercedes C280.'

'Smashing is not a good word when talking about cars and the colour of my baby is Designo Silver.'

Simon gulped. 'And you have another one.'

'Another what?'

'Mercedes, which is red.'

'Volcano red.'

There was a moment of silence during which Simon felt the appraising eyes of Gilbert on his sorry self.

'Two such mahoosively amazing cars *and* you are a famous writer whom everyone admires. My name is Simon, by the way, and I intend to write a book too.'

'God help us.'

'I could do with help,' took up Simon. 'Perhaps one day, one day in the future, a faraway future, I could own a Mercedes like you.'

'You managed to meet me today. Let me guess: you admire me. You envy my fast-earned fame and fortune. Have you got any idea how boring this is for me?'

'The Maybach 57 has the first V12 engine ever built in a—'

'Go on.'

'She runs like a bitch on heat. If she growls, you know you did it right.'

'Now you're talking.' A smile further enhanced Gilbert's face. 'Tell me more about your fetish for Mercs.'

'The way they're built, the presence they have on the road, gee, I can't find the right words.' A little snort through his nose. 'That's why I am trying to become a writer.'

'So that you will be able to afford one.'

'You nailed it.'

Gilbert laughed, a rare outright guffaw. 'Do you want to come with me on a little drive in the hot bitch?'

'What do *you* think?' Simon responded, with a fresh, freckled complexion and excited blue eyes.

By the time Bob had turned down the volume on the cassette player and Colette had pinged a fork against a glass, and the vicar stood up to speak, Gilbert and Simon were speeding down the A421 in the Sport convertible.

'Listen to this. I'll put her into overdrive and you'll hear rage.' They were overtaking a John Lewis distribution lorry. Simon realised that he was having an impact on Gilbert who seemed to enjoy showing off his car.

'The good thing is,' Simon said, 'we can speed. The village policeman is back at the party.'

'You know what?' Gilbert slowed down a little. 'You look like a pink, ginger-haired, dumb guy but you are actually quite smart.'

'It's a ruse to get what I want.'

'What do you want?'

'What you have.'

'OK, I'll make you a deal. You can take over my job in Stuttgart and work for Mercedes. I have decided to buy property in the Bahamas, where I intend to spend the next part of my life.'

'What kind of job with Mercedes?'

'I have a contract to write publicity material for their cars, evocative descriptions of what a Mercedes can do which other cars can't. With the birth of every new model, a glossy brochure comes out. There is a photographer hired to take pictures of the cars in the snow of Zermatt and the desert of Ouarzazate in Morocco. There's a psychologist who analyses what seduces men to Mercs. And there is an editor to sort out my writing. I think you're the right man to replace me. You look Germanic. That will go down well.'

'My heritage is actually Irish.'

'Whatever. You would have to move to Stuttgart. I stayed there during the week and did London at the weekends. I'll let you take over my German studio flat. Would that be a problem for you?'

Simon took some time to process this. He sat in the hand-sewn leather seat, eyes closed, nostrils flaring.

'Dav,' he said eventually.

'Yeah. I was introduced to her. Your fiancée.'

'She got the ring but did not say yes.'

'Perhaps I can talk Mercedes into paying for your spouse to accompany you.'

The Merc engaged in a wide double curve and executed the task with smooth élan, like a metal angel swinging centrifugally on the end of a silk ribbon, before Gilbert brought her back onto the straight. Patting the dashboard, he cooed, 'Good girl.'

'Dav...' Simon spoke up again, '... I've come to the conclusion, is in love with Colette and not me.' He added weakly, 'For Dav, everything about me is wrong.'

'So then, no spouse allowance. I have seen your Dav with the boho-dressed lady of Riverbend. I must say, everything points to lesbianism.'

'Shush. Please don't go on. I accept the job you are offering me. I love Mercs and will be able to learn how to write about sexual attraction to them. Besides, I like bratwurst.'

★

Under the tent, Audrey said to Colette with alarm, 'A police car has just driven up. What shall we do?'

'Nothing. I invited him. His name is Stanley. He is the constable in the local police station.'

Constable Stanley, in casual clothes and with a relaxed manner, approached the party.

'Thanks for the invite to me and my missus. We're separated.'

'Sorry, I didn't know. Let me introduce: Audrey, my mother, the daughter of the woman whose remembrance birthday we are celebrating today.' Colette gave a nasal laugh and, turning to her mother, said, 'Constable Stanley is a long-suffering man.'

'Is that so?'

'Mum, I called him a couple of times for nothing.'

'To be correct, it was four times, for suspected acts of terrorism. It cost the local police each time more than a hundred pounds.'

'Why, if they were false alarms?'

'My overtime and then the paperwork involved.'

'Would it help if I apologised for my daughter?' Audrey fluttered her lashes.

'Nice try, lady. Let me go and talk to Bob Worship over there.' The constable moved on.

'This man has no airs and graces.'

'He's a copper, Mum.'

'Forgive me for not having come across many policemen in my life.' Audrey stumbled through the uneven grass towards a table at which sat Liz, whom she called Elizabeth. It was a safe move as they had known each other for years and could reminisce about Margaret.

Colette went to Davina, sitting alone at a table with a drink. 'So, your appraisal went well then. Max will keep you on.'

'Max is the sort of man you can't help loving, while at the same time wishing you had never come across him. He is a wild horse. You don't know him.'

'I know his voice. He called after the Valentine delivery to enquire whether the important rose order for the special friend of his employee, Davina, had been delivered to satisfaction.'

'I am surprised. I didn't think he bothered to call clients. Perhaps it is because I told him about you.'

'Surprising you more,' said Colette, 'he has arrived and is pacing the garden in a rather proprietorial manner.'

The main course and plates were brought back to the kitchen, and homemade apple strudel with a bucket of vanilla ice cream and a Matterhorn-shaped pile of whipped cream arrived. The guests applauded and cheered.

The Italian upholsterer, who had successfully caught the ram, held him tight against his side. 'There's a lot of good wool on this beast,' he kept saying, before he had to let the struggling animal go.

After that, Colette lost sight of the sheep. Things were going well, several people were dancing. Even Stanley was seen, standing with Bob outside the tent, laughing and giving each other occasional friendly pats. Only Audrey looked uncomfortable, she who knew this place so well. She sought comfort from Colette again.

'The other day, I heard from Thomas – you remember the doctor of chemistry.'

'Not him again, Mum.'

'He phoned to say that he was engaged and wished me health and happiness in my future. You hurt his pride, that is for sure.'

'His bride can fix that now.'

'Not funny.'

Bob changed the tape to a foxtrot. A gust of wind sent paper napkins flying. The Pakistani child played with a 90 balloon. At the end of the table, the vicar was in animated conversation with the Baptist parents of Davina.

'Let's dance.' Davina offered her arm to Colette. The two young women shuffled on the grass and others joined in.

'I love it here,' Davina whispered into Colette's ear. 'You are so lucky.'

'Alone, this is not as wonderful as you think. To be honest, it is more like a nightmare, even though for me the kindness of Nonnie shines everywhere. I have to live in fear of Taliban terrorists.'

Davina's first reaction was to stop moving and give a short giggle. 'They have more important targets to get at than you.'

'I tried to tell you before, but two of them came here and tried to kidnap me, tape over my mouth, arms tied behind my back.'

'But they did not succeed. And that, Colette, means it did not happen, did it? You read that in Gilbert's novel, where she was ambushed and shot at. This is the

Bedfordshire countryside, not Paris where they killed all those young people and crushed that pregnant woman's unborn baby.'

The music stopped.

Checking Colette's face, Davina said more soothingly, 'Look, you're still shell-shocked. Without preparation, you have found yourself responsible for such a property and all its land. I couldn't do this on my own. Besides, you had a romantic attachment to an Islamic warrior.'

'Officer.'

'And now back home, you are afraid of the danger you exposed yourself to. That fear of yours takes shape in all sorts of imaginings. Besides, you share a property with a writer who has written a book about something similar to what happened to you. It has further fuelled your imagination.'

The women stood face to face. They reached out to each other until their hands met and joined. Thus they remained, as if about to dance again.

'Think positive. If all that land I am seeing belongs to you, then you can really go crazy with planting.'

'If you came here more often, we could plant flowers together: sub-tropical ones, exotic ones, carnivorous ones.'

The music from the tent played a new tune and the women started to turn, holding onto each other, faster and faster, both leaning outward. 'Dahlias, asters, lilies, gladioli.'

'Are we three years old?' made them slow down and let go of each other. There was some tottering until the giddiness wore off. Max stood there with a half-full beer glass in his hand. 'I'm Max. Thanks for the invite. Obviously, Davina forced you to extend it to me. Pleased to meet you, Colette. If I didn't need to hang onto my beer, I would now rattle your paw.'

'I warned you about his talking,' Davina said to Colette under her breath.

'Tell him about planting flowers on my land,' Colette whispered to Davina.

'You're sure you want him to know about it?'

'Women whisper, whisper like wispy witches,' Max whispered in just the way he objected to.

Davina spoke up, after Colette gave her a nod. 'If half of Riverbend's land were cultivated for flowers, fifty per cent of Blooms4You needs could be supplied home-grown.'

'Quite an idea. It had also crossed my mind.' Max bent down, gathered some earth and patted it in the palm of his hand before letting it drizzle out.

'During my appraisal, you asked me to come up with new ideas,' Davina said tartly.

'How does the owner of the land feel about it?'

Colette stood in her ankle-length dress, the dark-blue hijab on her head, the lashes securely glued. Everything about her said *Yes*: the little smile in the corner of her mouth, the excited grasping of alternate hands, and the wriggle of her body. She knew that Max took it all in.

'It would need to be set up professionally,' he said. 'Three gardeners at least, one doing the heavy work. Transport easier than getting supplies from Kenya or Israel. Winnie could do with a larger van and more responsibilities. Some large greenhouses would have to be built.'

'You already have three gardeners,' smiled Colette. 'There is Davina, myself and Bob, the neighbour who has the right-sized digger. He is strong and enthusiastic.'

'The one who keeps tightening the tent ropes.'

Colette nodded.

'A methodical and conscientious man. I like it,' mused Max.

'You do know there is one major problem with this,' piped up Davina. 'I don't live here. Simon, the one in the pink shirt over there, getting out of Gilbert's Mercedes, and I share a flat in West London.'

'Marriage plans?' came from Max.

'N… no.'

'Then over to you, Cutlet.'

'You can come and live in Riverbend. It's large enough for two,' Colette offered generously, ignoring Max's deliberate messing with her name.

'Thank you ever so much. Oh my God, Colette, how wonderful.'

'I take it, it is a deal.' Max watched Davina hopping on tiptoe. 'However,' he said darkly to get their attention, 'we are talking business. There will be no doing each other favours. No female emotions. And definitely no *Ringa Ringa Roses*. Money will be involved. Riverbend will become a major supplier of Blooms4You. Davina will advise me on what to plant. I will pay Colette for the flowers. Colette will pay a salary to Davina and Bob. Colette might think of collecting rent from Davina. Contracts will be drawn up by my lawyer.'

'Davina will stay in Riverbend as my guest,' Colette stated firmly.

'Better safe than sorry.' Max advised caution.

'The living arrangements are up to us.' Colette finalised the discussion.

'How exciting!' Davina's voice was shrill. 'I'll be part of a great start-up.'

'Don't call it a start-up,' shouted Max. 'If Simon gets anywhere near it, he's a complete…' Max remembered to hold back.

'… Dreamer.' Davina finished for him. 'Shall we tell Max about the skeleton in the cupboard?' She glanced at Colette and expanded, 'Gilbert de Villiers is living in Riverbend.'

'Only in the caretaker's room,' protested Colette.

'Are you and he an item?' Max focused on Colette.

'Most definitely not.'

'I don't think it's a problem,' Max said. 'I heard Gilbert tell people that he is moving to the Bahamas, in style I presume, to judge from the expensive Panama hat he brought to a simple country get-together.'

★

When any party breaks up, people linger in car parks or at doors, as if second thoughts have kicked in, which needed to be shared before parting.

Max, shoulders bent, head dipped, steered towards Colette who stood near the child's swing. 'Good to have met you. Think about the business we discussed. It will be a big commitment. If you have any doubts, let me know. Otherwise, I will be starting to plan through the summer for planting in the autumn.'

'I am on board,' Colette pronounced without hesitation.

'I believe you, Cutlet. You will have Davina as a companion in the large house. She is a pain in the neck but trustworthy. I suppose you already know that. Try to dress less like a timid Muslim. I'll need you to be a businesswoman if the project takes off.'

'I look forward to becoming a member of your team, Max,' Colette said softly. 'Mostly because you were right when you said that if you look closer, every flower smiles at you.'

'My little sister,' he said and walked to his car, cheekily parked in front of the house.

Not far from them, the vicar's wife was saying goodbye to Audrey. 'Your mother is much missed around here. We console ourselves with her granddaughter living in Riverbend now, but it is not the same. Colette doesn't come to church or participate in the community.'

'She is young. Give her time.'

'Bless her for having organised this party for her grandmother.'

'I should have inherited Riverbend,' blurted out Audrey. 'At the end of her life, my mother's brain was not as healthy as the lawyers thought it was. I knew. They didn't. What could I have done, huh? Colette got the lot.'

Trudy appeared, holding a greasy leather collar. 'They loved my sausage salad and the apple strudel.' She gleamed. 'I've got to get the collar back on the ram.'

'Was it your idea to get Bob to bring a sheep to the party?' asked Audrey. 'Sheep resent dogs.'

'If they don't get on, then how come the Afghan hound is still playing tug-of-war with the ram behind the house?'

'Well, darling, my taxi has arrived. You did well.' Audrey embraced her daughter. 'Your Nonnie would have been proud of you. Apart from the choice in food. You let Trudy rule. A mistake. Let me help you next time. Toodle-oo. Oh, one more thing—'

'Isn't the taxi waiting?'

Guiding Colette back into the shadow of the oak tree, Audrey asked, 'What happened to your bracelet, the one you were given by that good, good friend of yours in Kabul?'

'It got lost.'

'Don't cry.'

'I can't, you know that.'

'That established, you can't hide from me what happens inside you. The friend was a man. A mother knows. Did he love you? Will you see him again? At your age, you really need a man by your side. The chemist was a mistake, but you will be thirty in November.'

'Twenty-eight.'

'I love you, darling. Anyone else who loves you is naturally close to my heart. Please tell me. Is there any possibility that the man who gave you the bangle might become part of your life?'

'I wish.'

'Kabul, Afghanistan is not that far away with the improved airline services. Invite him to come to England.

I have been saving and could pay for his ticket. Gilbert, in his novel, writes about a woman not unlike you who went to work in an embassy in Kabul and fell in love with an Islamic warrior. A gripping story.'

'Mum, the taxi is waiting.'

'Your friend's name. Please open up enough to give me his name.'

'The taxi driver is now waving.'

'His first name then.'

'Abdul. It means servant of Allah.'

Audrey stepped back. She appeared to be teetering on her high heels near an abyss. 'Maybe we'll talk about this another time.'

★

When the guests had left and Trudy had dragged the sheep back to the farm, Colette climbed the steps to the house, her hand upon the sloping stone banister. On the top step, she sat down and bundled her knees together with her arms. In the distance, she could hear the voice of Trudy calling out for HanHan. 'Abdul,' Colette whispered. Mother had brought him right in front of her again, except that Colette seemed to have forgotten the shape of his mouth, the depth of the dark velvety eyes, the warmth of his well-shaped hand on her shoulder at the traffic lights. Weighed down by the sadness of remembering and, with it, the forgetting, she mumbled, 'Hannan, I love you as I did the moment you crossed your ankles under the school desk. I can't tell my mother. I can't go back and look for you. You can't come to England and live as my mother's son-in-law. Wherever you are, my beloved, may Allah the merciful please look after you.'

★

Trudy was clearing up under the birthday tent. Colette up at her desk felt slightly guilty for not helping. Contact with so many people had left much to sort out, for someone who spent most of the day alone as she did these days. She pieced together the course of events which had led to her committing Riverbend to become a market flower garden with everything such a business entailed. And she would become a manager, as well as an employee. The best thing about this was that Davina would come and share the house with her. For that alone, she, Colette, would shovel earth and plant bulbs for as long as it took. Davina had confided in her that Simon, her boyfriend, had decided to go and work in Germany, whilst Gilbert had trumpeted his plan to live as an expat in the Bahamas. It all clicked together so perfectly.

Colette relaxed her shoulders. 'Thank you, Nonnie,' she said. 'You did that for me and deserved your party today. I love you.'

On the flowery duvet, the dog twitched his ears, before deciding to dangle his head over the rim of the bed, eyes fixed on her.

'I love you too.' She sighed with satisfaction. She would become happy in Riverbend. It was a beautiful place. The sun was way down towards the horizon; cumuli had gathered, pink and mauve, to witness the event. Colette noticed Gilbert's red Mercedes appear from the garages. It suddenly came to a stop with a bump, down below, close to the bottom of the steps. Gilbert got out, tossed his Panama hat onto the seat and opened the bonnet, testing around the motor. Colette stood up to see more clearly what was going on. He seemed to be looking for the problem which had made the car come to a halt.

Trudy emerged from under the tent, emptying a wine bottle into her mouth. She threw the bottle from her and shouted at the top of her voice, 'Quitter! Coward!' She even broke into a run, still shouting, 'When we need help, his lordship takes off. You stay right here. You help with the dishes.'

Avoiding the ranting figure, Gilbert hopped back into his car and shut the door. Leaning forward, he looked upwards and threw a guilty glance up at Colette's window.

'Swinehead,' Trudy shouted. The motor started and backfired, producing a black cloud of exhaust. With a shriek, Trudy ran away from it and down across the lawn.

At that moment, there was a metallic screech, a yellow flash and a tremendous ear-splitting blast which shook the bedroom, the whole house. A roar of hot wind slammed into Colette, glass shards whistled past her, and she was thrown from the window towards the bed. A dog tongue licking her face was the last thing she was conscious of for a while.

When she came to, she found herself on her back on Nonnie's bed. The room was full of acrid smoke, making her cough continually. She tested her limbs before rolling off the bed to approach the gaping hole in the wall where a shredded bit of voile curtain dangled from a twisted rod. On Nonnie's desk were glass fragments like packing ice. Her stomach was cramped and the force of the explosion was still ringing in her ears. The stench of chemical smoke and taste of metal filled her brain. Dust coated her tongue.

Outside, beneath her on the gravel drive, the car bomb had reduced the large car to a smoking mound of twisted steel and debris, presumably cremating Gilbert at the same time. What about Trudy? Colette frantically looked around. Mon Dieu, Trudy? In the spreading grey of crepuscule, Trudy's shape in foetal position could be made out on the grass. Her legs were moving. Clearly, she had been thrown onto the grass by the impact but had survived.

A car bomb. A desperate last move of her Islamic enemies. There were no sane limits to their resentment. Were they still out there? From the ghost-like remnants of the tent, bunting hung motionless. Glasses, plates and bottles were scattered with the tables. The charcoal fingers of twilight crawled towards Colette over her land.

She turned to take stock of what was left of Nonnie's bedroom. The door to the landing had been blown away. A high-pitched whine from under the bed was that of a dog in pain. On all fours, she crawled across the floor, cutting her knees on the debris, but she felt no pain. Perhaps shock had cut her brain off from the feelings of her body.

'HanHan.' Colette clawed herself close to the bed. The destroyed room was suddenly filled by the siren of a police car and then a second. The telephone on the desk started to ring, but she was only able to give a sob. Why was HanHan not reappearing from under the bed? All she could see was the glint in his eyes.

With a loud crash, the lintel of the central window came down, shattering on the sill, spilling rubble outside and in. Before the brick-cloud had time to settle, the right-hand lintel came down the same way.

Loud voices came from outside, conjuring up a sense of doom and despair.

'Stand back from the window,' someone yelled. She knew that was for her. She checked the ceiling. Would that crash down as well? Under the bed was a good place. She went down flat and searched for the glint in the dog's eyes. 'HanHan,' she tried to say, but only sobs rose in her chest. She reached out and felt the dog's head, then tested further through the long tangled hair until her shaking fingers caught under his wide collar. She pulled the animal towards her. Once half of him was clear of the bed, despite her spinning head, she realised that HanHan was seriously hurt. Several rather large metal fragments were embedded in his body, and the fur partly covering the flesh wounds was stiff and red from blood. A blanched bone showed under the torn flesh of his front paw. She remained immobile for a while, breathing carefully and holding her heart.

'Help,' she shouted. And again with more strength, 'Help. Someone help us,' she pleaded ineffectively into an empty house. Outside, more strident sirens drowned the shouting voices. Giddy, she reached out to support herself against the doorframe, but slid back down to her knees.

'Can you get up?'

'It's you,' Colette whispered to Trudy who was standing over her.

'Are you hurt?'

'I'm not important. HanHan is hurt. Call an ambulance.'

'The pooch is probably kaput,' said Trudy. 'I checked. Two ambulances are already in front of the house and Constable Stanley has called in an army of police.'

'I can't hear clearly. I can't cry.'

'We know. Don't worry, Colly. The ambulance first aider will be here any minute.'

'I refuse to go unless we take Hannan to the vet on the way. He has been shot, twice. Promise me. He needs help. His parents will never accept me. His father is trying to get me killed. He needs a new front paw. It is all my fault.'

'Hold onto me, Colly. You're barely conscious. It will be all right. Just stay with me.'

★

A few days later, when Colette's cuts and grazes were healing, and HanHan returned from the vet, only a lugubrious black stain remained on the gravel at the entrance. She rocked gently on her swing, the ropes of which Bob had shortened. Forward – backward – forward. The time had come for her to read Gilbert's novel. He had given her a copy of course, which she had promptly thrown into the bin. Another had appeared in front of her bedroom door. That one was signed by him and was thrown back into his lodgings through an open window.

Not wishing to be seen buying the book in Bedford, Colette decided to go to Foyles bookshop in London. Wearing one of her wigs, she boarded the train and chose a seat on the right-hand side where she would be able to see the Blooms4You banner on the white building just before the tunnel. Was she not going to be a partner in that business, providing home-grown flowers? But the train rushed along the track and Colette missed seeing the banner. In St Pancras, it came to a slow stop. She stood at the folding doors.

'Are you getting off?' asked a woman behind her.

'*Oui, je vais descendre*,' Colette said absent-mindedly, in the language she had taught in Kabul.

When she emerged from Tottenham Court Road tube station, it started to rain, more like spitting only. She had brought Nonnie's black umbrella with the mother-of-pearl handle, but was reluctant to open it. When the sun had last come out for Nonnie, the old lady with her mottled hands had rolled the umbrella, fold upon fold, spirally, and then tidied it with the strip latch and press-button, the way Nonnie did things right. Colette pulled the blue hijab from her bag and wound it around her head. Feeling cossetted, which gave her confidence, she walked down the Charing Cross Road.

It smelled of damp, warm London. Thunder crackled above, an extended crackle with a short encore. The electrical charges playing in the sky overhead made people walk on faster, as if driven by a spiritual force, an elemental fear. A general atmosphere of unease spread over everything. Traffic seemed to move slowly and erratically, and an unfamiliar smell arose from the pavement. A sombre darkness grew, before an intense bolt of lightning jolted everything back to life for less than a second. Breath held for a little longer and the thunder crash followed. Colette felt strangely involved in the natural phenomenon. Down here, they all scrabbled about, driven by innumerable tasks to perform, some giving themselves importance by making up religions and laws, engaging in wars, while above them in the vast cosmos, the Gods still found a way to grumble, as they had long before mankind was created.

It started to rain in earnest with the typical intent of April weather. She undid the little button and sheltered under black silk. She jolted to a halt. Abdul Hannan was walking not far in front of her. The figure, shoulders alone, the angle of his chin to the side, his profile, the strong black hair peppered with raindrop pearls, the large, veined hand against the injured thigh as if to console the limb for having to limp after the healthy one. This was a cruel delirium. Pain threatened to strangle her, rose through her cheeks, and forced liquid to brim from her eyes. Thus clouded, she still perceived the ache of his injured leg caused by one of the Babur Gardens bullets. He had become too thin, too angular. He should really use a walking aid but his pride… She remembered how he had dared her with his dark smoky eyes. Only a few metres from her was the man she could reach out to again, smell, touch, hold in her arms and feel his tenderness flow back into her lonely body. She would share all his pain. He would tell her all about himself and she would tell him all about herself. She would dare her mother. They would find somewhere small to live in London and face everyday tasks and duties, and begin the ordinariness of being together. Empowered by their shared love, she would become beautiful and her hair would grow back. Had she not already been able to shed tears or were they just drops of rain? If the tears weren't rain, she did not need an umbrella. She let go and dropped the umbrella for someone else. She walked under the rain disoriented and was aware of her worn-out sandals which she simply stepped out of, one by one, to walk on barefoot, leaving them behind like rudderless boats in a river.

He had by this time made it to the crossroads: a choice, because he stopped.

It was up to her to decide whether to go up to him or to walk away. For the good of both of them, she turned, ever so slowly. Rocked by dry sobs, she walked away, accepting that purgatory was during lifetime and not afterwards.

This book is printed on paper from sustainable sources managed under the Forest Stewardship Council (FSC) scheme.

It has been printed in the UK to reduce transportation miles and their impact upon the environment.

For every new title that Troubador publishes, we plant a tree to offset CO_2, partnering with the More Trees scheme.

For more about how Troubador offsets its environmental impact, see www.troubador.co.uk/sustainability-and-community